A CURE FOR
MADNESS

ALSO BY JODI McISAAC

THE THIN VEIL SERIES

A CURE FOR
MADNESS

JODI McISAAC

Text copyright © 2016 by Jodi McIsaac

Published by Thomas & Mercer, Seattle

www.apub.com

Amazon, the Amazon logo, and Thomas & Mercer are trademarks of Amazon.com, Inc., or its affiliates.

ISBN-13: 9781503951624
ISBN-10: 1503951626

Cover design by Christian Fuenfhausen

Printed in the United States of America

For my brother

PROLOGUE

Peggy had often assumed she would meet a violent end at the hands of her son. She'd imagined the scenario many times, especially in the early days of what she called "the troubled years." A quick blow with his fists, a kick with his steel-toed boots, or a bullet to the head, should he ever find his father's hunting rifles.

But the man pointing a gun at her now was not her son.

"Terry, please, it's Bud and Peggy Campbell," she said, her hand on her husband's arm.

"What are you doing here?" The man stood on the path in front of them, blocking their way. The nearby streetlamp threw his shadow over Peggy like a ghost. His combed-over hair was askew, and his hands shook as he jabbed the revolver at her face.

"What are *we* doing here?" Bud sputtered beside her. His cheeks burned red under his thick gray sideburns. "We're going for a walk, that's what. What are *you* doing here? Put the gun down, man, and let's talk!"

"I know you," Terry muttered, moving closer to peer at them. The light glinted off the barrel of the gun. Peggy whimpered.

"Of course you know us!" Bud said. He pulled Peggy closer to him. "Haven't we known each other for twenty years now? Is this why you weren't at prayer meeting today? Out making a fool of yourself?"

"*Don't* call me a fool!" Terry bellowed. He shoved the gun in Bud's face, then back at Peggy, swinging it back and forth like a metronome while his eyes darted between them.

"Don't upset him, Bud . . ." Peggy whispered.

"Prayer meeting . . ." Terry mumbled. "I don't need that anymore. I have a direct line to God. He talks to me."

Peggy's eyes widened. This sounded all too familiar.

"Of course he does," Bud said. "And right now he's telling you to put the gun down. Please, Terry, you're frightening Peg."

At this, Terry's head jerked up. "No. You can't hear him! You're one of *them*!"

"What's wrong with you?" Bud asked. "You're talking nonsense! Have you been drinking?"

Terry shook his head jerkily. "No. No. I know what you are. I know what you're planning."

"We're not planning anything," Peggy said. "Just let us go." Under her breath she started to pray. "Dear Jesus, we ask you to help us. We call upon Your name—"

"Stop whispering!" Terry bellowed, spit flecking from his mouth. "I know the truth! They told me! Their ghosts came to me. They told me what you'd done! You're going to kill us all!"

"How is Lucille?" Peggy tried. "How are Mark and Georgia? Are they home from college for the summer?"

If Terry recognized any of these names, he gave no indication. The wildness in his eyes grew. "They're back," he said hoarsely. "They're speaking to me." He sank to his knees and moaned, "They won't stop talking! Shut up! Shut up!"

Bud tore his arm out of Peggy's grip and lunged forward. He dove for the gun, which was limp in Terry's hand. Terry bellowed. There was a roar, a scream from Peggy's own mouth. Bud landed at her feet.

She screamed again, but a powerful thud in her side cut it off.

She fell onto the path beside Bud. Her head connected brutally with the pavement. Her vision blurred, and she struggled for breath. Pain, worse than birthing her two children, tore through her, as if she was being ripped in half.

"Bud," she gasped. His lifeless eyes stared at the night sky. Another roar. Terry's body fell back into the shadows beneath the bridge.

Peggy heard sirens in the distance. It didn't matter. It was too late for Bud; too late for her. *Wes needs new underwear,* she thought frantically. *And the key sticks in the lock. Oh, Wes, who will look after you?* He had only the Lord to protect him now . . . and his sister, Clare.

Peggy's bets were on the Lord.

CHAPTER ONE

The secret to staying alive was to keep moving. At least, it had worked so far. I'd lived in Seattle for two whole years, longer than I'd lived in one place for almost a decade. I was getting itchy feet, and my roommate and best friend knew it.

"Just stay for a bit longer, Clare," Latasha would urge me whenever she caught me browsing for real estate in San Diego or Barcelona. "You're never going to meet someone if you can't sit still for five minutes. And what about your career?"

I wasn't worried about my career. Freelance copywriting had its perks. Give me a Wi-Fi connection and a cup of coffee, and I'm good to go. The health-care benefits were nonexistent, but that small inconvenience paled compared to the freedom it gave me. I could go wherever, whenever.

However, Latasha *did* have a point about my love life. I was thirty-one and single. Serious relationships seemed more trouble than they were worth. But my ovaries were twitching, and I'd recently checked "Interested in a long-term relationship" on my online dating profile. Seattle seemed as good a place as any to settle down. The best part? It was about as far away from my actual hometown in Maine as a person could get in the continental United States.

We were deep into our Saturday gaming night. Latasha and her book-club friend Amy had introduced me to the world of Arkham Horror, Risk, and yes, Dungeons & Dragons. My experience with games had previously been limited to UNO, Balderdash, and watching my brother play Phantasy Star II on our old Sega Genesis.

Tonight we were playing Warring Worlds Online. I was about to die. Apparently the secret to staying alive applied to fictional worlds as well. Stay in one place for too long, and before you know it, you're surrounded by enemies, without the tools or strength to fend them off.

"Dammit." I pushed my chair back from the table, which was covered in laptops and cords.

"Sorry, Clare." Latasha peered at my screen and then shot me a sympathetic look. "That's a shitty way to die." She ran a hand over her short-cropped black curls, which I had envied ever since we first met in college a dozen years ago. My hair was stringy, shoulder length, and—as my father had once put it—the color of soot.

I opened a second bottle of merlot in the kitchen and refilled Latasha's and Amy's glasses, then poured the rest of the bottle into mine.

"Weren't you going to call your brother today?" Latasha asked through a mouthful of Brie. Eating an obscene amount of cheese and crackers was a treasured part of our game nights.

"Oh yeah." I glanced at my phone. Ten o'clock. "It's probably too late . . ."

"Whatever," Latasha said, calling me on my bullshit. "You said he stays up half the night and sleeps until noon. Just call. You're always glad when you do."

"What's so bad about calling your brother?" Amy asked, consulting the hand-drawn map beside her keyboard.

"Nothing," I said quickly. "It's just . . . we don't have much to talk about. He's mentally ill."

Amy looked up. "Really? What kind?"

"Paranoid schizophrenia. He's been in and out of the psych hospital for the last few years."

"Where is he now?"

"He's in," I admitted. "But he gets out tomorrow—hopefully for good."

Amy frowned. "I'm so sorry. I had no idea."

I shrugged. "It's no big deal. It doesn't really come up that often."

"Is the hospital in Clarkeston? That's where you're from, right?"

"Yeah. My parents are still there, so they visit him a lot."

"Well, that's good. Have you seen him recently?"

I took a gulp of wine and shrugged off the wisp of guilt that floated down onto my shoulders. "A couple of years ago, last time I went home for Christmas."

"Sorry for asking so many questions," Amy said with an awkward laugh. "I've just never known anyone . . ."

"It's okay," I said. Amy began another round of apologies, which I promptly cut off. "Don't worry about it. Really, I don't mind."

This was partially true. The full truth was that in my day-to-day life, Wes didn't exist. Now that he was in the hospital and not wreaking havoc on our town and family, I tried not to think about him. My calendar reminded me to call on his birthday and Christmas, and every year I sent him a pile of books I thought he'd like—books dark enough to catch his interest, but not enough to give him any dangerous ideas. Epic fantasies were a safe bet. Wes thought himself a great warrior, a slayer of evil forces, and I hoped that reading about fictional heroes and villains might diminish his desire for the real thing.

"Has he always had this condition?" Amy swirled the wine in her glass.

"When we were children, everything was fine." That seemed like another world, some mythical realm of normalcy.

"How far apart are you guys?"

"Just a year." My head felt fuzzy. I took another long drink. "We were practically raised as twins. I skipped kindergarten and went straight into first grade, so we were always in the same class. Went to this tiny Christian school in the basement of a church—the kind that makes you wear a potato sack all day if the hem of your skirt doesn't touch the ground when you kneel."

"They did not!" Amy exclaimed.

Latasha snorted. She was draped over the armchair, her laptop abandoned, a plate of cheese resting on her stomach.

"That's not the worst," I said. "We had an entire semester of 'science' class on fermentation so they could 'prove' that when Jesus turned water into wine, he was really turning it into Welch's grape juice. Because we all know that alcohol is of the devil."

The girls laughed, and we lifted our glasses in a toast to my messed-up upbringing. But I couldn't bring myself to laugh, no matter how ridiculous it sounded now. Back then, I'd been a true believer. I'd bought it all. Wes? He hadn't given a shit. How times had changed.

"So when did you find out your brother had schizophrenia?" Amy said once she recovered. "If you don't mind me asking, that is."

I gave her a reassuring smile. "He was about twelve, I think. Started having behavioral problems. Stupid stuff, like stealing from our mom's purse, skipping school, whatever. Just . . . became a bit of a misfit. Then in high school he got into the wrong crowd and started doing drugs. He dropped out in eleventh grade. He just . . . completely changed. At first we thought it was the drugs—we didn't know anything about mental health. My parents blamed themselves. My dad even stepped down from his position as an elder at the church because of some stupid Bible verse that says if you can't control your own family, you're not fit to lead in a church. It was only when Wes got arrested that he got diagnosed."

"He was arrested?" Amy pressed.

"It's a long story," I said, avoiding Amy's rapt gaze. "I should really go call him before it gets too late."

"Take your time. We'll hold down the fort," said Latasha.

I climbed the stairs to my bedroom, taking my wineglass with me, and shut the door. The cell phone was heavy in my hands, and my heartbeat was annoyingly fast. It was always this way. I had overcome my childhood shyness and could speak in front of crowds and make small talk with strangers like it was the simplest thing in the world. But calling my own brother? That required some serious pep talking.

Growing up, we were as close as your average brother and sister, if "close" means always fighting and scraping and trying to get the other sibling in trouble. But we had each other's backs when it counted—most of the time. I remembered the day he climbed to the top branch of one of the sprawling maple trees in front of our old farmhouse. I'd been sitting underneath the tree, reading a book, trying to ignore the twigs and leaves he was raining down on my head.

"Clare!" he'd yelled suddenly.

"What?" I yelled back, not looking up.

"Help! I need help!"

"Yeah, right," I muttered, returning to my book. Wes had been on a torment-the-sister rampage recently, and I was certain that if I looked up I'd get a face full of something unpleasant. He'd probably found a bird's nest and was just waiting to crack an egg on my forehead.

"No, really, help me! I'm stuck!"

"You never get stuck." It was true. Everything Wes touched turned to gold; without seeming to put in any effort, he'd succeeded at everything he put his hand to. Sports, art, music, school, friends—they were all his for the taking, and he took and took and took. I, on the other hand, was born with two left feet, had the artistic ability of a three-year-old, and was so painfully shy that the person I talked to most was the reflection of myself in my bedroom window. The thought of Wes trying and failing at anything was ludicrous. He could probably fly down from the tree if he set his mind to it.

But curiosity got the better of me, and I looked up. Wes was hanging upside down, one foot wedged in the fork of a branch. Well, well . . . would you look at that. Of course, I wasn't thinking rationally; it didn't occur to me that he could break his neck if the branch gave way. All I was thinking was that he needed my help, and I needed some leverage. I gazed up at his flailing form.

"What are you doing?" he bellowed. "Go get Mom!"

"First tell me where you hid my diary," I spat up at him, clambering to my feet.

"What? I'm about to fall!"

"Where is it?"

"Jeez! It's under the sink in the downstairs bathroom!"

I hadn't actually thought he would tell me; I was still expecting him to perform some athletic feat of daring and land gracefully on the ground in front of me. But now—now I wondered what else I could get away with.

"Promise that I get to play your video games whenever I want, for a whole month."

"Are you crazy?"

I sat back down.

"Fine!" he yelled. "Just help me, please!" I noticed for the first time that his face was red and wet with tears. His blond hair, which usually fell smoothly over his forehead, highlighting his bright blue eyes, was reaching toward the ground, as though it was pointing the way.

Feeling a twinge of guilt, I finally took off toward the house, yelling for our mother. She sent me across the railroad tracks to fetch Uncle Rob, since our dad was at work. By the time he and I had raced back over the field, my mother had dragged our tall aluminum ladder from the shed and propped it against the tree trunk. She had climbed up into the tree and was trying to reach Wes.

Together, she and Uncle Rob got him down. His ankle was swollen and bruised, but at least his neck was intact—no thanks to me, he'd been quick to point out. Instead of video games, I'd gotten a red welt on my bottom in the shape of our wooden kitchen spoon. But I'd recovered my diary, so it hadn't been a total disaster.

You're not kids anymore. I turned my phone over in my hands. Then I dialed the number of the hospital.

"Riverside Psychiatric Facility. How may I direct your call?" The woman's voice on the other end was crisp and professional. I wished I could just talk with her instead.

"Wes Campbell, please. Room two sixty-three."

I listened to the phone in his room ringing. *Maybe he won't be there.* But where else would he be?

"Hello?"

"Hey, big brother."

"Hey! I wondered if you'd call."

"Of course! I'm sorry it wasn't earlier."

"Doesn't matter. What are you up to?"

"Just playing a game with the girls."

"Oh yeah? What kind of game?"

"Um . . . it's an online game. A fantasy kind of thing."

"Huh. On the computer?"

"Yeah." I picked at a loose thread on the bedspread. "I know you don't really like computers." That was a bit of an understatement. Wes had previously gone on vitriolic rants about how they were "fucking tools of the devil."

"Just be careful," he warned. I could hear the worry in his voice. "You don't know who's watching you."

"Wes, my roommate, Latasha, works for the NSA," I said. "I'm pretty aware of what they can do. But I don't really care if they watch me kill a few orcs and demons." I regretted the words as soon as they were out of my mouth. Even in his more lucid moments, Wes thought he was a demon slayer on a mission from God. I changed the subject. "So, you're leaving tomorrow, right?"

He grunted. I realized I had no idea where he would be going. "You moving back in with Mom and Dad, or what?"

He snorted. "Yeah, right. Dad's got an apartment lined up for me."

"Well, that's cool."

There was a long pause, and then he said, "Your roommate really works for the NSA?"

"Yeah."

"Have you thought about killing her in her sleep?"

"Wes! Jesus!"

"Hey, you shouldn't swear."

"You shouldn't suggest I murder my friend."

"Calm down; I was just kidding. But do you ever wonder if she's . . . you know, keeping track of you?"

"She's not keeping track of me. And if she was, I'd just feel bad for her. I have the most boring life in existence. Believe me, the government has more interesting people to stalk." I tried changing the subject again. "What have you been reading lately?"

"I just think it's weird that she happens to be living with you right now," he persisted. "Because I just met this former government guy here at the hospital. Maybe they're both plants."

"Latasha's not a plant. She's a systems analyst, not a spy. Who's the guy you met?"

"Winston Ling. A scientist. Got checked in a couple of weeks ago. He told me about a covert government project he was working on in a secret lab. Called it 'Project Amherst.' But something happened— something really bad." He had lowered his voice, and I could picture him looking over his shoulder, checking to see that no one was listening at the door.

"Like what?"

"He didn't say. Not exactly. Just said it all went wrong and something got out. Are you thinking what I'm thinking?"

"Probably not."

"Mutants. I bet that's what it was."

I was glad he couldn't see me rolling my eyes. I slipped into auto-pilot. This was the part of the conversation where Wes would tell me about his latest encounters in the spiritual realm and I would nod my head and say "mm-hm" and bite my tongue whenever the word "crazy" floated in the general direction of my vocal cords. I drained the contents of my wineglass. *This isn't his fault.*

"And then he killed himself," Wes continued.

I abruptly switched back to manual pilot mode. "What? Are you serious?"

"Yeah. Heard the nurses talking about it. Happened a week or so ago, I think. Wondered why I hadn't seen him around."

"Jesus."

Wes cleared his throat at my language.

"Sorry. What happened?"

"Made a noose out of the bedsheets. At least that's what they said. It's not unusual. People kill themselves a lot around here. Or go missing."

"Well, it's good you're leaving, then," I said in an attempt at levity.

"Don't you think that's strange, though? He was part of this secret government project, and then he 'killed himself'? Want to know what I think? I think they offed him to keep him quiet." His voice was rising, and I could picture his eyes getting wider, the veins on his face becoming more pronounced. I had to nip this in the bud.

"Listen, Wes. This guy was in there for a reason. Remember what it was like before you were on the right medication? How you'd think things were true, but it would turn out they were just in your head? This is probably the same thing. Everything he told you, it's just due to his illness. Chances are he wasn't even a real scientist. Don't worry about it. Just concentrate on staying well and enjoying your new life. Won't it be great to be able to come and go whenever you want and not have nurses hovering around you all the time?"

"You tell me."

I pressed my lips together. "I'm really glad they think you're well enough to leave."

"Are you coming home any time soon?"

"I don't know. I'll try, but . . . it's expensive, and I've got a lot going on with work."

"Sure."

There was an awkward silence—awkward on my end, at least.

"So I killed a demon the other day," Wes said.

I frowned into the phone. I thought his medication was supposed to control this sort of thing. Maybe there was only so much it could do.

"Oh yeah?" I struggled to keep the skepticism out of my voice. "How?"

"With my telepathy."

"You have telepathy?"

"Yeah. I mean, I can only use it to communicate directly with other telepaths. But God uses it to guide me to people who need my help."

"Okay. How does that happen?"

"Well, I was just reading in my room, and I heard this little girl crying for help. But it's not like there are any little girls in here, right?"

"I hope not."

"But I knew she was scared—I could just feel it, and I could hear her crying. She was scared because there was a monster under her bed."

"Okay . . ."

"Only, it wasn't a monster, it was a demon. They like to masquerade as monsters, y'know; that's why kids are afraid of the dark. They can sense the demons. And this was a big one. I reached out to her with my mind and told her it was going to be okay. Then I transported myself to her room, and I just opened my mouth and sucked in the demon. I sucked it way down into my gut and then burned it with my holy fire."

"Your . . . holy fire?"

"We all have it, everyone who has Jesus living inside them. Most people just don't know how to use it."

"Wow. So . . . what happened to the little girl? Was she kind of freaked out to see you in her room?"

"She never saw me; she just felt me. She knew I was there to protect her. I could feel her again after I destroyed the demon, and she wasn't afraid anymore. She was peaceful."

There was a knock on his end, and a pause. Then he said, "I gotta go. We're not supposed to be on the phone this late."

"Okay, well, it was nice talking to you," I said. "I love you."

"You, too. Watch out for that roommate of yours." He hung up before I had the chance to ask him what his phone number would be in his new place.

I picked up the empty wineglass and headed back down the stairs and into the living room, where Latasha and Amy were once again staring intently at their screens. "How did it go?" Latasha asked, handing me an open bottle of cabernet sauvignon.

"Oh, fine," I answered, refilling my glass. "He thinks you're spying on me."

"Him and everyone else," she said with a snort.

"I don't know if he's ready to be released, actually."

At this, Amy looked up, too. Her eyebrows were raised; Latasha's pointed down in a deep V.

I slumped into the armchair I had rescued from a garage sale after my move to Seattle. It was oversized and ancient, with black and red paisley cushions and round wooden legs. I loved it; Latasha tolerated it.

"He seemed all right for most of the conversation," I said. "But then he talked about crazy things. Like this guy he'd met—supposedly a scientist working in a secret government lab on something called Project Amherst. Maybe you should look into that," I joked lamely, nodding at Latasha. She gave me a wry smile.

"Anyway, Wes said the guy killed himself—but of course he thinks it's all part of a big cover-up."

"What? At the mental hospital?" Amy asked. "Aren't they supposed to have measures in place to protect against that kind of thing?"

"Honestly, I never know what to believe with Wes. But he was convinced it happened, and that's what makes me worry. And he followed that up with a story about how he can communicate through telepathy and saved a little girl from a demon under her bed by swallowing it and burning it with holy fire."

To their credit, neither Latasha nor Amy laughed.

"Your parents keep a close eye on him, though, don't they?" Latasha asked. "And you said it's taken them a few tries to get his medication right; maybe it just needs a bit more tweaking. Or maybe he's nervous about leaving tomorrow, and it's setting him off."

"Maybe," I admitted. How would he adjust to normal life again? Not that Wes would ever have a normal life. Work wasn't really an option. His current medication was strong enough to control the voices in his head—mostly—but it also wiped him out emotionally and physically. He slept at least sixteen hours a day. Being around people made him nervous—a painfully sharp contrast to the gregarious, outgoing boy he'd once been.

I opened my laptop. Time to escape. Latasha was right; Wes would be fine. My parents would see to that.

My phone rang, breaking the silence, and all three of us jumped.

"Is it Wes calling back?" Latasha said, glancing at the clock on the wall.

"Maybe. It's a Maine number, but I don't recognize it." I lifted the phone to my ear. "Hello?"

"Clare? It's your uncle Rob. I'm sorry for calling so late, but I've got some . . . difficult news."

CHAPTER TWO

I wished I could freeze time. I'd read the books, seen the TV shows. When someone called late at night and warned you they had difficult news, it always meant that your life was about to change in a horrible, irreversible way—and there was nothing you could do to stop it.

"Is it Wes?" I whispered, knowing it couldn't possibly be; I had just spoken to him.

"No. I hate to be the one to tell you this, especially over the phone . . ." He took a deep breath. "Your parents were killed earlier this evening."

His words, still echoing in my ears, prompted a sudden out-of-body experience. I watched myself sitting in my paisley chair, my mouth slightly agape. One hand was clenched around the phone; the other was digging into my leg. A long silence stretched out. The girls were staring at me, and I knew Rob was waiting for a response. But I had none to give. Words were useless.

"They were shot," he continued, his voice tight.

"By who?" I asked, staring at the hand on my leg as though it belonged to someone else. "Why?"

"We know the who, but not the why. His name was Terry Foster. He's known your parents for years. Went to their church. Didn't have a violent bone in his body."

My brain shifted slowly into gear. "Terry Foster . . . yeah, I know who he is. But this doesn't make sense."

"None of it makes sense. A jogger found them along the river, down by the train bridge. Terry must have ambushed them, then shot himself."

My mind was whirring, but I was having difficulty forming coherent sentences. "Are . . . you sure?"

"I identified them myself. All three. It was Terry's gun, and his prints were all over it."

"Does Wes know?"

"Not yet. I want to tell him in person, not over the phone, but I can't get in until morning. Unless you want to be the one to tell him?"

"No, you can," I said at once. "I mean, if you don't mind . . ."

His voice grew even more somber. "Of course. Listen, Clare, I can imagine how you're feeling right now. Do you have someone with you? You shouldn't be alone."

"I have friends over." Latasha and Amy's eyes were trained on me.

"Good. Listen, I'll start getting things arranged with the funeral home," Rob said. "You just concentrate on getting yourself back here, and we'll go from there. Do you need any help getting a flight?"

"No."

"There's one other thing. I'm sure you've talked about this with your parents. You're Wes's legal guardian now—did you know that?"

"Um," I stammered. "I knew . . . I knew that's what would happen if . . ."

"I know. No one could have planned for this. Your parents met with his doctor and social worker earlier today for his discharge meeting. They were going to pick him up first thing in the morning. But since you're his guardian now, you'll have to be the one to get him once you come home. Between you and me, I think it would be best if he stayed there a few more days, until we're sure he's going to handle this okay. But it's up to you."

"Okay."

"You going to be all right, kid?"

"Yeah. I don't know." I hung up and dropped the phone into my lap, unwilling to hold it any longer. My chest throbbed. Maybe I was going into shock—or maybe I was just a horrible person for not being overcome with grief.

"Clare?" Latasha asked. "What's happened?"

"My parents are dead," I said. I felt like an actor in someone else's play.

"Oh my God," Amy said, the horror I was suppressing reflected clearly in her face. "How?"

I relayed to them what my uncle had told me.

"They were shot by a friend of theirs? That doesn't make any sense," Latasha said.

I nodded woodenly. "I know, I should have asked more questions, I just . . ." I felt them then, the tears, way down in my chest. I tried to keep them there—I didn't want to cry, I didn't want to dissolve, I just wanted to figure out what the hell I was going to do, how I was going to handle this tectonic shift in my life. A wave of nausea hit me hard, doubling me over. One minute my biggest concern was whether I wanted to settle down in Seattle or move on. Now my parents were dead, and I was my brother's guardian. I had no idea what that meant.

Latasha's arms closed around me. She made gentle shushing sounds, as though I were a toddler on the verge of having a tantrum. "I'm sorry," she said. "Of course you don't know all the details, and this is hardly the time to talk about it." She put her hands on my shoulders and looked at me, her dark brown eyes wet with tears. "How can I help?"

I stood and paced around the living room, hoping movement would hold back the inevitable wave of grief. "I don't know," I said. "I don't know what to do."

"Do about what? There must be some way we can help," Amy said.

"I'm Wes's guardian now."

Latasha exhaled loudly. "Ah."

"I guess . . . I'll figure it out when I get there. I mean, I have to go home right away. I don't know for how long. At least for the funeral, and I have to make sure Wes is okay. It might take me a few days to set everything up, with his new apartment and all . . . and there will be family stuff to sort out."

Latasha watched me pace and ramble, but was strangely silent.

"What is it?" I asked.

"*Will* he be okay on his own?" Latasha asked. "Or does this mean you have to move back there, for good?" A pained expression spread across her face.

"No," I said firmly. "I'm never moving back there."

Latasha didn't respond. I turned my back and headed up the stairs, not knowing where else to go. I closed my bedroom door and sat down on the bed.

I pictured my parents' faces, smiling in a photo from the top of the Empire State Building. Taken on one of their adventures, it was the last photo they'd emailed me. My parents loved going for short weekend jaunts, and they'd dreamed of traveling to Europe once Wes and I were on our own. But Wes's illness was expensive. They never got their chance.

My breath hitched, and I let out a small gasp. All I had ever wanted, ever since Wes's problems started, was a normal life: a life with a brother who played football and dated girls; a life where I was just Clare Campbell, not the sister of the town freak; a life where we would grow up and have jobs and families and barbecues in each other's backyards.

It had all gone so incredibly wrong. Now I was an orphan—and my brother's de facto parent.

I shook my head and fought back tears. *Enough.* I told myself all the platitudes about death I'd heard over the years. *They're in a better place.* Except I didn't believe in heaven. *They're no longer suffering.* They hadn't been suffering in the first place. *This is all part of God's plan.* I really hated a God who would make plans like this. *It was their time to go.* This was the absolute worst possible time.

My hands balled into fists and pressed into my forehead as I sat doubled over on the edge of the bed. I couldn't keep the memories out now: memories of my mom's perfume as she bent over my shoulder to help me with my homework, of my dad waiting for me at the finish line of my first cross-country race, of my mom's face beaming as she brought out yet another spectacularly decorated cake for my birthday, of my dad and me sharing the newspaper over breakfast, pointing out articles of interest to each other. Gone. Gone. Gone.

Latasha knocked at the door. "You okay?"

I got up and opened it, letting my face speak for itself. She wrapped her arms around me and I finally dissolved, leaving great wet slimy patches on her shoulder.

"I guess I need to book a flight," I said, my voice muffled against her shoulder.

"I'll do it," she said. "I'll see what's available for tomorrow morning. You try and get some rest."

She kissed my salty cheeks and then closed the door softly behind her. A moment later the front door opened and closed, meaning Amy had left. I lay down on the bed, knowing rest would be a long time coming.

I reached for my phone and flipped through my emails, looking for the last one from my mom. She'd sent it a few days ago, and I hadn't responded yet. There was nothing urgent in the message, just small talk about her new hairdresser and how the pastor at church was taking a sabbatical and some young guy was coming in to take his place for the year, and how Dad had put up a few new bird feeders, these ones squirrel-proof, he hoped. She ended with her customary line: "It would be nice to hear from you once in a while, you know."

I hadn't responded. Not out of spite or anger. Life had simply gotten in the way.

I buried my face in my pillow. *Wes, oh Wes, how are you going to handle this?* What could I possibly say to comfort him? He and our parents had been locked in an eternal struggle of abuse and forgiveness—him doing the abusing and them doing the forgiving. They were the rocks he had thrown himself against time and time again. Who would absorb the impact now?

***

Latasha woke me the next morning, a cup of coffee in her hands. "You've got a flight to catch," she said. "Time to pack."

I sat on the edge of the bed, clutching the coffee cup to my chest. Latasha sorted through my clothes, searching for something suitable for a midsummer funeral. Given that I worked from home, my wardrobe consisted primarily of jeans and T-shirts in various states of rattiness.

"You're the best," I croaked. Latasha had been full of surprises ever since I'd met her in our freshman year of college in Clarkeston. She'd seemed so posh, so confident, that I'd assumed she was on the student council or part of some cringe-inducing sorority. But, as it turned out, she was president of the local chess club and an active member of the robotics society. I was an English major, operating under the illusion that I would become a great journalist one day, traveling the world in search of the stories no one else was telling.

When winter arrived that first year of college, Latasha proudly brought out her hand-knitted Ravenclaw scarf and offered to make me one. I declined. But I was intrigued by this beautiful, brilliant, bizarrely confident girl—so much so that we fell into bed together after an excess of wine just before Christmas break. We went home to our respective families, hungover and confused, and returned two weeks later to an awkward conversation in which both of us confessed we hadn't really enjoyed the experience.

We'd been best friends ever since.

Latasha continued on her brilliant path after college, earning a graduate degree from MIT and now working as a systems engineer for the NSA. When she first got the job, years ago, I teased her about working for Big Brother. But then Chelsea Manning and Edward Snowden happened, and the joke got old—or it just wasn't funny anymore. Nowadays, she didn't like to tell people what she did for a living. More often than not they would laugh awkwardly and say, "Well, there's no need to introduce myself, is there? You probably already know everything about me."

"It's not like that," she would reply, but no one believed her, and you could almost see them edging away, as though she might plant a tracker on them if they got too close. On the rare occasion someone found her job fascinating instead of creepy, they hounded her with questions she wasn't allowed to answer and tried to impress her with the technical spy knowledge they'd gained from reading cyber-thrillers.

Now, as I watched her pack my clothes, I felt grateful such a person had come into my life.

I roused myself enough to go to the bathroom, take off yesterday's makeup, and drag a brush through my hair. By this time the coffee was cool enough for me to gulp it, and some of the cobwebs cleared.

I returned to the bedroom with an armload of makeup, shampoo, and my hair dryer. Latasha stood over an already-full suitcase.

"Thank you," I said. "This feels so . . . surreal."

"I bet." Latasha looked down at the suitcase, then up again. "You know, I just wanted to mention . . . I mean, I wasn't sure if you knew . . ."

"Knew what?" *No more surprises, please.*

"Did you know Kenneth moved back to Clarkeston?"

Huh. My stomach gave a strange jolt. "No. When?"

"A few months ago. I saw it online. I was going to mention it, but . . ."

"Yeah." I knew why she hadn't. Kenneth and I had been close—very close—in college back in Clarkeston. Everyone used to assume we were together, but it wasn't like that. At least, it wasn't for me. And then I'd gone and fucked things up. We hadn't spoken since I'd left Clarkeston.

"Anyway," Latasha was saying, "you probably won't even see him. I just thought I should give you a heads-up."

I took the suitcase from her and started stuffing my toiletries into the outer pockets. "Thanks, but it doesn't matter. That was another world ago."

***

Several hours later I was watching the country pass beneath me and taking shallow breaths of recycled air. I'd changed planes in New York and was on what my dad would have called a "puddle jumper" en route to Clarkeston.

Normally, I loved flying. It had always seemed magical to me that a metal tube could transport you to another part of the world in just a few hours. After college I'd set out to experience what the rest of the world had to offer. I'd waited tables in London and Belfast, backpacked through Germany, and faked an interest in missions so I could stay with friends of my parents' pastor in Thailand and China. All the while I wrote travel articles, and miraculously even sold a few. Each time I boarded a flight to a new destination, I was filled with a sense of lightness so intense I could have flown there myself. There was adventure ahead and, above all, freedom.

But this flight was going in the wrong direction. My chest tightened, as though bricks were being laid one by one on top of my rib cage. Invisible bars descended around me, landing with an ominous thud.

I closed my eyes and focused on my breath, as shallow as it was, and told myself I was being ridiculous. This wasn't forever. I wasn't returning to my younger self, to all those years of turmoil and confusion and anger. I was a grown woman, going home for a short visit. And then I would be able to leave.

My thoughts drifted to Kenneth. What was he doing back in Clarkeston? Last I'd heard he was in Boston, having finally achieved his dream of becoming a doctor. He'd been collateral damage; another casualty of my need to escape. If I saw him, what would I say?

"Not a fan of flying?" my seatmate asked sympathetically.

I opened my eyes to look at her. She had a kind face, like someone's grandmother. Her hair was set in an old-lady perm and dyed a very unnatural shade of red. Her cheeks were wrinkled and covered in blush, and she wore a straight orange skirt with a matching blazer over a yellow blouse. It was like sitting next to someone on fire. She patted my hand, which was still gripping the armrest.

"Not really," I lied, giving her a swift smile and then turning to look out the window.

"It's very safe, you know," she told me. "Much safer than driving a car, or even going for a walk, they say."

I nodded and reached under the seat in front of me for my book.

"That's a good idea." She nodded approvingly. "Distract yourself. What is it you're reading?"

I showed her the cover of Justin Cronin's *The Passage*.

"Goodness, that's a big one," she said. "What's it about?"

"Um . . . vampires. Sort of."

She frowned at this. "I never did understand the whole vampire fascination. But my granddaughters are all Edward this and Jacob that. Is it that sort of thing?"

"Not really."

"I would hope not, at your age. I've just been to visit them, and they're growing up too fast. Are you headed to home or away from it?"

Wasn't that the question? "I grew up in Clarkeston. I live in Seattle now."

"Ah, visiting family, then?"

I pressed my lips together. "Kind of."

She raised her eyebrows. "I see. The complicated kind. Have you been back recently?"

"Not really." I opened my book again as a signal to end the conversation, but she plowed onward.

"Do you have children of your own?"

"No."

"They are both a blessing and a curse," she said, nodding sagely. "Who did you say you were visiting?"

Perhaps brutal honestly would do the trick. "I'm going to bury my parents. They were murdered yesterday." I held her eyes for a little longer than was socially acceptable.

Her wrinkled mouth formed a little "O." Then she placed her hand on my arm, gripping it tightly when I flinched and tried to move it away. "You poor thing," she whispered. "What happened?"

"I don't know," I said, twisting my arm so that it released from her grasp. "They were shot by a friend, I think. I'll find out more once I'm home." At least, I hoped I would. I couldn't figure it out. Why would an old friend have killed them in cold blood? I'd met Terry a few times. He and his wife had come over to play cribbage with my parents. He'd seemed as normal as the rest of them.

My seatmate looked scandalized. "You don't say? One of those folks who's gone sick in the head, do you think?"

"Who?"

She tutted. "Insane, we used to call it. I know it's not the politically correct term anymore, but I call it like I see it."

"Do you mean . . . mental health problems?"

"It wasn't like this in my day. 'Depression' was no excuse for not doing a hard day's work and looking after your family." She huffed loudly. "It's probably all these cell-phone waves. Or parents who don't give their children the right kind of discipline, if you catch my meaning. An entire generation raised on computers, with both parents working—well, it's not hard to see why things have started to break down."

I stared at her incredulously, completely at a loss for words, but she seemed to take my silence as agreement.

"Anyway, as you said, you'll find out more once you're home. But don't be surprised if it turns out to be one of these 'mental health problems,' as you call it. You see more and more of it these days. Do you have siblings?"

"A brother," I croaked out, having found my voice.

She sighed loudly. "Well, that's good. He can take care of you."

I actually smiled at her. It wasn't a happy smile, although the thought of my brother taking care of me would have been amusing before today. I smiled because I pitied her and her narrow, fearful worldview. And because if I didn't smile, I would disintegrate in the seat beside her and have to endure her "comfort" for the next several hours.

"My brother is mentally ill," I said. "So I'm the one who will be taking care of him."

I was almost finished with my book by the time we began our descent.

The pressure in my ears grew, along with the pressure in my chest. It was like breathing through a thick blanket. I tried to keep reading, but Cronin's monsters could no longer distract me from what lay ahead. The problem was, I had no idea what lay ahead.

I looked out the window at the tops of the trees. It was hard to believe we were nearing any sort of civilization; from our vantage point up in the air, we might have entered the Mesozoic Era, when the world was little more than foliage. Clarkeston wasn't one of those iconic Maine fishing villages you see on postcards. It was a midsized college town near the Canadian border, about two hours inland. When Wes and I were kids our parents would take us to the coast on summer weekends, to play in salt water and sand dunes and swaying grasses on rocky beaches. Maybe that's why I loved Seattle—it reminded me of home, without reminding me of home.

Too soon, the jarring rumble of asphalt beneath our seats signaled that the trip in the magic tube was over. I had been transported to another world.

The rickety stairs leading down to the tarmac creaked as I descended, as though they might give up the ghost at any moment. Every time I came home I was amazed how rural it felt—the weeds growing out of cracks in the runway; the tiny, one-gate airport surrounded by forest; the John Deere hats and fanny packs on the passengers around me. I peeled off my sweater in the July heat, wondering if Latasha had packed mosquito spray.

I'll just borrow some from Mom. Then my heart contracted and I stopped cold just outside the terminal entrance. *Shit.* I moved to the side to let a family go in ahead of me and texted Latasha.

Arrived. About to meet my uncle.

She texted back right away. Take care of yourself. Keep me posted.

The terminal was exactly as I remembered it. Large windows lined one wall, where people could watch the planes and wait for their friends and families to arrive. There was one small carousel for luggage. A back-lit billboard advertising the town's oldest hotel stood behind it. Against one wall was a rack of tourist brochures and postcards. It was small, quaint, and quiet, just like the people here.

"Are you going to be okay, dear?" My seatmate from the plane had appeared beside me. She had clearly gotten over the shock of hearing about my brother. "Is someone here to meet you?"

"My uncle is coming, thank you," I said. I took a bottle of water out of my bag, wishing for something stronger.

"You know, if you grew up here, then you probably know my husband," she said, indicating the stout, gray-haired man who was walking toward us, blowing his nose into a large beige handkerchief.

I did a double take. "Mr. Sweeney?"

"Hello, hello," he said, looking at me curiously after kissing his wife.

"This is probably one of your old students, Richard," the woman said. "Though I suppose you can't remember them all."

"Yeah, I took English 201 and 301 with you," I said. He held out his hand, having stuffed the handkerchief back into his pocket, and I shook it. "Clare Campbell."

"Clare . . . Clare . . ." he muttered. "Yes, of course. Very bright. Wanted to be a writer. How did that work out?"

"Well, I'm a copywriter now," I said. "So . . . it sort of worked out."

"Clare's parents were murdered yesterday," the woman said to her husband in a scandalized whisper. "The poor dear has just come home."

"Oh, of course. I heard about your parents. Tragic," Mr. Sweeney said. He pulled out his handkerchief again. At first I thought he was going to offer it to me for my nonexistent tears, but then he bent over in a coughing fit so severe flecks of spittle flew everywhere—including onto my face.

"Are you okay?" I asked. "Here, would you like this?" I offered him the water bottle.

He looked at me as though I had just offered him a bottle of rat poison. "What's the meaning of this?" he spat, backing away. His eyes, congenial and warm just a moment before, narrowed into sharp slits.

"It's just . . . for your cough . . ." I said, confused.

I was saved by a gruff voice behind me. "Hey there, Clare Bear." It was Rob, with the same salt-and-pepper hair, beard, and moustache he'd always worn, along with the little wire glasses he'd had since I could remember. He was maybe a little thicker around the middle, and his hair was a little thinner, but other than that he was the same old Rob, my mother's big brother. He was wearing blue jeans and a red button-down plaid shirt. Without any more preliminaries, he wrapped me in a bear hug.

Rob knew a thing or two about grief. He'd lived just across the train tracks from us when we were growing up, raising his daughter on his own after my aunt Karen died of cancer. Tracey and I were the same age, and we had counted her as our third sibling. Then Tracey died in an accident—a fall in one of the outbuildings, what we called the hen pen. Wes had been the one to find her, broken on the concrete floor. He'd become obsessed with her memory. Our parents had moved us into town the next year, and Rob had followed a few years later. He threw himself into his work at the car dealership until he retired last year.

"You'll be okay, then, dear?" Mrs. Sweeney asked.

"Yes, thank you."

She patted me on the cheek before I could move out of reach. Mr. Sweeney stood behind her, still glaring at me, twisting his handkerchief as though trying to tear it to pieces.

"Thanks for coming," I said to Rob. "How are you?"

"It's been a shitty day," he answered. Now that I looked closer, I could see signs of aging and stress that hadn't been there before—or that I hadn't noticed. Deep wrinkles framed his eyes, and his cheeks sagged. His skin looked thin and papery. "But who cares about me? How you holdin' up?"

I shrugged. What was I supposed to say? Fine? Horrible? Scared out of my wits? I settled on "Fine."

"Yeah, me too," he said sarcastically. We were silent for a moment, watching the luggage carousel move in its perpetual circle as passengers gathered around it with their friends and families.

"Did you talk to Wes?" I asked. "How'd he take the news? I tried calling him before I boarded the plane, but there was no answer."

"He didn't take it too well. Not surprising. While I was there they came and got him—said they needed to do some more tests before he was released. That's probably why he couldn't take your call."

"Oh, Jesus."

"I don't think Jesus is on our side."

In another world, I would have said, "Don't let Mom and Dad hear you say that." Rob had been as religious as the rest of our family for most of his life, but the loss of his wife and daughter had taken its toll. He was the one relative I could be myself around.

I tried and failed to suppress a yawn. My head felt as though it had been injected with quicksand. My thoughts, which had been racing all day, had slowed to a crawl. *You're slower than cold molasses*, my mother used to say.

Rob put his arm around me. "C'mon. Let's get out of here."

I nodded. "I want to see Wes."

"Not tonight. Visiting hours are over. I told them we'd be back in the morning. I'm guessing you'll want to go to your parents' home eventually, but I'm not letting you sleep there on your own tonight. You can come home with me. We'll figure out which end is up in the morning."

"Can we get pizza?" Rob's idea of gourmet was to order delivery from Pizza Hut rather than throwing a frozen pie in the oven.

"It's being delivered in half an hour," he said, squeezing my shoulders.

The ride in Rob's rust-colored old pickup was mostly silent. The truck reminded me painfully of my dad's pickup, the one I'd learned to drive in. Same worn-out seats and sweaty-man smell. There was even a cassette player in the dash. I gazed out the window at the turn-of-the-century clapboard houses and huge lots—such a contrast to the tony townhomes and postage-stamp yards of Seattle. There was just so much *space* here. So why did I feel so trapped?

"How are things in Seattle treating you?" Rob said, breaking the silence.

"They're great. Work is steady, but I passed off my active contracts to another copywriter I know. I won't have to do any work while I'm here."

"You got a boyfriend?"

"I date now and again, but there's no one serious."

"Why not?"

I shrugged. "Just haven't found the right one, I guess." It was the standard line I used to give my mom whenever she pressed me on the issue.

"But you're happy?"

"I am." At least, I had been. I didn't know what I was now. "How about you?"

He snorted. "What, am I happy, or am I dating?"

"Both." I looked at him curiously, waiting for his answer. We'd never spent much one-on-one time before; we usually visited each other in the context of a family gathering. I wondered if I'd crossed a line.

"Well, I don't know. I guess I'm happy," he said. "Depends on how you define happiness, I suppose. I'd be a lot happier if . . . well, you know. If Karen and Tracey were still around. Not to mention your folks."

I put my hand on his arm, which was clenched on the steering wheel. "I'm sorry, I didn't mean—"

"Don't you be sorry for anything," he said gruffly. "Anyway, about the other thing . . ."

"The other thing?"

"Well, there's this lady, Diana, who comes into the coffee shop in the mornings, same time as I do. We've started . . . just chatting, you know? She's a widow, and she's new in town, so I've been taking her out places, showing her around."

"You've got a girlfriend!" I smiled, the first real smile since I'd heard the news.

"Well, I don't know if you'd call her that—"

"Whatever it is, I think it's wonderful. You deserve the best."

He grunted but was saved from further commentary when we pulled into the driveway of his apartment building.

He insisted on lugging my suitcase up the stairs.

"Keeps me fit," he puffed. "Never take the elevator if I can help it."

No sooner had he put my suitcase down on the futon in the spare room than the doorbell rang with the pizza delivery. We sat down at the Formica table in the kitchen, and he turned on the TV in the corner of the room.

"Maybe you should ask your new lady friend to help you decorate," I said, my cheeks stuffed with pepperoni, as I eyed the sparse surroundings.

"Ha ha," he retorted, stealing an olive off my plate. "I'm—what do you call it? A minimalist. I thought you would like that sort of thing. Very modern."

I grinned. "It's perfect." We smiled goofily at each other for a moment, but then I was jolted back to reality when I heard my parents' names.

"Police are still investigating the double murder and suicide that happened in downtown Clarkeston on Saturday night," the newscaster said. "Local residents Bud and Peggy Campbell were allegedly shot and killed by another longtime resident, Terry Foster, who then allegedly shot himself. According to sources close to the couple, Foster was known to them, and he even attended the same church, Northside Baptist Church."

Pictures of my parents and of Terry Foster came up on the screen. I was suddenly more tired than I'd ever been in my life.

"Want me to turn it off?" Rob asked quietly.

"Yeah."

He grabbed the remote and jabbed it at the television, turning the screen mercifully black. I stared down at my plate, no longer hungry. "Do they know why he did it?"

"If they do, they haven't told me yet. But I'm guessing the police will want to have a chat with you, in case you have some information that could help them."

"I don't," I said. "I hadn't even talked to them in . . . well, too long."

"Don't beat yourself up. At any rate, the police chief is a friend of mine. He's a good man. They'll find out what really happened, and why."

He fixed me with such a piercing gaze that I felt I had no other option than to nod in agreement. "So . . . I guess we should talk about . . . whatever happens next," I said.

"Eventually. But it can wait until morning. Why don't you get some sleep? We'll be in better shape to make decisions tomorrow."

I stood and kissed him on the top of the head, muttering, "Thanks."

I washed the day's sweat and tears off my face and brushed away the taste of pepperoni. I was exhausted, but as I climbed under the covers of the futon, my mind lurched from one disturbing thought to the next.

Did they suffer, or were their deaths immediate? What possible motivation could this man have had to kill them? Were they specifically targeted, or would he have killed anyone who had crossed his path that night? Had my father died protecting my mother?

If only the attack had happened at home, he might have been able to defend them. When we were kids, his hunting rifles always hung on a rack behind his desk. I admired the gleaming wood, though I didn't dare touch them. Dad used to take Wes and me hunting in the woods behind our home in the country, back before we moved into town. I could still remember the way the recoil had knocked me backward, flat onto my bottom, the first time I ever fired. Wes had stood there and laughed—until the same thing happened to him.

After Wes started causing trouble, my dad removed the firing pins from all his guns. He locked the pins and the ammo in the safe, then hid the guns under a pile of thick blankets in the basement crawl space. It wasn't the best hiding place, but when I asked him why he didn't just get rid of them entirely, he told me that he couldn't. A man needs to be able to defend his home and family. That was always his mantra. Defend your home and family. Work hard for your home and family. Sacrifice for your home and family.

That was the other reason I couldn't sleep.

Others would ask Latasha's question about moving back home. I was asking it myself. Was it now my obligation to move back to Clarkeston to keep an eye on Wes? To make sure he settled peacefully back into society, drive him to doctors' appointments, buy him shoes when his wore out, and make sure he took his medication? My parents had done all this for him for years and would have done it again once he was released from the hospital.

Was that the price of love, of family, of duty, of honor? I stared up at the stippled ceiling, as if hoping an answer would come to me from the stars. But there were no answers. There was only fear, and grief, and, above all, guilt.

CHAPTER THREE

I awoke to the smell of coffee and the agony of the impossible decisions ahead of me.

"Morning," Rob grunted as I padded out into the kitchen and ran my fingers through my hair.

"So it is," I replied, glancing at the clock on the microwave: 10:21 a.m. Damn jet lag. He handed me a mug of coffee, black. I thanked him and headed for the fridge for some milk. I sat down at the kitchen table, and we regarded each other soberly.

"How'd you sleep?" he asked.

"Fine."

"Ready to talk logistics?"

I nodded. He let me take a few drags of caffeine, then began. "There are a few things that need to happen. I'm the executor of the will, so I'll need to go see their lawyer, Al Irvine. You're welcome to come with me."

I nodded again, and he continued.

"I've spoken to Pastor Steve at the church—he's the one filling in while Pastor Dean is on sabbatical. Kid looks like he's barely old enough to shave, let alone conduct a funeral service, but Dean is in Zambia and won't make it back in time."

I scowled at this. My parents would have wanted their longtime friend and pastor to conduct the service. Well, my father would have. My mother had always joked that she wanted her remains cremated and scattered around the world, in all the places she'd never had a chance to visit. I guessed neither of them was going to get their wish.

"Sure, whatever," I said.

"If it works for you, we'll have the wake the day after tomorrow and the funeral the day after that, on Thursday."

"Do we have to have a wake?" I knew the answer even as I asked the question. The prospect of hours of small talk and commiseration with my parents' thousand friends, most of whom I barely knew, was about as appealing as the time Mom dragged me to one of her quilting circles.

I half expected Rob to reprimand me, as he might have done when I was a kid, but instead he smiled sadly. "I felt the same when Karen and Tracey died. But if I hadn't done it, I'd be regretting it now. It's an important part of saying good-bye. Even for you."

I mumbled my assent.

"The coroner told me he has to cremate the bodies, so there won't be a viewing, but people will want to come pay their respects."

I looked up. "Why does he have to cremate them?"

"He didn't say, really. Cited some kind of health regulation. Are you okay with that?"

I shrugged. "It's fine. That's what Mom would have wanted anyway."

"So here's what I recommend," Rob said. "Leave Wes where he is for a little while. Let's go see the lawyer. Then we'll go to the funeral home and make sure everything is ready there. We'll need to write up an obituary. I can do it if you want, but you're the wordsmith. Why don't you take a crack at it, and I can fill in any blanks. *Then* we'll go see Wes."

I shook my head. "I want to see Wes first."

Rob looked as if he was going to argue, but changed his mind. "Okay," he said. "Then that's what we'll do."

"I think—please don't take this the wrong way, but I'd like to see him on my own first. I mean, he's free to go, right? I'll pick him up, and we'll spend a little time together. I just want to make sure he's okay before I do any of that other stuff. He's been in and out of there so many times."

And it all started because of me. Of course, there had been other arrests since that first one. It wasn't entirely my fault . . .

"The least I can do is pick him up and bring him home," I said.

"You can take my car," Rob said. "I'll take the truck and meet with Al and the funeral director. Let me know when you've got Wes. Sound good?"

I got up from the table and wrapped my arms around his neck. "I'm so glad you're here," I said, kissing him on the cheek.

"Hey, Clare," he called out as I was about to leave. "When I went to see Wes yesterday, the hospital seemed . . . busier than usual. Nothing to worry about, I'm sure. Just thought I'd give you a heads-up."

***

I drove along the river that bisected the town. I passed the train bridge but averted my eyes. *Not now.* This side of the river boasted the downtown, the college, the high school, an art gallery, a theater, and government offices, as well as beautiful turn-of-the-century mansions lining the riverbank. I had no idea who lived in them, but they were meticulously maintained, with fancy cars in the driveways and manicured lawns. Why anyone who could afford a BMW would choose to live in Clarkeston was beyond me. We had lived on the north side, with the used-car lots and the abandoned cotton mill. It was the Clarkeston equivalent of the other side of the tracks.

A few minutes later I pulled into the parking lot of the hospital—half regional hospital, half regional psych ward. We were lucky to have it here in our town, I supposed. It was a beast of a building, all gray concrete and hideous orange trim. I'd only visited Wes here once before, two years ago.

He'd been in and out over the past several years. Not long after his first release, he broke into my grandmother's house and kicked in the walls with his steel-toed army boots, convinced she was hiding the bodies of dead children, victims of a child-trafficking ring. My grandmother called the police, and Wes was sent back.

The sensation of being caged that always plagued my first few days at home grew stronger as I stepped toward the entrance of the psych hospital. My feet were like magnets being pulled toward the center of the earth. Every step was an act of will. Once I had Wes, there would be no giving him back.

I was unprepared for the scene that assaulted my senses the moment I entered through the glass doors. Busier than usual was an understatement. The waiting room was crammed with people—some sitting, some standing. One middle-aged lady writhed on the floor, but no one was helping her. A small boy crouched in a planter in the corner, his arms wrapped around the thin trunk of a fake tree. His mother pleaded with him to come out, but he was deep in conversation with someone else—the tree, perhaps. Several people were gathered around the receptionist's desk, trying to drown out the moaning and screaming with their own shouts and complaints. The receptionist was telling them to take a number and a seat. Her eyes were red-rimmed, and her face stretched into an unsightly yawn as she repeated the same information to each new supplicant.

"I told you, you need to fill out these forms," she told a man with deep gullies around his eyes.

"The doctor said you'd be able to get her in right away," he protested. "Please, I just can't deal with her anymore."

"Fill out the forms," the receptionist repeated.

"What's wrong with him?" The young mother was now at the desk, having left her son in the planter. "He was fine a few days ago. What's going on? What's wrong with *all* these people?"

"Ma'am, I'm not a doctor. I have no idea," the receptionist said, handing her a clipboard.

"I don't want to fill out forms, I want someone to tell me what's wrong with my son!" The mother threw the clipboard down on the receptionist's desk and moved in closer. There was a general murmur of assent behind her, and other voices joined, in demanding answers.

I couldn't believe what I was seeing. This was more than busy—it was chaos. What was happening? I took advantage of the turmoil around the front desk and squeezed through the crowd and around the corner to the elevators. I knew from my last visit that they were keyed, but the door to the stairwell was open. I slipped in, closing it gratefully behind me. The bedlam of the waiting room faded as I climbed the stairs to the second floor.

Apparently the stairwell was the only peaceful place in the building. The second floor was a hive of frantic activity. Intercoms blared requests for doctors and supplies. A man strapped to a gurney against the wall shouted, "It's the end! The devil has come for us! Repent!" A sweaty orderly grabbed the gurney and ran with it down the hall. The man's voice only grew shriller.

I pressed my back against the wall. Two nurses shouted at each other from behind a long counter, to be heard over the intercom. One wore a stiff white mask around her mouth and nose. Another nurse was slumped in a corner, crying.

I made a beeline for the desk, dodging a bin of linens that nearly took my arm off.

"Hi, I'm here to see—" I began, but the woman at the desk waved a hand at me and shouted into a phone.

"You heard me; I want the director on the line right now. Half of my nurses are telling me they won't work in these conditions. And I don't blame them. He's where? Well, tell him he can't dodge this one. We're falling apart at the seams here. Fine. You do that."

She dropped the phone in disgust, then gave me a furious look. "Who the hell let you in?"

Was I not supposed to be here? I opened my mouth to answer but was cut off by the sound of a scream. A teenage girl tore down the hall, ripping off her clothes as she ran. Two masked orderlies raced after her.

I turned back to the nurse. "What's going on here?" A chill shot down my spine, giving me goose bumps.

"You need to leave, now. No visitors."

"I can't leave. I'm here to pick up my brother, Wes Campbell. He's being discharged today."

She looked at me suspiciously, but then directed her frustration at her keyboard. "Name?"

"Wes Campbell. I'm his sister, Clare."

She continued to glare at her screen.

"Really, what's going on?" I asked. "Why is it like this?" Last time I'd been here it had been a ghost town.

"I'm not at liberty to say," she said curtly. She looked at me again. "Our notes say that Wes is to be discharged into the care of his parents. Are they with you?"

I dropped my gaze. "No. It's just me. They were killed over the weekend." It felt so odd to say that out loud. Couldn't the rest of the world feel the void where my parents' lives had been?

"I'm so sorry to hear that," the nurse said, her tone softening.

"Thank you. So . . . my brother?"

"I'm afraid it won't be that simple. You're his new guardian, I take it?" I nodded. "Then we'll have to schedule a meeting with you, his social worker, and his psychiatrist before he can be released."

"Why? Didn't my parents already have that meeting?"

"Yes, they did. But if he's being released into your care, then you need to have all the information they did."

"Okay. When can we have this meeting?"

She frowned back down at her screen. "We had a cancellation; otherwise it would have to be next week at this rate. I can squeeze you in this afternoon. Does two o'clock work?"

"Sure. Can I see Wes in the meantime?"

"That's the other thing. Your brother has been moved."

"Where?"

"Looks like he's over in the main hospital wing."

"Why?" I demanded, my voice getting louder. "Is he hurt?"

"You'll have to ask his attending physician," she said, the tension returning to her voice.

"And who's that?"

"You'll have to ask at the desk. Section E. North wing." She leaned in closer. "Normally I'd need to escort you off this floor, but as you noticed we're rather occupied here. Take the elevator up to the fourth floor, then walk all the way down the hallway. There will be a set of doors at the end. Put the code five-three-one into the keypad on the wall, and the doors will unlock. Make sure there aren't any patients around; we don't want any escapees. I'll let them know you're coming." She started fielding anxious questions from someone else who had been hovering at the desk.

I took the stairs up two more flights and then sprinted down the hallway. My mind kept swirling with the same questions over and over again: Why had they moved him? Had something happened to him? I thought back to Wes's story about the scientist who had killed himself. Had Wes . . . ?

I punched the code into the keypad so fast I got the numbers wrong and had to do it again. I took a deep breath in an attempt to calm myself, but adrenaline had taken over. Rob had warned me that the hospital was busier than usual, and it was, but that didn't explain what I'd seen. Something was very, very wrong here.

"I need to see my brother," I said, breathless, to the first person I saw. "Where is he?"

The startled orderly pointed me to yet another nurses' station. This section of the hospital seemed less chaotic than the psych ward, thank God, but there was still something . . . off. A single nurse sat behind the counter, her fingers flying over a keyboard. Several others buzzed in and out of rooms like angry bees. The nurse behind the counter glanced away after noticing me, as though hoping I'd disappear. She slipped out from behind the nurses' station and tried to walk around me, but I stepped firmly in front of her.

"I'm here to see my brother. They told me he was moved here. Wes Campbell."

"If you'll just wait over—"

"I can't wait! Is he okay? Did something happen to him? I don't even know why he was moved. No one would tell me."

"Your name?"

"Clare Campbell."

"Have a seat, Clare, and someone will be with you shortly." Her tone brooked no argument, so I sat in one of the chairs lining a small nook near the nurses' desk. The plastic squeaked uncomfortably beneath me. My insides twisted as I imagined all the possible scenarios.

I watched the nurses, their eyes shadowed and rimmed red. There was no idle chitchat or discussions about grandchildren or summer vacations. There were two other occupants of our tiny waiting room, but both were staring at their phones and avoiding eye contact.

Finally a nurse stopped in front of my chair. Her navy scrubs had gray and white kittens gamboling across them. "Clare Campbell?"

"That's me." I peeled myself off the plastic chair.

"This way." She walked briskly down the hallway, more drill sergeant than nurse. She opened the door to a small office, and I stepped inside after her, expecting to see Wes. But no one else was there. My heart jolted.

"I understand you're concerned about your brother," she said, closing the door behind us.

"Is he okay?"

She smiled tightly, deepening the wrinkles in her cheeks. "Yes. There's nothing to worry about."

I relaxed. So he wasn't mortally injured, and he hadn't tried to kill anyone—himself included.

"So where is he?"

"You can see him in a minute; don't worry. I just wanted to touch base with you first, since I understand you're his guardian now. Is that right?"

"Yes. Can you tell me what happened? Why did he get moved?"

She waved a wrinkled hand through the air. "Nothing happened. We just wanted to run a few more tests on him before he was released, make sure everything was okay."

That's what Rob had told me, but they hadn't explained it to him either. "Why? He was supposed to be released yesterday. Wouldn't any tests have been done before then?"

The nurse's smile faltered, then recovered. "Well, I don't know all the details, only that his physician ordered the tests. But I assure you it's nothing to worry about; all perfectly standard."

"What were they for?"

Her hand fluttered again, dismissing my concerns. "Basic blood work, the usual. Seeing how he's reacting to his new medication."

"Yeah, but why move him over here? Couldn't you do that on the psych ward?"

She put her arm around my shoulders—I flinched—and opened the door. "I understand you've having the family meeting this afternoon. I'm sure all of your questions will be answered then."

"So is Wes free to go?" I wanted my questions answered *now*, not later.

"We're still waiting for the results, so it could be as late as tomorrow. But again, they'll have more information for you in the meeting. Now if you'll just follow me, Wes is in a room right around the corner."

I followed her down the hallway until she stopped in front of a white door marked 416B. She reached inside one of her kitten-festooned pockets and withdrew a small gold key on a white plastic keychain. I frowned. I didn't know hospital doors had locks on them. But knowing my brother, maybe it was a sensible precaution. She turned the key in the lock, then rapped on the door before entering.

"Your sister is here, Wes."

Before I could say anything, I was engulfed in a ferocious hug. I returned the embrace as best I could, ignoring the chains and piercings pressing uncomfortably against me. Then we stepped apart, and I got a good look at my big brother.

He'd gained a little weight since the last time I'd seen him. His round, still-boyish face was marked with tattoos on both sides of his temples and cheeks—crosses on one side, tribal markings on the other. His first tattoo had been a black spider on the side of his skull. He'd attempted to do one on the other side himself; I still couldn't tell what it was supposed to be. He must have been fifteen at the time, and our parents had nearly lost it. But they soon got used to it, as one tattoo followed another—some professional, some not so much. *I'd rather buy tattoos than food*, he used to say. But it didn't look like he was starving, at any rate.

He was attempting a Mohawk with what was left of his hair, thinned by years of drug use, malnourishment, and now medication. He'd gained some new piercings since my last visit: the other eyebrow, and the space beneath his bottom lip. His tangled beard, naturally blond but dyed orange to match the fauxhawk, almost hid the tattoo that read "Tracey" across his neck. Years after her death, Wes had become convinced she was communicating with him from the spirit world. I wondered if he still believed that.

"Hey, sis," he said, showing black and yellow teeth.

"Hey. How are you?"

He shrugged. "I'm a fucking guinea pig, and Mom and Dad are dead. How do you think I am?"

I glanced nervously at the nurse, who had pursed her lips.

"I'll leave you two alone for a minute," she said. Then she pointed at what looked like a doorbell on the wall. "If you need anything, just ring this."

"Yeah, right," Wes muttered as the nurse left, leaving the door ajar.

"Are you sure you're okay?" I asked. "All they told me was that they needed to do some more routine tests before you could leave."

"Routine, my ass. They didn't do this any of the other times I was discharged."

"Well, maybe that's because this time you're getting out of here for good," I suggested hopefully.

"That's for sure. I'm never coming back to this hellhole."

I sat down in a chair beside the bed, but Wes stayed standing. It seemed to be a rather nice hospital room, with a single bed, two chairs, and a bevy of tubes and equipment hanging from the walls. There was even a window looking out on the parking lot below. But why the lock on the door? Maybe they all had locks on them and I'd never noticed.

"How are you feeling about . . . Mom and Dad?" I asked tentatively.

He responded by baring his teeth and growling. "Let's just say that the motherfucker who shot them is lucky he killed himself. Otherwise he'd have me to deal with."

I shot a nervous glance toward the hallway. "You can't say things like that. That's how you got yourself here in the first place, remember?"

His face darkened even more, and I flinched. Wrong thing to say.

He stomped over to the window. "So when are you getting me out?"

"I don't know exactly. I have to meet with your social worker and psychiatrist first. The meeting's this afternoon, though, so hopefully you can leave later today. But the nurse said we had to wait for the test results, so you might have to stay here one more night."

"Fuck that. Let's just go right now."

"I don't think that's a good idea."

He huffed. "Still following the rules, eh? How long are you home for?"

"I . . . I don't know," I said, caught off guard. "I haven't booked my return flight yet."

"You staying with Uncle Rob?"

"I did last night. I don't know where I'll stay tonight. Maybe I'll go home."

He nodded approvingly. "That's where I want to go. If they'd stop doing experiments on me, that is."

"They're not experiments. They're just tests to make sure you're healthy," I pointed out.

He snorted. "Whatever. I know what's really going on."

I was about to ask him what was really going on but caught myself in time. I didn't want to get into it. We'd have plenty of time for conspiracy theories later.

He slammed his hand against the window, making me jump, then pressed his forehead to the glass. A foggy patch appeared near his mouth.

I glanced back toward the open door. The kitten nurse was headed toward us.

"How are we doing in here?" she asked.

"Fine," I said. Wes just glared. "Um, I'm going to get myself a coffee. Do you want anything?"

"Yeah. Coffee. Black," he said.

"Is that all right?" I asked the nurse. "Can I get some food and bring it in here?"

She nodded. "That's fine, but Wes needs to stay here."

"I'll be right back," I told him. He had already turned back to the window, both hands pressed against the glass as though in surrender. I stepped into the hallway and waited while the nurse locked the door.

"Why are you locking it?" I asked, pitching my voice low so he wouldn't be able to hear me.

"We don't normally have psychiatric patients on this side," she explained. "It's just a precaution."

"Has he tried to get out?"

"Twice today," she said, giving me a significant look. "I left the door open while you were in there because I thought it might make you more comfortable, but I had a security officer keep an eye on it."

"Sorry about the trouble," I muttered. "Can I get you anything from the cafeteria?"

She raised an eyebrow and shook her head. "Just come back to the desk when you're ready to see him again."

I took the elevator down to the main level, my head swimming. This was already more complicated than I'd anticipated. Jet lag and stress and grief pulled on my nerves. I wondered if it was too early for a martini. *Later*, I told myself.

My phone buzzed in my purse, and I pulled it out. It was Latasha.

"Hey," I answered.

"How is it going?" she asked. "I've been worried about you."

"Thanks. It's okay." I told her about the chaos at the hospital and Wes's unexpected tests.

"I'm sorry to hear that," she said. "Did your brother seem . . . okay?"

"As okay as he ever does. Oh, shit."

"What?"

"Nothing. I'm fine. Everything is fine. I just . . . have to go."

Kenneth Chu was walking toward me.

CHAPTER FOUR

"Clare." His body was rigid. He wore a white lab coat and held a tablet tight in one hand. A stethoscope hung from his neck.

I tried to smile, but my face was stiff and uncooperative, even as my stomach churned and my heart rattled against my rib cage. Latasha had warned me, but I hadn't really thought I'd see him. The years had been kind: he'd lost some of his college roundness; his body was lean and his high cheekbones more pronounced. His dark hair was brushed back off his forehead. His eyes were the same—soft, warm . . . and piercing.

"Hi," I said.

"I heard about your parents. I'm sorry."

"Thank you."

"I wondered if you would come back."

Ouch. I looked away.

"I didn't mean it that way," he said quickly. "It's just—"

"It's okay. How are you?"

"Fine. Busy."

"Latasha told me you'd moved back home."

He nodded. "How's Latasha?"

I managed a small smile this time. "She's great. Soaring career and all."

"Great."

We stood awkwardly for a few seconds. I gestured toward the cafeteria. "Well, I was just going to get a coffee. I should—"

"Yeah. Fine."

I took a step away, then stopped and forced myself to look at him. "I know this is several years too late. But . . . I'm sorry. About what happened. I've regretted it."

He pressed his lips together. "Which part?"

I looked at the floor, unsure of what to say.

"Never mind," he said. "It doesn't matter." The shadow of a smile flitted across his face. "It was a long time ago, Clare. We've both moved on. At least, I know I have."

"Of course you have," I stammered. "I didn't think—"

"You didn't think I'd pine after you forever?" His laugh was forced. "I did, for a while. Too long, maybe. But I'm over it now. What's it been, nine years?"

"Something like that."

"Long enough. So why are you here? In the hospital, that is?"

"Oh. Wes. My brother. He's being released today."

Kenneth raised a dark eyebrow. "I didn't know he was here. Is he injured?"

"No, he's been in the psych ward . . . for a while."

"Ah. I see. Sorry."

"It's fine." *Fine. Great. Sorry.* So many meaningless words. *What happened to the two of us?*

You know exactly what happened, my bitchy inner voice told me. But despite the way we'd parted, it felt good to see an old friend right now. "Do you want to join me?" I asked, gesturing toward the cafeteria.

He looked at his watch. "I could probably spare a few minutes. The coffee here isn't great, but at least it's caffeine."

"That's all I need. Jet lag is not my friend." We ordered our coffees and sat down in a couple of gray metal chairs around a small table.

He was right; the coffee was pretty bad. I made a mental note to get a fresh cup for Wes before I went back up, and to add plenty of sugar.

"How long have you been back?" he asked.

"Just a day," I said. "Got in last night."

"It's a horrible reason to come back home. I can't imagine how you must be feeling."

"Not great," I muttered.

"And Wes being released . . . was that supposed to happen before . . ."

"Yeah. They were going to pick him up. But I'm his new guardian now, so they have to do the family meeting with me before they can let him out, and they did some extra tests, and it's all a little . . . overwhelming."

"I can imagine," he said. "And it's been really . . . busy here lately, so things are probably taking longer than usual."

"Why *is* it so busy?" I asked. "I especially noticed it over in the psych ward. I've never seen the hospital like this. It's frightening."

He frowned into his coffee cup. "There's been a rise in . . . erratic behavior, for lack of a better term. Remember how I have an aunt with schizophrenia? And there's your brother, of course. It reminds me of that, in a way—as if there's been an increase in schizophrenia, but that doesn't make sense. This past week in particular has been intense. A colleague told me that they called in the CDC a few days ago to help figure out what's happening here."

"The Centers for Disease Control? That seems a bit over the top, doesn't it?"

He shrugged. "It's their job to step in when the state health department feels overwhelmed or out of its league. There's a staff meeting later today, so hopefully we'll get an update."

"What are the symptoms like? You said erratic behavior; what do you mean?"

He hesitated. "I shouldn't be telling you this, but when I heard about your parents . . . well, you deserve to know. Some of the people who've been admitted in the past few days are completely withdrawn. Talking to themselves or to people who aren't there; unable to remember loved ones. Typical symptoms of dementia, except these patients aren't old. But most of the patients are more like . . ."

"Like Wes."

"Like Wes at his unmedicated worst," he admitted.

"So you think the man who killed my parents . . ."

"I can't say for certain, of course, but it fits the pattern."

I must have looked stricken, because Kenneth leaned in and said, "Hey, you've got enough to worry about. You just focus on taking care of yourself."

We avoided each other's gaze for a few seconds. Then he said, "I know this is the last place you want to be." There was bitterness in his voice, but it was soft, like an echo. "But . . . it's good to see you again. I just wish it were under better circumstances."

"Yeah. Me too."

"How are you really?" he asked. "Before all this, I mean. Were you happy?"

I remembered Rob asking me the same thing as we drove from the airport. "I was," I answered, truthfully. "I don't know how I'm going to feel . . . going forward." A sense of unease hovered in my chest. "And you? Are you happy?"

"As happy as a recently divorced single father can be, I suppose." His eyes crinkled when he smiled.

I flushed. "I didn't know. I'm sorry."

"It's okay. It was my fault. Workaholics don't make good husbands, or so I'm told. It's part of the reason I moved back here with Maisie. She's five. My mother helps look after her. And I'm trying to be around more. This current . . . whatever it is, it isn't making that easier. Do you have kids?"

"Me? God, no. I can barely keep houseplants alive."

He smiled. "I remember that. I bought you a cactus for Christmas one year, and you managed to kill it."

I stood up. "I should go. I told Wes I'd bring him a coffee."

"I should go too," he said, glancing again at his watch.

He waited in silence while I bought another coffee, then walked alongside me to the elevator.

"Well," I said. "It was good to see you."

He pulled a card out of the inner pocket of his lab coat and handed it to me. "Listen, I know this is a really hard time for you. If there's anything you need . . . well, my cell number's on the card."

The doors opened and I stepped inside. I slipped his card into my pocket. "Thanks, Kenneth."

I closed my eyes as the elevator ascended. That was . . . not as bad as it could have been. Awkward, yes. But it had felt good to see him again.

When the doors opened on Wes's floor, I had to double-check that it was the right one. A half-dozen men and one woman were huddled behind the nurses' desk, peering at a computer screen over the shoulders of a harried-looking nurse. Two of them were speaking quickly into cell phones pressed to their ears. They were all wearing suits, as though this were a board meeting.

"This can't be right," one of them was saying. "Can you run that again?"

The nurse at the desk huffed. "I've run it three times," she said. "I don't believe it either, but there it is."

I slipped down the hall to Wes's room. The security guard outside recognized me and let me in. Wes was sitting in the chair near the window, reading a worn copy of *Fahrenheit 451*.

"Sorry for the wait," I said. "I ran into Kenneth downstairs."

"Who's Kenneth?"

"My old friend from college, remember? You met him once or twice."

"Oh yeah, that guy. The one you dumped the same time you left me."

"It wasn't like that."

"Whatever. You don't look too happy about seeing him," he said.

"It's not a big deal. There are more important things going on right now."

Wes nodded thoughtfully. "Yeah, I get that. Relationships are tough."

"We don't have a relationship," I insisted. "Do you have a girl-friend?" I asked, both to change the subject and because I was suddenly curious. I had never given much thought to Wes's love life.

"Oh yeah. She's awesome. Her name's Brandy."

"Where did you meet her?"

"Church. One of the times they let me go home for the weekend."

"You met someone at Mom and Dad's church?" I found that hard to imagine; I couldn't think of one person under the age of sixty in our parents' church.

"Nah, I went to the Meeting House downtown. It's a cool place. You can be yourself there, y'know? If you want to dance, you can dance. If you want to prophesy, you can prophesy. No one gives a shit what you look like. Anyway, I say she's my girlfriend, but we're waiting for each other."

"Waiting . . . to have sex?"

"Nah, man, we've done that! But the problem is that she's married, and she doesn't believe in divorce. And I'm not a home wrecker. So we can't be together in the physical realm. But we're still together in spirit."

"Um . . ." I was beginning to wish I hadn't asked . . . but I also had a morbid sense of curiosity. "So how does that work?"

"Well, you know I'm telepathic, right?"

"Uh, right."

"So is she. So we can talk to each other without being together. She loves me and I love her, but we have to wait until it's the right time to be together."

"But what if she doesn't ever get divorced? What if she grows old with her husband?"

He shrugged. "It's all in God's plan. He'll take care of it."

I sincerely hoped God's plan didn't involve this woman's husband dying mysteriously anytime soon.

"You want a book? I brought some over with me from my room." Wes held out a stack of paperbacks. I took them and examined the titles. Most of them were thrillers and mysteries, a genre I'd never really read. But I still had an hour to kill before the family meeting, and there wouldn't be much point in leaving and then coming back.

"Thanks," I said, picking one at random and giving the rest back to Wes. "I'm just going to call Uncle Rob first and let him know what's going on."

I stepped outside the room and dialed Rob's cell.

"Hello?"

"Hey, it's Clare."

"Hey, Clare, I was starting to worry about you. Everything go okay?"

I filled him in on the change of plans, which he seemed to take in stride. "Ah, bureaucracy. Everything takes longer than it needs to, and we have the pleasure of paying twice as much for it. Speaking of which, you'll want to talk to your parents' insurance providers sooner or later."

"Let's add it to the list," I said. "Everything okay on your end?"

"As okay as it can be. You want to head back here after your meeting? Don't suppose you've had a chance to think more about the obituary?"

"Not yet. I'll come by later and work on it."

"I'll see you later then. You remember how to get here?"

"Yeah. See you later."

I went back into Wes's room and sat in the unoccupied chair. I opened up the book I'd chosen at random—*Terminal Man* by Michael Crichton. But I couldn't get further than the title page. I kept glancing up at Wes every few seconds, as though I couldn't quite believe he was really sitting here in the same room, calmly reading. In less than an hour, I'd be in a meeting with his social worker and psychiatrist. I knew they'd have questions for me. But I had no answers.

I didn't want to disturb him, so I sat there pretending to read, but all the while my mind was jumping from my parents to Wes to Kenneth and back again. I started composing an obituary in my head, but it all got jumbled up and I didn't want to get emotional, not now, when there were so many decisions still to be made.

Finally I could take it no longer and stood up. "I have to go to that meeting now."

Wes grunted. "Tell them to let me the fuck out of here."

I tried to look encouraging. "I'll do my best. I'm going to go to Uncle Rob's afterward . . . so I'll see you in the morning, okay? Everything should be clear for you to leave then."

"Yeah, whatever." Wes shifted his chair so that his back was to me and returned to his book.

As I stepped into the hallway, I heard his voice. "Clare."

I stuck my head back inside. "Yeah?"

He turned in his chair to face me. His light-blue eyes were wide and earnest—and afraid.

"Don't leave me here."

I nodded at the security guard, who locked the door.

CHAPTER FIVE

I was the first to arrive. A harried nurse ushered me into the conference room and told me to have a seat at the oval table. I pulled a pen and a small notebook from my purse and poured myself a glass of water from the pitcher on the table.

I had no idea what to expect. My parents had attended many of these meetings over the years, but I'd never gone with them. I hadn't even asked what it was like. I tried to anticipate the questions—or directives—I was about to receive.

"We think it would be best if your brother moved in with you."

"You are now responsible for hundreds of thousands of dollars in hospital bills. How would you like to pay?"

"You and your brother should live in your late parents' house, as a familiar environment will be best for him."

"If your brother commits another crime, we will hold you legally responsible."

I stood and paced the room. What would they say when I told them I wasn't staying around? It wasn't like Wes was incapacitated or needed help with basic things like feeding himself or bathing. He was perfectly capable of looking after himself. Mom and Dad had probably even set aside money in their will for him. He could have *all* the money in the will, as far as I was concerned.

My frantic thoughts were interrupted by a knock at the door. The same nurse who had directed me to the room came in holding a clipboard and a stack of papers. She sank into a chair and exhaled loudly, as though she was glad for the rest. Then she pushed the clipboard toward me.

"You need to sign these papers."

I stared at her. "But what about the meeting? What about the social worker and the psychiatrist?"

"They've been called away. Normally, we would reschedule, but . . ."

"But what?"

"I don't know if you've noticed," she said irritably, "but we're a little understaffed right now. Your parents met with the team last week, correct?"

"Yes, but they're—"

"Then all you need to do is sign these papers and your brother is free to go in the morning, after his test results come in."

I picked up the clipboard and leafed through the papers. Seemed like regular bureaucratic verbiage. Nothing in there about selling my soul to the devil or moving back to Clarkeston.

"Do you know what kind of medication he needs?" I asked.

The nurse consulted a file on the table in front of her. She said a name I didn't recognize.

"Sorry, can you spell that?" I asked, getting my pen out.

An alarm went off in the hallway, a shrill double beep that made both of us jerk around. The nurse scrambled to her feet.

"What is that?" I asked.

"A patient has escaped." She scooped her papers back into her arms and headed for the door.

"But—"

"Just check down at the pharmacy," she said, one hand already on the doorknob. "They'll have his medication history for you. Once this is over, we can reschedule the meeting if you still want it."

"Once what is over?"

She closed the door behind her, and I was left in the empty conference room. I picked up the clipboard again. One scribble of ink, and Wes would be my responsibility. But I had to do it. I couldn't leave him here indefinitely. The least I could do was set him free.

I signed the papers and crept out of the room. The alarm stopped suddenly, only to be replaced with a constant stream of announcements over the intercom, only half of which I could make out. The nurses' station was completely empty—they were probably all out looking for the rogue patient—so I laid the clipboard on a keyboard where they would be sure to see it.

I should go back to Wes. But I couldn't bring myself to go back up there. Not yet. I headed toward the pharmacy, then changed my mind. That, too, could wait.

Rob's car was a welcome refuge. I sat in the parking lot for a long minute before starting the engine. I'd missed several calls from Rob, but I didn't return them. I'd see him soon enough. I drove slowly, lost in a sudden heaviness that had wrapped itself around me like a wet blanket.

I spurned Rob's advice and took the elevator instead of the stairs when I reached his apartment building.

He took one look at me and frowned. "You look beat."

"Funny, that's exactly how I feel."

"I'm afraid rest will have to wait for a few more minutes. Officer Danley is here to ask you a few questions to help with the investigation of your parents' murder."

"Oh . . . okay."

A uniformed officer stood in the hallway, arms crossed. He held out his hand. "Pleased to meet you."

"Thanks." I wasn't a big fan of the Clarkeston police, but I did want to help figure out what had happened to my parents—or, more to the point, *why*.

We sat in the living room and he began by asking me where I lived, what I did, how often I spoke with my parents. I answered in short, clipped sentences, too tired to go into much detail.

"Did you parents have any enemies? Any old rivalries? Business troubles?"

I shook my head. "No, none that I know of. Most of their friends were from church."

"Did you know they were in debt?"

I looked up at this. "No," I said, surprised. "I mean . . . I've never really thought about it. But I'm guessing Wes's care isn't cheap." *There goes any inheritance for Wes.*

"This might be a difficult question, but do you think your brother had any reasons for wanting your parents dead?"

My hackles rose. "Are you insinuating Wes was behind this?"

"I'm just examining all possible motives," Officer Danley said in what he probably thought was a mollifying tone.

"Well, you can stop examining that one. Wes had nothing to do with this. He loved my parents. He would never hurt them."

The officer looked down at his notes. "I have a note here that says Wes once put your mother in the hospital with a broken jaw."

I must have looked like a fish gasping for water. "That's not . . . they never told . . . *when?*"

He raised an eyebrow at me. "About four years ago. They never told you?"

"We're not . . . we weren't super close," I mumbled. Had Wes really attacked our mother so savagely he'd broken her jaw? Where was I four years ago? China, maybe. Or Thailand. "Listen, Wes has his violent outbursts, but he would never, ever do something like this. You know he was in the hospital when they were killed. I talked to him on the phone that night! And you know who did it: Terry Foster. Why are you even looking for someone else?"

The officer just looked down at his notes.

"Have you spoken with this Terry's family? What do they have to say?" I pressed. I wanted to ask if they knew what was happening up at the hospital, if they thought there was a connection, but I didn't want to get Kenneth in trouble.

"We have," he admitted. "But I can't discuss that part of the investigation."

"Of course you can't."

"Miss Campbell, I'm sorry if I upset you. I'm just doing my job. We need to find out exactly what happened that night. That's what I'm trying to do."

I glowered at him but didn't retort. "Is there anything else?"

"I think that will do for now. Can we contact you if we have any more questions?"

I nodded and stood up.

The officer handed me his card. On his way out, he paused to speak quietly with Rob in the hall.

Once he was gone, I asked, "How did it go with the lawyer and all that?"

"Fine," Rob said. "Everything's being taken care of. Except for you, apparently. You need some sleep."

I didn't even try to argue with him. "Don't let me sleep for too long . . ." I muttered as I made a beeline for the futon in the spare room.

"You sleep as long as you need to."

***

It was almost six o'clock when I woke up, groggy but famished. There was a note from Rob on the table.

Went to help my friend Diana put together some furniture. Call me if you need anything. The car is still here if you need it.

I checked the fridge, but it was empty save for a bottle of ketchup, a jar of mayo, and three cans of cheap beer.

I stumbled into the bathroom and caught a glimpse of myself in the mirror. I winced. A shower was definitely in order.

Once dry, I pulled on my jeans and an old The Clash T-shirt, then drove downtown. I needed street tacos. I hoped Rosa's was still open. How many times had Latasha, Kenneth, and I gone on a late-night taco run to fuel our study sessions?

The ache in my chest grew as I drove under the canopy of leaves that arched over the road. I passed the brick-faced building where my dad had once worked. The farmers' market we'd gone to almost every Saturday to buy fresh-pressed apple cider and warm Belgian waffles. The 200-year-old cathedral Wes had broken into once, convinced that a dear friend of his was being sacrificed in a satanic ritual. That had been arrest number two.

The tiny hole-in-the-wall shop was still there. Two green plastic chairs and a stained wooden table stood on the sidewalk—the extent of the patio. A well of nostalgia rose up in my throat as I parked and stepped out into the muggy heat.

The door opened, and I automatically moved to the side. Then I saw who it was.

"Kenneth."

He looked nonplussed for a few seconds; then a wry smile cracked his face. "Looks like we both needed some comfort food."

"I guess." Why did I feel so self-conscious? It wasn't like I'd followed him there. "I thought you'd still be at the hospital."

"I'm done for the day. Thought I'd get something here before picking up Maisie at my mom's."

"Oh. Well, I should let you go, then."

"Sure."

"Unless . . . you have time to stay? For a few minutes?" Was I pushing him too far? Maybe he'd just been acting polite at the hospital. Maybe he was annoyed I was back in town. But I couldn't help it. I needed a friend.

He hesitated, then sat down in one of the plastic chairs. "I'll wait while you order. Try the shrimp tacos. They're new."

I ducked inside and returned a few minutes later with a Styrofoam container filled with shrimp tacos.

"How are the arrangements going?" he asked once I sat down.

"Fine, I think. Actually, I don't really know. My Uncle Rob is taking care of most of it, which is amazing." I told him about the visit from Officer Danley.

"I'm sorry you had to go through that," he said. "I'm sure they're just trying to be thorough."

"I know. But it bugs me when people jump to conclusions about Wes. I mean, I can see how it looks, and I know he has a history of violence. He doesn't think like you and me. But hell, they *know* who did it. Do they really think Wes convinced Terry to shoot our parents? That's insane. Wes is a gentle soul on the inside. He really is."

"He's lucky to have you," Kenneth said. "And how was the family meeting?"

"Nonexistent, actually." I told him what had happened.

"I'm sorry; that's quite unprofessional. You deserve to have a full picture of your brother's condition before he's released to you. But I can't say I'm surprised."

"Why not?"

"The doctors you were supposed to meet with were at the same meeting I was attending. All senior personnel were there."

"With the CDC? What'd you find out?"

He looked down at his hands. "I'm not supposed to say anything . . ."

I leaned in closer. "Come on, who am I going to tell? I don't even live here anymore. You said it might have something to do with my parents' death. And if it could affect Wes, I should know."

"It won't affect Wes. At least, no more than anyone else. But I'm really not supposed to say. They don't want to start a panic."

"Have you ever known me to panic? C'mon, you can trust me." The reproach in his eyes made my cheeks burn. *Of course* he didn't trust me. He had every reason not to. "Never mind," I muttered.

"Hey," he said. "I'm over it, remember? And I do trust you not to call up half a dozen reporters. Nothing is conclusive. But they did give us some surprising numbers. Intake at the psych ward is up fifty-seven percent this week alone, and they think the number of unreported cases could be much higher."

"That's a pretty huge jump, isn't it?"

He nodded. "Then they gave us their theories. It could be an environmental issue, like tainted meat or something in the water supply. They're testing that out now. They've already ruled out rabies. But what worries me most is the third possibility."

"And that is . . . ?"

"Well, it seems unlikely, but it's possible that a virus or bacteria is causing these symptoms."

I gaped at him. "What?"

He held up his hand. "I know; it sounds crazy. And it's just a theory."

"Who knows about this?"

"Right now just the CDC and the senior medical officials at the hospital. And you." He raised his eyebrows significantly.

"I'll keep it quiet, I promise. But aren't you freaking out?"

"No, because the likelihood of it being contagious is extremely low." He paused and wiped his hands with a brown paper napkin. "I shouldn't have told you; I really don't want you to worry."

"When will they know for sure?"

"A couple of days, hopefully. But seriously, Clare, I don't want you to worry about it. You have enough on your plate. How are you feeling about . . . everything?"

"I'll be fine," I said. "I don't want to dump all my stuff on you."

"Fair enough. But what about Wes? Will he be okay without your parents?"

Isn't that the million-dollar question? "I hope so."

We spent the next hour getting caught up, swapping stories about the last several years of our lives. I felt myself slipping back into the familiar, easy rhythm of being with Kenneth. It felt . . . normal. Like the way things should be.

He talked a lot about his daughter, Maisie, but said very little about his ex-wife. Finally I asked, "So what happened with your marriage? If you don't mind . . ."

He shook his head. "I should have seen it coming. Like I said, it was my fault. For the most part, anyway."

I found that hard to believe, but then again, I'd known Kenneth when we were young and carefree. I had no idea what he was like as a husband, as a father.

"It's simple, really," he continued. "I was so focused on my goals and career that I forgot Rachel had ambitions of her own—or maybe I just thought mine were more important. I learned that one the hard way. She said she needed to focus on herself for a while. After she left, Maisie and I were on our own. I had to get my priorities straight in a hurry."

"I'm sure you're a great dad," I said.

"I'm trying to be. She's worth it. How about you? Anyone special back in Seattle?"

"Nah. No one serious. Unless you count Latasha. We're just room-mates," I added hurriedly when he raised his eyebrows.

He smirked. "I always wondered about you two. Well, tell her I said hi. But I should get going—it's one of my few free evenings to spend with Maisie."

"Okay." We said good-bye, and I watched as the brief sense of normalcy I'd felt drove away with him.

My phone rang on the drive back to Rob's. Latasha. I turned on the speakerphone.

"Hey, Latasha."

"Hey there. How you holding up?"

"As well as can be expected." I filled her in on Wes and the chaos of the hospital.

"Are you kidding me? What's going on there?"

"I don't know." I wanted to tell her everything, but I'd given Kenneth my word. "I saw Kenneth. He says hi."

"You saw him? Where?"

"He works at the hospital. And then I just ran into him at Rosa's."

"Oh God, Rosa's. Was it . . . incredibly awkward? You guys haven't seen each other since you left, right?"

"It *was* awkward. But we're both adults. I told him I was sorry. He said he was over it. That's about it."

"Damn. Well, tell him hi back if you see him again. What are you doing tonight?"

"Writing an obituary, I suppose."

"I wish I could be there with you."

"Me too. I—hold on a second."

"What is it?"

"Someone's flagging me down. Looks like they ran out of gas or something. I'll call you right back."

Ahead of me, a car was on the shoulder, the hood raised. The car had clearly seen better days, but I couldn't immediately see anything wrong with it. A young woman who couldn't have been more than twenty stood beside it, waving her hands in the air. She had shoulder-length dirty blonde hair and a strategically ripped plaid shirt.

I pulled over in front of the car and got out. "Need some help?" I asked. I didn't know the first thing about cars, but maybe I could give her a lift to the gas station or make a call for her. I didn't like the idea of leaving a young woman stranded on the side of the road.

She pushed her hair behind her ears.

"They cut my brakes, the motherfuckers," she said as I approached. I stopped walking.

"I'm sorry?"

"My brakes! They've been cut!" she repeated, baring her teeth. "Those fucking bastards want me dead." She pushed her hair back again. Her hands trembled.

"Who wants you dead?"

"I don't fuckin' know! Probably everyone. Do you have a phone? I need to call the fucking governor and tell her what I think of this shit."

"Um . . . I don't think the governor can help you. But I can call a tow truck if you'd like."

"Like that'll help," she spat.

"Why do you think your brakes were cut?" This was starting to sound too much like a conversation with my brother. Maybe this girl was just troubled . . . Then a sudden thought struck. Could she be one of the people Kenneth had told me about? He didn't think that whatever was happening to them was contagious, but what if he was wrong? *That's impossible*, I told myself. *Craziness is not contagious.*

"I already told you. They want to kill me!" She started kicking the tires so hard with her Converse sneakers I was surprised she didn't break a toe.

"Hey, take it easy," I said. "Don't hurt yourself. Let's get you some help."

The young woman wheeled around without looking at me. She stared at the ground and started to kick up puffs of dirt, as if she couldn't bear to stand still. "Don't need help," she muttered. "Need to talk to the governor. Or the president. Do you have his number?"

"No, I don't. But I can call someone for you. How about your parents? Or a friend?" I didn't take my eyes off her, but I started to back away, moving toward my car.

"Hey, aren't you going to help me?" she yelled, sticking out her chin.

"I need to get my phone so we can call your parents."

"Are you crazy? They're probably in on it!"

"Then let's call someone else," I said. The metal door of the car pressed against my back. Turning, I eased it open and got into the driver's seat. I closed the door gently, not wanting to spook her.

It didn't work. As I reached for my phone, she threw herself against the passenger door. She scrabbled for the handle, screaming.

My hand flew to the automatic locks just in time, but the resulting click sent her into a frenzy. She tore at the handle like a rabid animal and then slammed her hands and face against the window, her eyes bulging.

"You motherfucker! You want me to die?"

I shook so hard I dropped the keys on the floor. I'd been on the receiving end of this kind of rage before.

She stopped thrashing at the window and climbed onto the hood of the car. Then she kicked at the windshield with her heel. A dull thudding noise echoed throughout the car.

I grabbed the keys and pushed them into the ignition, twisting them so fiercely the engine screamed in protest. But I couldn't bring myself to put my foot on the gas. I didn't want to risk running over her. Even if I just knocked her off the hood, she could hit her head or break an arm. Finally, I rapped on the windshield with my knuckles, and she stopped kicking.

"Your car is on fire!" I shouted. It wasn't, but I was counting on the fact that she was in some sort of delusional state.

It worked. She screamed and jumped off the hood of my car and ran toward her own, which was still sitting innocently on the shoulder. As I peeled back onto the road, she flapped at the imaginary flames with her hands.

Once a safe distance away, I pulled over and got out of the car. I gulped the fresh air and leaned against the cold metal, waiting for my heart—hell, my whole body—to slow down. *Jesus Christ, what* was *that?*

I called 911. A recorded voice told me they were experiencing higher than usual call volume and I should stay on the line. I frowned. Then the voice said, "If someone you know is exhibiting uncharacteristic or erratic behavior, call the health hotline at . . ." Kenneth hadn't been joking. If it was bad enough to put on the 911 recording, why hadn't there been a public announcement?

I hung up and dialed the hotline, only to be greeted with another message. "Thank you. Our operators are currently on other calls. Please stay on the line, or press two to leave a message, including a call-back number."

I left a brief message, with the location of the girl and a description. I didn't leave my number.

The sense of peace I'd felt at the restaurant had been shattered. For the space of an hour, I'd actually thought that maybe everything would be okay. Now, reality came rushing back in with brutal force. Nothing was okay. It never was, in this place.

CHAPTER SIX

The girl from the side of the road haunted my dreams that night. Only she kept changing into Wes, and then into my mom, and then suddenly there were more of them, pounding at my car windows and tearing at the metal as I cried and begged to be left alone. Rob woke me up. I'd been screaming for my mother.

I've been watching too much Walking Dead, I thought, shaking my head as I climbed the stairs of the hospital in the morning. I'd kept my head down as I snaked my way through the lobby. Reporters and cameramen had joined the patients and their families in demanding to know what was happening to their town.

Behind the desk on Wes's floor, a nurse was swearing into a phone as the intercom blared overhead. I pressed my back against the wall and watched, wondering if she was dealing with one of the new psych patients. When she stopped barking into the phone, I marched up to the desk.

"I need to talk to someone about Wes Campbell. I'm his sister. He's being discharged today."

The nurse looked at her computer. She wore a mask around her mouth and nose, like the nurse and orderlies I'd seen yesterday. Just a precaution, or did they know something I didn't?

"Yes, everything looks fine. He can go."

That threw me off a little. "That's it? What about his test results? The nurse yesterday told me we had to wait for them."

"Everything came back normal," she said. "And you signed the discharge forms yesterday, so he can leave. God knows we could use the bed."

"Can I at least get a copy of the results?"

But then a woman's voice boomed, "Someone give me a hand here!" I craned my neck to see down the corridor. A doctor in a stained white lab coat was wrestling with a large bald man who was trying to throw her off. The nurse in front of me muttered, "Not another one," before springing out of her chair and bolting down the hall.

I swiveled around, looking for someone else to help me, but everyone on the floor seemed to be running, shouting, or furiously typing into computers and tablets.

"Excuse me, can you—?" I called out to one passing nurse.

"Not now," she snapped, brushing past me.

Things were getting worse. *Get Wes. Get the hell out of here.*

Wes's room was locked. It took me another five minutes to track down a nurse with a key. She gave me a harried look as she fumbled with her key chain. "Not the way to run a hospital," she muttered. "No protocols for something like this . . .

"Good luck," she said as she turned and marched swiftly back to the nurses' station, where three separate phones were already ringing.

I pushed the door open. "Hey."

"Morning," Wes said. He was sitting on the edge of the bed, a brown duffel bag at his feet. I closed the door behind me. His room was an oasis of calm compared to the chaos of the ward.

"We can leave."

"Cool."

"Is that all you have?" I asked, indicating the bag.

"They don't let you bring much." He bent over and fiddled with his shoes.

"Wes, you know how you asked me how long I was staying? I've decided. I'm going back to Seattle after the funeral."

He didn't look up, but his hands suddenly went still. "That soon? You just got here."

"Yeah. It's just . . . you know I don't love coming back here at the best of times. No offense. But I've moved on, you know? I don't belong here. I need to get back home."

"This *is* home." His eyes stayed trained on the floor.

"Not for me."

He slid off the bed and shoved his hands into his pockets. "I don't get you. You took a plane across the entire country, and now you're going back? It makes no fucking sense."

"Wes, I came to do what I had to do. Say good-bye to Mom and Dad and make sure you're going to be okay." I took a deep breath. "You're free now. Mom and Dad got you an apartment, right? You've always taken care of yourself before. You don't need me to look after you."

Finally, he looked me in the eyes. "You're right, I can look after myself. But I thought you'd stay around for more than a couple of days. Hang out for a while."

"There's nothing for me here."

"Only because you're not looking! All you've ever wanted is to get away from them, get away from me, get away from this fucking town! But can't you show a little decency?"

"Please tell me you're not lecturing me on doing the right thing . . ."

"Yeah, I've fucked up pretty good in my life; I know it. That doesn't mean you're off the hook."

I didn't know what to say. I didn't want things to be like this between us, especially not now. It was all just too much. I slumped down onto the bed beside him and put my head in my hands, tears leaking through my fingers.

Immediately, he put his arm around me. "Hey, I didn't mean to make you cry."

"You didn't," I said, my hands muffling my voice. "It's just . . . everything. Last night this woman attacked me on the road. And I don't know how to make any of these decisions about Mom and Dad, I've just been letting Rob do it all, and the police are asking me these horrible questions, and I . . . I have all these awful memories. I hate this place. I can't do this, Wes. I can't stay here."

He pulled me closer. "You can," he said gruffly. "Yeah, I can take care of myself. But I do need you, and I think you need me, too. Just stay for a few days longer. We shouldn't be apart right now. We're all we've got."

I couldn't tell him this, but that was why I was crying.

**

He picked up his bag, and we slipped through the frenzy of nurses, doctors, patients, reporters, and anxious families. As we reached the glass entrance doors, a flurry of movement outside caught my eye. A woman about my age stood outside, in jeans and a long beige top. She was yelling at someone and waving her hands, her back to me. Her movements were erratic and jerky, as though she were having a mild seizure. Then the automatic doors opened, and her voice flooded into the entryway.

"Get away from me!" she screamed.

A distraught man stood beside a car, its driver and passenger doors gaping open. The faces of two children were pressed against the backseat window, their eyes and mouths wide. The man pleaded, "Emma, baby, please, you're not yourself. Just come see the doctor with me."

"No!" she spat. "I know what you really are!"

"Emma, you're scaring the kids. Please calm down!" he begged.

Emma? I looked closer. It was Emma Ross, one of my best friends from high school. What was she doing?

"What did you do with Adrian, huh?" Emma raved. "Where's my husband?"

"*I'm* your husband. I'm Adrian; I haven't changed. You're sick. You need help. Please, for the kids . . ."

A crowd was gathering. Reporters had flipped on their cameras. A couple of orderlies started forward, but they stopped in their tracks when someone barked out an order: "Everyone get back! No one go near them. Security is on the way."

Emma continued to scream, her voice growing higher. "Those aren't my kids, you bastard! Tell me what you've done to them!" She put a hand into her purse and pulled out a can of hair spray, which she pointed at her husband.

"What . . . what are you doing?" he stuttered. The blood left my face. *I* knew what she was doing. Wes had nearly killed himself once this way. She pulled a lighter from her pocket and flicked it.

"Stop!" I yelled. When I tried to run toward her, Wes grabbed my arm and yanked me back. "Let go!"

"I'll go," he said. He raised his hands in the air and took a step forward. "It's okay. I'm not going to hurt you."

Emma glanced at him, distracted.

"You know those voices in your head?" Wes said. "I hear them, too. But they're not real. They're lying to you, and you can't let them take control."

Emma was staring intently at Wes now, but her finger was still on the nozzle of the hair spray.

"Wes, don't get too close," I urged.

The kids in the backseat were crying now.

"Put it down, Emma!" Adrian yelled, and Emma's attention was ripped away from Wes.

"I want my husband back!" she screeched, and then she pressed the nozzle of the hair spray and lifted the lighter in front of it. Wes dove to the ground as a jet of fire burst through the air toward Adrian, who ran away from the car, where his children were now screaming in terror.

But Emma had found her mark. The flames caught Adrian's shirt-sleeve. He yelled and dropped to the ground to smother them.

She followed, her makeshift blowtorch still raging. A loud pop exploded through the air, and Emma and Adrian were engulfed in a ball of flame.

Everyone around us was screaming now. I ran toward Wes and helped him to his feet, but both of us were knocked to the ground seconds later. The uniformed members of the security team thundered past us. They all wore white masks over their noses and mouths. Had the CDC's worst-case scenario come true?

Someone grabbed my arm and helped me up. It was Kenneth. I hadn't even noticed him there. "Come on. They've got this," he said, his face ashen and his eyes fixed on the horrible scene. He, too, was wearing a mask. He gave Wes a hand, helping him to his feet.

One of the men had thrown a heavy blanket on each of the victims. Emma wasn't moving; Adrian was moaning loudly. "Let's go," Kenneth said, and he led us back into the hospital lobby, where he guided me to a chair. Wes sank down into the seat beside mine.

My hands shook in my lap, and my breath was ragged. "I know her," I whispered.

"Who is she?" Kenneth asked, sitting down across from me. He rubbed my arms with his hands, as though I had hypothermia.

"Emma Ross. We were friends in high school," I said, my voice faint.

"Oh, Clare . . . I'm so sorry," he said.

"We kept in touch on Facebook," I continued. "She was pregnant."

The muscles in his forehead convulsed, but he didn't speak. What was there to say?

"The masks," I whispered. "Why are you all wearing masks? Is it . . . true? Is it contagious?"

"I don't know," he said. "But if it is . . . God help us."

***

Wes and I drove out of the hospital parking lot in silence. I'd given Kenneth my cell number, and he'd promised to call if he learned anything new about Emma's condition. A semblance of calm had returned now that the chaos of the hospital was behind us. But I knew it was an illusion—and a temporary one at best.

"Where are we going?" Wes asked, once we were on the main road.

"Your choice: we can stay with Uncle Rob or go back to Mom and Dad's. I guess I should go there at least once before I head back to Seattle."

"I want to stay at Mom and Dad's. I want to see the place again. Say good-bye, y'know?"

"Okay. Maybe we can find the keys for your new apartment. We can get you set up."

He was quiet for a minute, then said, "Maybe I'll live at Mom and Dad's."

"You would want to?" I tried to picture Wes rattling around the place, lounging about the living room with its doilies and Royal Doulton figurines, cooking drugs in the pristine kitchen. "Besides, I imagine we'll have to sell it. To pay for the funeral and stuff."

He shrugged. "I have good memories there."

I didn't reply. I gripped the steering wheel tightly, on the lookout for any signs of trouble around us.

"Hey, can we stop for some smokes?" he asked.

"Yeah, I guess." I pulled up to a convenience store. "I'm assuming you don't have any money?"

"Nope."

I handed him a bill and said, "I'll wait here."

He hopped out and went inside. A minute later he came back with a pack of cigarettes and a bag of Swedish Fish. He tossed them in my lap. "Still like these?"

I picked up the bag. "I do. You remembered . . ."

"So, how are we going to get into the house?" Wes asked.

"I have a key."

"Oh. 'Cause I was going to say I could break a window or something."

I grinned despite myself. He grinned back.

We stopped at Rob's apartment to get my stuff. He was out, but he'd given me a key. I left him a note saying we were going to spend the night at Mom and Dad's.

We drove a bit farther, and then there it was, an unremarkable split-level with yellow siding and white trim, on a street filled with other unremarkable homes. My chest constricted as I took it in. The bright pink impatiens my parents planted every year were in full bloom, and the bird feeders my dad hung on the crab apple tree in the front yard were still filled with seed. *They've only been gone three days*. It felt like so much longer.

We parked in the driveway, behind their Ford Fiesta. The fluffy orange cat from next door ran over as soon as she heard the car; Mom was notorious for giving treats to all the neighborhood cats. The cat walked in circles on the small landing in front of the door, meowing.

I glanced at Wes, who made no sign that he was about to get out. His blue eyes were fixed on the house, his mouth grim. "I used to sneak out that window," he said, eyeing one of the two dormers above the garage.

"I know," I said. "Until Dad nailed it shut and you started sneaking out of mine."

He snorted. "You snuck out, too."

"Not out the window, though. I wasn't as brave as you. I used the patio doors."

"Mom knew about that."

"She did not."

"Yeah, she said something about it a while ago. Said you always used to leave your nightie on the patio so you could change back into it before coming back inside."

I stared at him in disbelief. "Then why didn't she stop me?"

He shrugged. "Dunno."

"Jesus." What else had she known? Had she known all my secrets?

"You shouldn't swear," he reminded me.

"You swear all the time," I shot back.

"There's a difference. I say words like 'fuck' and 'shit.' They're just words. I don't take the Lord's name in vain. It's dangerous."

"Dangerous how?"

"There are spiritual forces in the world. Jesus's name has power against them. If they know you don't take it seriously, it makes you vulnerable."

I put my hand over his. "You know I don't believe that."

"You should. I'm praying for you."

"Thanks," I said, trying to sound sincere. Then I opened the car door, more to change the subject than anything.

He grabbed his bag from the backseat, and I got my suitcase from the trunk. I knelt on the landing and gave the cat a few rubs. She purred happily and wound herself around my legs. "Hey, Fluff Bucket," I whispered. It was the nickname my mother had given her years ago. "You don't seem very sad; I guess no one's told you the news." My throat grew tight as I stood up and fumbled with my keys.

"How come I don't have a key?" Wes asked.

"Because you steal things and sell them for drugs," I said matter-of-factly.

"That was years ago. I'm different. I got serious about my Christianity."

"Mm-hm."

"Whatever. I'll be right in; I'm going to have a smoke."

I pushed open the door and braced myself for the onslaught. The smell hit me like a truck: a mixture of old carpet and wood shavings and tanning oil. My parents had never been much for redecorating, and the entryway looked pretty much identical to how it had looked when Wes and I were in the fourth grade. Peach-colored wallpaper, beige linoleum, and one of those old coiled rugs in brown and yellow.

My dad's hat still hung on one of the hooks on the wall. They must have chosen a warm night for their ill-fated walk; he was seldom without his hat, an old-man newsboy in burgundy. My stomach ached at the sight of it.

My eyes went automatically to the patch in the wall where Wes had kicked a hole with his steel-toed boots. I couldn't remember exactly what they'd been fighting about; maybe it was the first time he'd stolen from them. But they'd never bothered to properly repair it—they'd just plastered it over and left it like that. Their decision not to cover it up had never made sense to me.

"You okay?" Wes asked from behind me.

"Yeah. It's just weird . . . being here without them."

"Yeah. Super weird."

Pictures of us as kids covered the walls and the mantelpiece in the living room. Dressed up for Sunday school, at a family picnic, holding our awards for earning the highest marks in our grade at school. We had tied one year. There was my grad photo, hideous as it was, and the photo my mom had forced Wes to have taken even though he'd never graduated from high school. In it, his face was smooth and tattoo-free, and his blond hair was full and brushed back. The smile on his face verged on a smirk, but it was charming all the same.

I walked into the kitchen and pulled open the fridge out of habit, then closed it. I couldn't eat the leftovers of the dead.

"Want to order pizza or something for lunch?" I asked Wes, who was coming up the stairs.

He shrugged. "Sure."

I pulled out my phone and searched for pizza places in Clarkeston, then started filling out the online order form.

Wes watched me warily.

"What? You still like meat lovers?" I asked.

"You're ordering pizza over the Internet?"

"It's not a new thing."

"Yeah, but now the government knows what kind of pizza you like."

I checked his expression to see if he was joking. He wasn't.

"Fine. I'll make the order over the phone if it makes you feel more comfortable."

"Hey, I'm not trying to be difficult," he said. "I just don't trust the Internet."

"It's okay." I dialed the number and placed our order.

Some papers lay on the counter, along with a silver key. "Here's your rental agreement," I said, handing him the papers. I held up the key. "Want to go check it out?"

"Later," he said. "I want to stay here for a bit."

My phone rang. I answered the call and headed into the other room. "Hey, Rob."

"Hey, kid, got your note. How you holding up?"

"Fine."

"Everything go okay at the hospital?"

I knew I should tell him what had happened, but I frankly didn't have the energy. "It was kind of crazy there. But I got him in the end. We're at Mom and Dad's now."

"Sorry I missed you this morning."

"No worries. Where'd you go?"

"To the paper office. Gave them the obituary notice."

"Oh, shit, I'm sorry. I was supposed to do that last night."

"Don't you worry about it. You're doing enough. Do you need anything? Do you guys want to come over?"

"No, we just ordered pizza, and Wes wants to hang out here for a bit. We might go check out his new apartment later; I'll let you know if you we do. Thanks, though."

"Okay. Well, in case I don't see you, the wake is set for tomorrow morning at ten at Bishop's. You okay with that?"

"Yeah. Whatever works."

"Okay. Call me if you need me."

"I will. I gotta go."

I hung up and headed back into the kitchen, where Wes was sitting almost meditatively at the table. "What do you want to do now?" I asked.

"Dunno. Play chess?"

"You play chess?"

"Yeah, I learned in the hospital. You play?"

"Not well. But I think Mom and Dad had a board around here somewhere . . ."

I went into what had once been the dining room but was now the pile-everything room. Our old piano was still there. Neither of our parents played, which made me wonder why they'd kept it. There were two tall cabinets where my mom had stowed photo albums and games and all the dishes she'd inherited from my grandmother. They were too "fussy" to use, she'd said, so she'd kept them tucked them away.

I found the chessboard hidden underneath Sorry! and Monopoly. We set it up on the kitchen table.

Strategy had never been my forte. Wes was creaming me when I was rescued by the doorbell.

"Pizza's here," I said, jumping to my feet.

We ate slowly, talking little. Once we were finished, he sat back in his chair and burped loudly. "I wrote some songs. Wanna hear 'em?"

"Sure."

He ran downstairs and returned with our father's old guitar. I opened my mouth, then forced it shut. Dad had loved this guitar. But he didn't need it anymore, so what did it matter if Wes played it?

He pulled a folded piece of paper out of his back pocket and smoothed it out on the table. The lyrics were written with heavy black pen in his angular scrawl.

"I only know power chords," he said. I moved my chair back a few inches.

"Ready?" He grinned.

"Ready," I said, smiling at his enthusiasm.

Then he began. I wouldn't call it singing, exactly. More like screaming—or rasping. Still, I could make out the words.

Jesus! Jesus is the way!
Bow down to him, all you sinners!
Leave your sins behind! He will forgive you!
Don't delay! Accept his spirit today!
You must turn to him! Or else burn, burn, buuuuuuuuuurn!

He ended by jumping off his chair onto the floor, still beating at the guitar as he rolled onto his back and kicked his legs in the air. Then he dropped the guitar and grinned up at me, panting.

"Pretty good, eh?"

I struggled to find words that were not outright lies. "Um. Wow. It was a really dynamic performance."

"I know! I was thinking of calling up my old bandmates to see if they want to get together again."

I had a feeling that Wes's old bandmates were probably married with children and careers by now. "Do you want to see what's on TV?"

"Yeah. But first I want to talk to you about something," he said, suddenly serious.

"About what?"

"Is there any hot chocolate?"

"That's what you want to talk to me about?"

"No. I just . . . it will be easier with hot chocolate."

I opened the pantry and found a container of instant hot chocolate, the kind with the little marshmallows in it. I put the kettle on and sat back down at the table. "What's up?"

"Let's wait until it's ready."

"You're not going to throw it at me, are you?"

Wes smirked. "No."

I cleaned up the chessboard and the dishes we'd used for the pizza. Then I rescued the screaming kettle from the burner and poured the boiling water into two mugs of sugary powder, adding some milk from the fridge to cool it off. I dug around in the pantry and found a bag of mini marshmallows. The ones in the mix were never enough. They were hard as rocks, but the hot chocolate would soften them up.

"Remember when we used to sit here at night after Mom and Dad went to bed?" I asked. I handed him his mug and sat down at the table.

"Yeah. I'm glad you remember."

Of course I remembered. It had been back in that strange phase when I'd thought everything was normal—or, at least, that every family was like ours. At the time we'd thought Wes was just a screw-up. We'd known so little about mental illness and had never thought it would rear its head in our family.

He'd been doing drugs and living on the street half the time. His mood swings had been wild and often violent, and you'd never know what version of him you were going to get. In desperation, our mother had forbidden Wes and me from speaking to each other; she was worried his behavior would rub off on me.

Or maybe she'd wanted to protect me. I traced the grain of the table with my finger. Whatever her motivation, it had only made us more determined to see each other. So we would sneak downstairs at midnight, drink hot chocolate heaped with mini marshmallows, and talk about absolutely nothing. More often than not, Wes had been stoned or high. Acid had been his drug of choice back then, and he'd dropped it more than once a day. I'd make faces at him from across the table while he was tripping and then giggle when he freaked out, seeing God knows what in my expressions.

So stupid. So naïve. I'd had no idea that what he was doing would help destroy him, damaging us all in the process.

"So what's up?" I asked again.

"I want to talk to you about why you left," he said, his stained fingers gripping his cup.

Not now. Not this.

"When?" I asked, feigning ignorance. "Yesterday at the hospital?"

"No," he said. "You know when."

"Oh."

"When you left for London."

"I don't want to talk about that right now, Wes. It's just . . . too much, with everything else."

"You never want to talk about it. And if you're taking off in a few days, we need to talk *now*."

"You know why I left."

"Not really."

"C'mon, Wes, that was nine years ago. You couldn't expect me to stay here forever."

He let go of his mug and grabbed my hands. I tried to pull back, but his grip was as tight as ever. "Clare. They'd locked me up. You knew it wasn't right."

"There was nothing I could do. I tried."

"Did you?"

I yanked my hands away and stood up. "Jesus Christ, Wes! And no, I'm not going to apologize for swearing. You know what happened. What did you expect me to do? I just wanted to get away from this shit hole of a town, and that was my chance! Did you want me to stay around here for the rest of my life so I could baby you and make excuses for you, like Mom and Dad always did? Is that what you wanted?"

He ignored this. "You never told your boyfriend Kenneth what happened, did you?"

"He wasn't my boyfriend. And what the hell does that have to do with anything?"

"How come you never told him?"

"Because I didn't need one more person who didn't believe me."

"*I* believed you. And then you left me to fend for myself."

"I did no such thing. You were well cared for. You know that."

"Well cared for? Are you fucking crazy? You don't know what it's like in there, with them watching your every move and force-feeding you pills you never agreed to take. Doctors poking you whenever and wherever they want. I was a fucking lab rat."

"You were sick. You needed help."

"I needed *you.*"

"I was twenty-two. I deserved to have a life. I still do." My jaw was clenched so hard it was starting to ache. The pressure behind my temples was pushing all patience aside. He was not going to guilt me over this. I did what I had to do. It was self-preservation, and I didn't regret it.

"I deserved a life too," he said. "And you let them take it from me."

"Nobody took anything from you! It wasn't my fault. I didn't ask you to beat up that asshole. You almost killed him, for Christ's sake! What did you think they were going to do, let you go?"

Wes stood up now as well, and I automatically backed up a few paces, until my back was pressed against the kitchen counter.

"Tell me he didn't deserve it," he snarled.

Of course he'd deserved it. "You needed help, and I'm glad you got it."

"You're glad I was out of the way, you mean," he said. "Admit it. I was the only one who defended you, and you left me to rot."

I forced myself to meet his eyes, but I was shaking. It was as if I'd been transported back to a time when I could avoid confrontation by running upstairs to my room with pink walls and pink carpet and a pink bedspread, slam the door behind me, and throw myself onto the bed. It was this place; it was messing with me. I *needed* to go back to Seattle, where I was a grown-up. Here I would always be a child.

Most people would have quailed under the look Wes gave me, especially combined with his tattoos, piercings, chains, and metal studs. And it's not that I felt no fear. I knew he could kill me with his bare hands if he felt like it, and my heart quivered a little at the fire in his eyes. The difference was that most people never considered whether or not their siblings would kill them, and it was a question with which I was very familiar—comfortable, even, despite what I'd said about Wes's gentle nature.

The buzz of my phone broke our impasse. It was a text from Kenneth.

The CDC is having a press conference in a few minutes. I think all our questions are about to be answered.

"Hang on," I said to Wes, who was still glaring at me. "We can talk about this more later, but something important is happening right now . . . something I want to see."

I turned on the TV in the living room and tried to figure out the remote.

"What's going on?" he asked as I flicked through the channels.

"The CDC is having a press conference," I said. "Centers for Disease Control. They think there's something wrong here in Clarkeston—an illness or something in the water. It's why the hospital's been so crazy."

I found a news station and sat down on the sofa. Wes sat beside me, still glowering. But he seemed willing to let things rest—for now.

On the screen, a thin, white-haired man in a dark blue suit approached a podium with the state of Maine's seal on it.

My phone rang. It was Latasha. "You watching the CDC thing?" she asked.

"Yeah, Kenneth just texted me. How did you—?"

"Saw it online. Shhh, it's starting."

"Thank you," the man said to whoever had introduced him. He was identified on the screen as Dr. Harry Normand, director of the Centers for Disease Control and Prevention. He cleared his throat.

"As some of you are aware, we have been investigating the rise of unusual behavior in and around the town of Clarkeston. We were asked by the Maine Health Department to investigate the increase in patients presenting at the Riverside Psychiatric Facility. This issue was brought to our attention only days ago. During this time, our scientists have been working exceptionally hard, often in hazardous environments, and for that, they certainly have our thanks."

He paused and looked down at his notes.

"We have investigated many potential causes and have now identified the agent of this condition as a pathogen—an infectious particle called a prion. Now, I want to say right up front that this is good news: we know what's causing it, so now we can determine how to treat it. We will be releasing new information through the CDC website as soon as we have it."

"Oh my God. Kenneth was right," I breathed into the phone. Latasha said nothing, but I could hear her fingers flying across the keyboard.

Reporters shouted out questions, but Dr. Normand held up a hand. "Let me explain what we know; then we'll get to questions. This is the first time we've identified this particular type of pathogen. It's neither a virus nor a bacterium. Rather, it's a misfolded protein. There are other diseases caused by prions, but what makes this one unique is that it is, to our knowledge, highly infectious."

There were more shouts from the reporters, which Dr. Normand waved down, this time with more difficulty. "We do not know where it came from, but finding its source is one of our highest priorities right now."

He consulted his notes again. "The prions attack the brain tissue of the infected person. The disease they create is characterized by rapidly progressive neurological deterioration, which can result in personality changes; impaired memory, judgment, and thinking; severe depression; bizarre behavior; hallucinations; paranoia; and delusions. It does not cause a fever or other flu-like symptoms, and infected individuals often remain physically healthy."

"Hoooooly shit," Wes said, his eyes wide.

"For now we are calling the disease created by this prion Gaspereau, after the lab where the pathogen was identified," Dr. Normand continued.

"How does it spread?" one reporter shouted at the same time another said, "Is it fatal?"

"Fortunately, it does not seem that Gaspereau is fatal," the doctor replied. "As I said, the infected individuals remain in perfect physical health. However, since some of the symptoms can lead to violence, there is a link between the growth of this disease and the recent rise in the violent crime rate in Clarkeston."

Wes and I exchanged glances. I hadn't told him about my suspicions regarding the man who'd killed our parents. But it seemed Kenneth had been right.

"The pathogen that causes Gaspereau is transmitted in the same fashion as the common cold virus, most readily by respiratory droplets that are released when an infected person coughs or sneezes. These droplets may then land on the mouth, nose, or eyes of those nearby. It can also be spread when a person touches an infected surface and then his or her own mouth, nose, or eyes." He cleared his throat. "The incubation period is relatively short, approximately twenty-four to seventy-two hours between contact with the pathogen and the first appearance of symptoms."

I'd never seen a press conference go to shit so quickly. Reporters clamored toward the platform, shouting questions and waving their recorders. A few slipped out the doors in the back—whether to file their stories or get the hell out of Dodge, I didn't know.

"Has a vaccine been developed yet?" shouted a reporter.

Normand shook his head. "As Gaspereau is caused by neither a virus nor a bacteria, a vaccine is not a plausible solution at this point, nor are antibiotics."

"Are you saying there's no cure?"

"We are working toward developing a solution as fast as possible," Normand responded.

"Is there the possibility of the pathogen going airborne?"

"Right now, there is no evidence of such a possibility," Normand said. "But we do encourage all those in the infected area, which right now is limited to the town of Clarkeston and the surrounding countryside, to wear a mask whenever they go out in public."

"How long has the CDC known about this? Why haven't we heard about it before?"

"Our test results were only confirmed today; as soon as we knew, we organized this press conference. We are doing everything we can to keep the public informed and safe."

"Is he serious?" Latasha said. I jumped. I'd almost forgotten she was on the line. "A disease that makes you go mad and spreads like the common cold?"

"He looks pretty serious," I said.

"Clare, you get your ass on a plane right now," she said, a note of panic in her voice. "Bring Wes; he can stay here. But for God's sake, get the hell out of there."

I tore my gaze away from the screen to look at Wes. He was looking back and forth between the television and me, his eyes full of confusion. When he spoke, his voice was low and quiet.

"Is he saying . . . schizophrenia is contagious?"

CHAPTER SEVEN

Back at the press conference, Dr. Normand cleared his throat. "I'd like to invite Governor Angela Preston to speak now." Visibly relieved, he left the podium, and a woman in a gray suit stepped forward. She reminded me of the staff at the hospital; it looked as though she, too, hadn't slept for days.

"Thank you, Dr. Normand," she said. "And thank you for everything you and your team are doing." She opened a folder and read from prepared notes.

"Our government has been closely monitoring the situation in Clarkeston ever since the increase in these symptoms was brought to our attention by health authorities a week ago. We have been working closely with hospitals and the CDC to find the root cause of this situation, which, as you've just heard, we now know. This newly discovered disease has progressed much faster than anyone could have anticipated. Now that the CDC has determined what is causing Gaspereau, our government will take all measures necessary to ensure the safety and health of our citizens and prevent the further spread of this disease."

The reporters still in the room shouted more questions, but Governor Preston was having none of it.

"Sit down," she snapped. "We're all adults here." Reluctantly, the reporters resumed their seats, their phones and recorders still held high in the air.

She drew a deep breath and looked as though she couldn't quite believe what she was about to say.

"I am immediately authorizing the implementation of our state's pandemic response plan, which right now is limited to the Clarkeston region. We will meet this challenge with information, efficiency, and cool heads." She emphasized this last part and glared at the reporters.

"Because of the rapid rate of infection and the current lack of a treatment, the best thing we can do right now is contain the spread of the disease. In order for this to work, we need everyone to take part. Here are the rules. Again, this is just for those living in or near Clarkeston.

"Number one. Stay home as much as you can. If you are caring for an infected person, we ask that you do not leave your home—and most importantly, that you do not allow the sick family member to leave. If you need medication or food, there is a hotline—I think it's coming up on the screen now—you can call, and someone will assist you. If someone around you becomes violent and you are worried for your safety, call 911. If you must leave the Clarkeston area, you'll need a signed doctor's note declaring that you are free of the disease.

"Number two. If you have to go out, avoid public gatherings. Keep your distance from others. Essential businesses will be kept open, and other businesses are being considered on a case-by-case basis. If you are an employer, consider allowing nonessential employees to stay home. The less contact we have with each other, the less this disease can spread.

"Number three. Wash your hands and wear a mask. The pathogen is not airborne, but by wearing a mask you will be less likely to touch your mouth or nose if you do come in contact with infectious particles. That's all I have for now; regular updates will be forthcoming."

The cameras followed as the governor left the room, surrounded by security. I stared, aghast, at the television as the news anchors dissected Dr. Normand and Governor Preston's announcements.

"Oh my God, Clare," Latasha said. "Are you okay?"

My stomach had solidified. The tips of my fingers were numb.

"I should never have come home," I whispered.

"You had no idea this would happen," Latasha said. "No one did, apparently."

I wanted to freak out, have a full-on nervous breakdown right there in my dead parents' living room. But I couldn't. Not in front of Wes. My mind was racing; had I had any contact with someone with Gaspereau? *That girl on the side of road—how close had she been? I was almost face to face with Emma. All those people in the waiting room . . . But I haven't touched anyone. Have I? Has Wes?*

"I don't buy it. Someone messed up," Latasha said.

"What do you mean?"

"I don't buy that no one saw this coming. There are armies of scientists out there whose sole purpose is to track down and identify new threats. How did this go unnoticed? How do they not have a treatment?"

I had no answers. My head was still spinning. I concentrated very hard on a spot on the floor, fighting the panic.

"Do you know anyone who's sick?" Latasha asked. "Do you think . . . you've been exposed?"

"I . . . I don't think so," I said. "I mean, I feel fine. But . . . Kenneth, he works in the hospital, and he wasn't wearing a mask until today. Hardly anyone was. What if he gets it?"

"He's a doctor. I'm sure he's taking precautions," she said, but she couldn't hide the worry in her voice. "Did you . . . get close to him?"

"No. I . . . he touched my arms. That's it. But . . . he seemed fine . . ."

"Oh, Clare . . . be careful. I'm so scared for you."

"Me too," I whispered. "I'm going to try to get a flight home. I'll keep you posted."

I hung up. "Come to Seattle with me," I said to Wes. "You can hang out there until this blows over. I'll see if Uncle Rob will come as well."

"What are you talking about?" He tugged on his scraggly beard.

"Didn't you hear them? An infectious disease that makes you, well—crazy?"

"Crazy like me, you mean?"

"I didn't mean it that way. You saw Emma at the hospital. That wasn't her. And the man who killed Mom and Dad—he must have had this disease. It's the only thing that explains it. Why else would one of their friends turn on them like that?"

"Maybe. But what about Mom and Dad's funeral?"

"It's—they're gone, Wes. They won't care. It's more important that we protect ourselves."

"More important to you, you mean. I'm not going anywhere. And you promised—you said you'd stay until after the funeral."

"That was before I knew what was really going on! Wes, you can't want to stay here. I'll pay for your plane ticket and everything."

"I don't care. This is my home. And I'm not going to run away because of some little virus. I've faced worse—demons and rogue angels. You think I can't face this?"

I pinched the bridge of my nose. "Fine," I spat. "You stay here as long as you want. But I'm leaving on the next flight I can find."

"Whatever. I'm going out for a smoke."

I heard the front door slam as I opened my computer. Then I called Rob.

"Did you hear about the CDC press conference?" I asked.

"No," he said. "What was it about?"

I explained it as best I could.

"Damn," he said. "Well, that explains a lot."

"You've noticed something was wrong?"

"Well, yeah, I thought something strange was going on, but I couldn't put my finger on it. Figured it was bad drugs or something. But can you see your old Sunday school teacher Mrs. Ackerman doing drugs? And yet she's been shuffling around, talking to her herself, saying things that make no sense. Greg took her to the hospital, but they sent her home—said there's nothing wrong with her physically. And Ronnie Hildebrant locked himself in his bathroom, wouldn't come out for all the pleading in the world. Stuff like that."

"Listen, I'm going back to Seattle. I'm sorry, I know I should stay, I just—"

"I get it. Hey, don't worry about it. Your parents would want you to be safe."

"I tried to convince Wes to come with me, but he won't. But you are more than welcome to come—you can stay with me for as long as you want."

"That's very generous of you, Clare, but I think I'd better stay here."

"Why?"

"Well, you said there's not a treatment, but I'm sure they'll find one soon enough. And in the meantime, they'll probably need some extra help. Maybe I'll volunteer with the Red Cross, like I did during Hurricane Bob."

"Are you sure? You don't have to be a hero."

"This is my home, Clare Bear. I know almost everyone in this town. I gotta help out where I can. But you do what you need to do. People will understand."

I told him I'd come say good-bye and return his car before I left.

Finding a flight was easier said than done—it appeared I wasn't the only one who wanted to leave. The fact that there were only two flights out a day didn't help. The next available flight left the next evening.

I booked it. I'd just need to get a doctor's note. How long would the lineups be for those? I texted Kenneth.

Just saw the press conference. Holy shit. I'm going back to Seattle tomorrow—any chance I can get a doctor's note from you?

Wes came back into the house, reeking of cigarette smoke. "So I guess you'll at least be here for the wake," he said, peering over my shoulder. I closed my computer without answering. He took a piece of pizza out of the fridge and chewed it loudly, sitting cross-legged on the floor. Then he nodded at the television. "You really think that's what killed Mom and Dad?"

"I do," I said. "It's the only explanation that makes sense."

He laughed—a manic, out-of-control laugh I'd always hated. When we were younger, it had usually meant he was either making fun of me or had pulled some kind of prank I had yet to discover.

"What?" I asked sharply.

"It's just . . . such a tiny thing, right? I bet you can't even see one of those Gaspereau things without a microscope! Something so little killed our parents!" He rolled onto his back, still laughing, his knees pulled up against his chest.

I scrambled to my feet. My patience was done for the day. "What's wrong with you? It's not funny!"

"I know it's not," he said, still chuckling. "It's a fucking tragedy, that's what it is."

"Then why are you laughing?"

"Because it's either that or shoot myself in the head. What would you choose?"

"Jesus, Wes, don't talk like that." I checked my watch. I had to keep moving. "I'm going to go to the store. If you're not coming to Seattle with me, you should at least have a good stock of groceries."

"Cool. I'll come with you to get them."

"I think you should stay here."

"Whatever. What if everyone's rioting? I can be your bodyguard."

"I don't think they'll be rioting just yet," I said, but I wasn't sure. How *would* people react to this news? How many people had seen or heard about the press conference? It must be all over the Internet by now. Were they panicking? I was so close to panic myself I could barely contain it. It was simmering inside me, waiting to boil over. *Move*, I told myself. *Just do something.*

"Come if you want," I said, snatching up the keys and my purse. "But don't touch anything, and don't get too close to anyone."

I peered through the window before going outside, as though expecting angry hordes to be stampeding down the street. It looked as sleepy as ever. I should check in on elderly Mrs. Johnston across the street when we got back, assuming she still lived there.

I turned on the radio in the car. Every station was talking about Gaspereau. The closest grocery store was only a few minutes away, but I took a longer route toward the Walmart, thinking they'd be more likely to have boxes of gloves and masks.

It had been less than an hour since the announcement, but the gigantic parking lot was nearly full. I pulled into the first spot I could find and jogged toward the entrance, spotting an abandoned cart on the way. I poured my travel-size bottle of hand sanitizer on the handle before touching it.

"What are we getting?" Wes asked, puffing as he caught up.

"Masks. Water. Lots of food." I steered the cart inside the store. The greeters at the door weren't smiling.

"Can you buy me some more smokes?" Wes asked.

I gave him a dirty look. "Fine. Anything else?"

He responded by throwing a huge bag of Twizzlers into the cart.

It was like shopping on Black Friday. Carts jostled against each other, but the people pushing them kept their heads down. A few were already wearing masks, but most weren't. I headed for the pharmacy section first.

Wes ran on ahead. "This what we need?" he yelled, holding a box of white masks over his head. I nodded, and he tucked it under his arm like a football. We grabbed several loaves of bread, a tub of peanut butter, and a bag of apples. The produce was already pretty picked over, but I threw in a bag of wilted carrots and some onions. I knew Mom and Dad kept a lot of meat in their freezer, so I skipped that section. The cart became harder to navigate as Wes and I loaded more things into it—boxes of cereal, cans of vegetables, jars of pasta sauce, a couple of multipacks of hand sanitizer, and a huge container of hot chocolate. People were streaming into the store in droves now. Several aisles away, someone was shouting, "If you're sick, get out! We don't want you here!"

"Let's go," I said, struggling to turn the cart toward the checkout. Wes grabbed the front of it and gave it a yank. For once, I was glad he looked the way he did; people gave him a wide berth.

The cashiers were putting people through as fast as they could, but most of them looked as panicked as their customers. A manager was going up and down the aisles, explaining the situation and handing out masks. As we stood in line, two cashiers from other registers grabbed masks and walked out of the store.

"What the hell is going on?" Wes asked.

"People are stocking up—probably planning to hunker down in their homes so they don't get infected," I said. "Which is what I highly recommend you do."

"Fuck it, let's just go," he urged me.

"I have to pay, Wes. I'm not a looter."

A young man ran by us and grabbed the batteries out of the top of my cart.

"What the hell?" I yelled after him, but at this point I didn't dare abandon my cart. If I left for even a second, everything we'd gathered would be gone. I grabbed onto the back of Wes's shirt to keep him from chasing after the guy. "Just leave it."

As the line inched forward, lights flashed outside the store. Two police officers came in and stood inside the entrance. Was the same scenario was playing out all across town? There must have been more than two hundred people in the store; if they decided to go on a looting spree, two cops wouldn't do much to stop them.

Finally, it was our turn to pay.

"Help me with the cart," I asked Wes after the last bag had been loaded in.

Someone tried to grab a bag, but Wes bodychecked him and yelled, "Nice try, motherfucker!"

We pushed our way to the doors, jockeying with the other shoppers as though this were a survival game of bumper cars. As soon as we emptied our treasures into the trunk, our cart was whisked away by a heavily pregnant woman. Around us, car horns blared as drivers jockeyed for parking spots. The screech of tires and a grinding crunch made me whip around—two cars had collided. Their drivers got out and started hurling obscenities at each other.

"Move your fucking car!" a man bellowed at me from his SUV. Wes rolled down the window and gave him the finger, and I quickly put the car in reverse before someone brought out a baseball bat—or worse, a gun.

Neither of us said a word until we got home. We sat in the relative calm of our parents' driveway. I flexed my fingers, which were sore from gripping the wheel too tightly. Finally Wes lit up a smoke and said, "Well, looks like the world has gone to shit."

I couldn't argue with him there.

***

We stayed up late and watched *Forrest Gump* on the old VHS player. I stayed glued to my phone, tracking the news as it spread across the country. But there were no new developments, no new announcements from the CDC. Finally my phone pinged with a response from Kenneth.

Re: the note. Are you sure you haven't been exposed?

Yes, I answered.

Let's touch base tomorrow before your flight.

That was it. I texted a response but got nothing back. He was probably overwhelmed. I couldn't help but worry. He was on the front lines. Surely they'd all be wearing protective gear by now—but what if it was too late?

Finally, beyond exhausted, I dragged myself to bed. My parents had changed nothing in my old room, except now the closet was full of my mom's sewing supplies instead of my clothes. The bed was still there, made up with my old bedding. "For guests," she would have said. But I knew the truth: she'd kept it there for me. I didn't want to sleep there, but I was too tired to look for an air mattress, and I knew from experience the sofa would kill my back. So I lay in my childhood bed in the midst of all that pink and tried without success to stop the hamster wheel spinning in my mind.

Eventually, exhaustion must have won over, because I was startled awake by the ringing of the doorbell. I sat upright so quickly my head spun. Maybe it was just a dream. The doorbell rang again—it wasn't. I checked the time: eight o'clock.

I stretched and yawned, thinking it must be Rob. I pulled on some jeans under my nightgown and topped it with a hoodie.

The bell rang again.

"Coming!" I tried to yell, but it came out in a squeak. I peered through the peephole, but it wasn't Rob standing on the front step. It was a man I didn't recognize, wearing a dark suit. He had a white mask over his mouth and nose.

"What the . . . ?" I muttered as I fumbled with the lock and opened the door a crack, leaving the chain in place. "Yes?" I said, squinting at him.

"Good morning, Ms. Campbell," he said. "I'm sorry to disturb you at home. My name is Dr. Stuart Hansen. I'm with the Centers for Disease Control and Prevention." When I didn't respond, he said, "May I come in?"

I took off the chain opened the door wider, letting him into the foyer.

Dr. Hansen nodded at me. "Thank you. I'll keep my distance. You understand."

"Yeah, social distancing. I saw it on the news yesterday."

"Ah, well then, that makes my job a bit easier," Dr. Hansen said. "You already understand the seriousness of the situation. I'm in charge of directing operations here in Clarkeston for the CDC. I'm here to speak with you about your brother. You're his legal guardian, correct?"

"That's right."

"I'd like to bring Wes in for some more tests."

I scowled, suppressing a yawn. "More? He already had an extra round of testing, and the nurse said the results came back fine."

"I assure you that he is well, and there is nothing for you to worry about," he said. "I would also like to give you my condolences on the recent loss of your parents."

How did he know about that? "Thanks. But what does the CDC want with Wes?"

Dr. Hansen cleared his throat. "This is off the record, of course. As part of our investigation into this new, er, phenomenon, we ran some additional tests on your brother while he was in the hospital's care. It was an ideal time to determine the similarities between the brain of someone with Gaspereau and that of someone with schizophrenia, since the two conditions seem to have similar symptoms."

I took a step back and crossed my arms. "Okay, that sounds wrong on a whole lot of levels, but keep talking."

"What we found was . . . intriguing. We'd like to do some follow-up tests as soon as possible. Right away, in fact. He shouldn't have been released when he was. It was a clerical error in the . . . confusion. We don't yet have all the information we need."

"But he's not infected with Gaspereau, right? Why do you still need him?"

Dr. Hansen pressed his lips together and stared at the floor. "He's not infected, no. Quite the opposite. It's all theoretical at this point . . . but I believe your brother may hold the key to helping us develop a treatment for Gaspereau."

I uncrossed my arms and stared at him. "Are you serious?" I asked. "You might be able to find a cure?" The smell of Emma's burning hair came back to me. What horror were her children going through? If there was a cure . . .

"It's far too early to tell," he said hastily, "which is why I need your brother to come in for some additional tests."

"Nope. Not gonna happen," Wes said from the top of the stairs. *Shit.* How long had he been listening? Dr. Hansen followed me to the bottom of the staircase. Wes was sitting on the top step, his hands gripping his knees. "I told you at the hospital, I'm done. Now fuck off. Get out of our house."

"Hey, Wes, I didn't know you were up," I said. "This is Dr. Hansen."

"Dr. Frankenstein, you mean."

"Hello there, Wes," Dr. Hansen said with a sidelong glance at me.

"Dr. Hansen was saying that they'd like you to go in for a few more tests. It might help them find a cure for Gaspereau," I said, unsure of how much Wes had overheard.

"And I was saying get the fuck out of my house," Wes retorted, getting to his feet.

"We just want what's best for everyone," Dr. Hansen said in a tone that was probably meant to be soothing but came out wooden and condescending. "Don't you want to help stop this disease before it spreads to the rest of the country?"

Wes's footsteps fell heavily on the stairs. "I said"—stomp—"get out." Stomp. "No more"—stomp—"doctors."

He reached the bottom. I stepped between him and the doctor, who hadn't yet retreated. "Wes, maybe we should hear him out," I said, holding my palms out, facing him. "Remember, the guy who killed Mom and Dad probably had Gaspereau—this might stop that from happening to anyone else!"

"Don't believe them!" Wes snarled. "I remember these guys—what was supposed to be a simple blood test turned into scans and all other kinds of shit. I told you, I'm just a guinea pig to them! I'm not going anywhere."

"Can you wait outside?" I said to Dr. Hansen. "Let me just talk to him for a minute."

The doctor didn't look thrilled, but he nodded and backed out of the entryway, closing the door behind him. I could still see his shape through the frosted glass.

"Listen, it's not a big deal," I told Wes. "He said it's just a theory at this point. Don't you want to help? What if they're able to find a cure?"

He snorted. "You're so naive."

"I'm not naive; I'm realistic. Come on. When was the last time you contributed to society? Helped someone?"

"You have no idea. I help people all the time, where it really matters—in the spiritual realm."

"I'm talking about *this* realm, where people are really suffering and dying and doing horrible things in spite of themselves because of this disease. What do you even do all day? Just sit around? Maybe this is your chance to give back to the world. Do something for someone else for a change."

I knew I risked setting him off. But I couldn't stop, now that I had started. It felt too good to finally say out loud what I had been thinking for years. "Look at all the things people have given up for you—how much Mom and Dad sacrificed. Did you know they had to remortgage the house? Do you have any idea what it's cost our family? How about showing a little gratitude? You could help a lot of people here. Make your life mean something."

"Are you saying my life doesn't mean anything?" he growled. His expression had darkened; his eyes narrowed.

"Of course not. It's just . . . it could mean more."

A knock on the door. "I'm sorry, but time really is of the essence," Dr. Hansen said, stepping back into the foyer.

"He still doesn't want to go," I explained, leaving Wes at the bottom of the stairs and meeting Dr. Hansen by the door.

"I'm afraid your brother has no choice," he said to me in an under-tone. "It's a matter of public safety."

Wes overheard this. "No choice? You're gonna drag me there? I'd like to see you try." He pulled a kitchen knife from his waistband behind his back and brandished it at the doctor.

"Oh my God!" I cried. When had he taken the knife? I should have locked them away. "Put that down!"

"Wes, if you come with us quietly, we'll just do a few more simple tests and then you can head back home," Dr. Hansen said. "You don't want to go back to the psych ward, do you?"

"I'm never going back there," Wes said, his face turning red and blotchy. "You'll have to kill me first."

"Please, just stop," I begged. "You're making everything worse. Just . . . give me the knife. Please." I edged toward him, hoping he wouldn't slash the blade across my face. I locked eyes with him, convey-ing as much compassion and understanding as I could muster. "Just give it to me, and we'll talk, okay?"

There was so much fear in his eyes I almost hesitated before taking the knife he held out to me. I tossed it across the room, out of reach.

"Thank you," Dr. Hansen said to me. Then he opened the door. "Wes, if you'll just come with me . . ."

"What the fuck!" Wes shouted. "I told you I'm not going anywhere with you!" Then he bolted through the living room.

To my surprise, Dr. Hansen sprinted after him, speaking into a small radio in his hand. "He's going out the back." Stunned, I followed just in time to see Wes heave the patio door open and vault over the railing to land in the backyard.

"Oh God," I breathed.

Two men in army fatigues were on him before he could get up. "Stop! Don't hurt him!" I cried out. I thundered down the patio stairs toward them.

Wes was fighting the men, but they were stronger—and better trained—than he was. They wrestled him toward the front yard.

Lights went on in the homes across the street. An ambulance and a couple of dark cars were parked in front of our house. As though on cue, they flashed red, white, and blue lights, filling the street with color.

"Clare!" Wes yelled. "Help me!"

Before I could say anything, Dr. Hansen reappeared at my side. "I'm sorry for this, Clare. We have to use whatever means necessary to end this. You're doing the right thing. He'll be well treated, I assure you."

I'm sure we all have moments in our lives that we cannot look back on without regret, without physical revulsion, without a burning in our cheeks. My modus operandi has always been to try and pretend these moments never happened, to wall them off with the other unpleasant aspects of my life. But there's also something powerful about embracing the worst parts of yourself, the parts you hope no one ever finds out about. To admit that you are not all light and hope and bravery, that you are both hero and villain in your life's story.

Deep down, I was glad they were taking him. If the government was going to be responsible for Wes, that meant I didn't have to be. I was free to get the hell out of Dodge and start pretending this entire episode had just been a crazy, fucked-up nightmare. I could return to Seattle, where everything was as it should be.

And so I let them take him without putting up a fight . . . even though I knew he was afraid, even though I knew there was something deeply wrong with the whole situation. I watched as they dragged him into the back of an ambulance, as his body sagged after being stabbed with a needle. I nodded blankly at Dr. Hansen's assurances that he would keep in touch, and took his card. He thanked me again for my cooperation and held out a gloved hand. In a tiny, useless act of rebellion, I didn't shake it. Instead, I went back inside and closed the door.

CHAPTER EIGHT

I spent the next hour roaming around the house, visiting each empty room and wallowing in the memories they offered up like gruesome sacrifices. A poem I had written as a child was taped on my mother's mirror.

I love you, Mommy
I love you a lot.
If I had money,
I'd buy you a yacht.

Why had she kept such a thing? Beside the poem was a sketch of one of our old cats that Wes had drawn, back when he had a steady hand. Such small mementos of a simpler time.

I headed toward the basement but stopped at the top of the stairs. As a little girl I had refused to go down there alone, convinced that ghosts would come out of the fake wood paneling and murder me. That had been years ago, but now the house seemed truly haunted. I chided myself for entertaining such infantile fears and forced myself down the stairs, flicking the light switch on the wall. The basement was dark and chilly, so I grabbed an afghan my grandmother had made from the back of the sofa and wrapped it around my shoulders.

I ducked into the crawl space to see if my dad's guns were still hidden there under a blanket. They weren't, which was a relief. It would be best for everyone if Wes came back to a gun-free home.

My dad's office and workshop were in the back, filled with relics from careers as a salesman, a woodworking shop owner, a trucker, and the manager of a small shipping company. Everything was covered in a thin coat of wood dust; apparently he had been using it more as a shop than as an office lately. A framed picture of my brother and me at Disney World hung on the wall. I looked about thirteen years old, and Mickey Mouse had each of us wrapped in one of his arms in a group hug. I didn't remember the moment, but in the picture I looked like I was enjoying it. Even Wes appeared to be happy.

The safe sat in the corner of the office. I squatted next to it and tried to remember the combination. It took me three tries to get it right, but eventually the handle snapped down and I yanked the heavy door open. I pulled things out one by one: a roll of gold coins, some strange-looking silver coins, and a stack of hockey cards. *Whoa.* Three Wayne Gretzky rookie cards in mint condition. How much would they be worth now?

Then I found the will. I opened it up and started to read before setting it down again. There were decisions to be made that were more pressing than the contents of my parents' will.

Rob answered on the first ring. "Morning, Clare. Did you get a flight?"

"It's not until tonight," I said. "Wes had to go back in for more tests this morning."

"Really? Why?"

"I'll explain later. What should we do about the wake? The governor said no public gatherings . . ."

"Bah. I don't care what they say, and neither will half the town. They can wear masks if they'd like, but I still think we should give people a chance to pay their respects. Besides, it's been advertised in the paper, so some folks are going to show up. Would be a shame if we canceled it—especially if you're still here. We can always see how the wake goes and then make a decision about the funeral."

Wes will be mad he missed the viewing. He wanted to say good-bye . . .

I groaned. As much as I hated small talk, the thought of being trapped alone with the ghosts in my parents' house was even worse. "Okay. I'll meet you there in an hour."

***

Rob and I were alone at the funeral home for the first hour of the viewing. Well, alone with the two urns containing my parents' ashes. Rob had blown up a picture of the two of them sitting on his deck last summer. My mom's head was leaning in to meet my dad's, and they both wore peaceful, satisfied smiles. It was a good picture; it was how they should be remembered.

Rob asked about Wes, and I told him about the visit from Dr. Hansen. I left out the part about them dragging Wes out of the backyard by force, but my face burned at the memory.

He whistled softly, the sound slightly muffled by the mask I'd insisted he wear. "I wonder what other tests they're doing."

I shrugged, ignoring the queasiness in my stomach. "He said the procedures would be simple. If it helps them find a cure for Gaspereau . . ."

"I guess. But I can't see Wes being too happy about it."

"Well, I'm sure he'll understand eventually, if it works. The greater good and all that."

I was saved by the arrival of my parents' young replacement pastor and his wife. They were wearing masks, and they made an awkward

109

kind of bow instead of shaking our hands. "I'm so sorry for your loss," Pastor Steve said. "Your parents were wonderful people."

"I've been crying nonstop since it happened," Pastor Steve's wife added. "I'm sure you have been, too." She looked about twenty, with waist-length blonde hair and so much foundation it was rubbing off on the edges of her mask. She went to hug me but then checked herself. "I'm sorry. I wish I could." I, for one, was glad she couldn't. "Is your brother here? The one who is . . . different?" She looked around the room, as though hoping he might pop out from behind the curtains.

"He doesn't really like crowds," I said, and she nodded sympathetically. This was not a woman with whom I would willingly share my secrets.

"You know, the Lord works in mysterious ways," she said, leaning in to whisper, as though we were co-conspirators in the Lord's plan. "Everything happens for a reason. We just won't know what it is until eternity."

I wondered if social isolation protocols precluded me from punching her in the face.

Rob must have read my intent, because he quickly intervened. "How are you liking the new church, Sylvia?" he asked, and she turned her tear-filled eyes on him.

A soft touch on my arm made me jump. It was Kenneth. Beside him was a little girl with deep brown eyes and shoulder-length black hair. A streak of hot pink peeked out from underneath the black strands. She wore a pink medical mask around her mouth and nose, but her eyes were dancing.

"Hey!" I exclaimed, too brightly. This was the only good surprise to land on me in a long time. "You came."

"Hi," he said. "We shouldn't be here, but I wanted to see you after . . . everything. How are you doing?"

"Thank you for coming. And you must be Maisie." I squatted down to her level.

"Hi," she said. "I'm sorry about your parents."

"That's so sweet. Thank you. Your dad's told me lots about you."

"He's told me lots about you, too," she said. I raised an eyebrow at Kenneth, who looked flustered.

"So how's it going?" he said, indicating the rest of the mostly empty room.

"So far? Torture."

"I thought you might feel that way, which is why I brought you this." He presented me with a travel mug emblazoned with the logo of Reid's Coffee Shop.

"Coffee?"

"With whiskey," he whispered, winking as he handed it to me.

"My favorite drink," I said, lifting my mask enough to take a big gulp. I winced as it burned a path down my throat. "You're the best," I croaked.

"Small crowd," he observed, looking around. Pastor Steve and Sylvia were standing with my uncle over by the urns, admiring the wreaths and bouquets of flowers that my parents' friends and family had sent in lieu of their presence. We sat down in the blue padded chairs that lined the room. Maisie pulled an iPad mini out of her backpack and settled back into her chair.

"She's adorable," I whispered.

"Thanks. I made her myself."

"I've been worried about you. How is it going at the hospital?"

"Insane—quite literally. They wanted me to pull a double shift, but I've got this little monkey to think of." He ruffled Maisie's hair. She smiled up at him, then returned to her game.

"What are they doing? How are they handling this?"

"The CDC is in charge, and they've sent in extra supplies— protective gear and sanitation units. Everyone's getting retrained on pandemic procedures."

"What about the people who are sick?"

He looked away. "They're trying . . . different things. How's your brother?"

"Fine, I think." I told him the same story I'd told Rob, again making it sound as if Wes had gone willingly.

Kenneth wasn't so easily convinced. "You do know you have a choice, right?" he said. "He doesn't have to undergo any medical procedures without your consent, if you're his legal guardian."

"I know," I said, staring at my coffee mug.

"Did the doctor say what kind of tests they're doing?"

"No. He just said it might help them find a treatment."

He was quiet for a moment, then asked, "So you leave tonight?"

"Yeah."

"Isn't the funeral tomorrow?"

"I don't think we'll still have it, to be honest. I mean, if people are afraid to come to the wake, no one's going to risk going to a funeral. We can always have a memorial service . . . later."

His gaze was intense, and my pulse quickened. He opened his mouth to say something, then closed it. After another moment, he said, "Well, I brought you this." He reached inside his jacket and pulled out a folded piece of paper, then handed it to me.

It was a note declaring me Gaspereau-free. His signature sprawled across the bottom of the page.

I carefully refolded it and placed it in my purse. "Thank you."

He nodded. "I should go. I have to take Maisie to my mom's before I head back to the hospital." His eyes lingered on my face.

"Of course." I pushed down a twinge of disappointment. I wanted him to stay, to help me make sense of all this. But I was the one with a plane to catch.

He stood. "Time to go, Maisie."

The little girl jumped off her seat. "Bye, Clare!" she said brightly.

"Bye, Maisie. I'm so glad I got to meet you."

"Me too."

Kenneth took his daughter's hand. "It was good to see you, Clare. Have a good flight. And enjoy the coffee."

"Thanks again," I said. "Maybe . . . stay in touch?"

His eyes crinkled. "I'd like that."

I watched him go, resisting the urge to call after him. Then I saw, in horror, that Sylvia was coming back toward me, a sparkling glint in her eye. "So who was *that* young man?" she asked, though he was probably ten years her senior.

"An old friend," I said icily.

"Well, that's nice. We need friends to support us in times like these."

"Yes, we do," I said. "Excuse me. I have to go to the bathroom."

I took my time. When I returned, Pastor Steve and Sylvia had left and a few others had arrived.

"It was kind of them to come," Rob said, reading the expression in my eyes.

"It was," I admitted. We waited, mostly in silence, and made small talk with my parents' friends. A few of them shared fond memories of Mom and Dad, but the talk inevitably turned to Gaspereau.

I stood in a circle with three ladies from my mom's women's group from church. After they gave condolences, one of them said, "I went to refill my prescription this morning, just in case they run out. I've never seen anything like it."

"I heard that the army is going to completely quarantine the town," another whispered.

"But what if we run out of food?" the third asked, looking anxious.

"I thought the governor said they would deliver food and supplies if you just called the hotline."

One of the women snorted. "Who would do the delivering? I can't imagine them sending Meals on Wheels to people's homes. What if someone in the house was infected?"

"I'm sure it won't get that bad," I interjected. "The government knows what it's doing. And they're working hard to develop a treatment. Maybe it will all be over soon."

The oldest of the ladies shook her head. "It's a different world now, Clare. Some of us lived through the war. We know how to go without, how to make things stretch. My mother had to feed a family of six on half a dozen eggs and a pound of cheese a week. These days, everyone wants to get as much as they can for as little as they can. They want the government to give them everything."

The other ladies nodded in agreement, then started comparing stories of how their own parents and grandparents had coped during World War II. I politely excused myself to greet some newcomers.

There were never more than five or six people in the room at a time, and no one stayed for long—it was hardly the wake my parents would have wanted, or deserved.

Between thanking people for their condolences and controlling my tongue in response to their ill-expressed platitudes, I thought of Wes and how he was doing, whether they'd had to keep him sedated, and what kind of information they might be able to gather from their tests. What if it didn't work? What if they were hurting him? Was he scared? In pain? *Maybe it will be over soon. And Wes will be a hero.* If they really did find a cure, he'd have no choice but to forgive me.

Finally, the last visitors left, and Rob came over to me. I'd been staring through a small stained-glass window in the outer wall, seeing nothing. He pulled his mask down. "Well, kid, I think we're done for the day." I nodded. "When I talked to Pastor Steve earlier, he agreed that we should postpone the funeral until this is all over." I nodded again. "Why don't you come home with me, and I'll order in some early dinner? Your flight doesn't leave for a few hours, right?"

I turned away from the window. "Sure. Thanks for looking after all this, and for everything else. Still won't come with me?"

"Nah. I'm good here."

"I know this is a lot to ask, but can you check in on Wes?" I gave him Dr. Hansen's number and told him where the apartment key was. "I don't know how long they'll need him, but . . ."

"I'll look out for him, don't worry. Ready to go?"

"Almost. I just . . . want to say good-bye to them alone for a minute."

"Take your time," he said. "I'll head home; come on over when you're ready."

It was strange, standing there between the remains of my parents. The words of Emily Dickinson came to me: "After great pain, a formal feeling comes." Perhaps that was why my eyes were dry, why there was no great outpouring of sorrow. In that moment I didn't feel anger, sadness, or even loss. There was only numbness, a strange acceptance that this was the way things were.

There was a polite cough from behind me, and I turned to see two latecomers. I recognized the couple as friends of my parents. They, too, wore masks. How odd that only a day had passed since the announcement and I was already used to the sight. They joined me in front of the urns.

"We're so sorry for your loss," the woman said.

"Thank you . . . Carol and Alvin," I said, glad to have remembered their names. "You played cribbage with them, right?"

"That's right," Carol said. She shook her head. "Such a tragedy. We're just praying this doesn't happen to anyone else. All those infected people, it's dreadful . . ."

"Do you know anyone else who's been infected?" I asked.

"Oh, yes. Donna Ray from the Missions Society, and one of my daughter's old high school teachers—Mr. Sweeney. He got sick just a day or two ago. He was probably one of your teachers. Do you know him?"

CHAPTER NINE

All the air was sucked out of the room. "Mr. . . . . Sweeney?" I gasped.

Carol nodded, mistaking my shock for sorrow. "Yes. Tragic, isn't it? Such a lovely man. His wife is sick now, too. She was traveling. Came back at the worst possible time. Must have caught it from him."

"Excuse me," I said, and bolted for the bathroom. I locked myself in a stall and leaned against the door.

Oh my God oh my God oh my God. Mr. Sweeney has Gaspereau. I remembered his strange behavior at the airport, how he'd coughed into that beige handkerchief, specks of spittle flying everywhere . . . including on my face. I'd thought nothing of it at the time. When was that? The man on TV had said that the incubation period was twenty-four to seventy-two hours. I pressed my head between my hands and forced myself to calm down enough to think. I'd arrived on Sunday night, and it was now Wednesday afternoon . . . almost seventy-two hours later. I didn't *think* I had any symptoms—but if I did, would I know? Did people with Gaspereau know they were thinking and acting bizarrely? What if I had it and had given it to Wes or Rob or Kenneth? I ripped off my mask and heaved over the toilet.

I wiped my mouth with a handful of toilet paper. Hands still shaking, I called Kenneth on my cell.

"I wasn't expecting to hear from you this quickly," he said, but he sounded pleased.

"Kenneth, I think I might have Gaspereau," I blurted out.

"What? How? I just saw you. You said you haven't been exposed."

"I know, but I just found out that someone who coughed on me has it." I told him about meeting Mr. Sweeney at the airport. "His wife has it, too, which means he must have been contagious. Kenneth, I'm freaking out here."

"Where are you?"

"I'm still at the funeral home. What do I do?"

"Listen, I know you're probably worried about spreading it—if you have it, that is. But remember, it's not airborne. Just keep your mask on and try to avoid touching things for now. Come on up to the hospital and we'll test you."

"Kenneth . . . I can't. I can't go into one of those little isolation rooms. It'll make me crazy."

"If you test positive, you might have no choice, but between you and me, we're running out of isolation units already. I shouldn't do this . . . but if you come over now, I'll do the test myself. A year ago we'd have been screwed, but the British recently developed a blood test for prions, and thank God. I have a buddy in the lab who can run it through for me quickly. Then at least we'll know."

"Okay. Thank you. I'll head over right now."

I left the funeral home without even noticing whether Carol and Alvin were still there. In the car, I sent Rob a text, saying I'd be late. I didn't want him to worry or try to come see me.

In town, hardly anyone seemed to be taking the government's advice to stay at home. There were long lines at the gas stations, and every grocery and convenience store was overrun. I kept running through the symptoms in my mind: Was I having paranoid thoughts? Had I done or said anything bizarre? Would I even recognize it if it happened?

I pulled into the hospital parking lot. A large sign had been erected that read "Gaspereau Triage." An arrow pointed toward the front of the hospital, where a school bus sat blocking the entrance. I got out of my car and walked toward the bus. It was hard to believe what I was seeing. Military vehicles surrounded the bus, and armed soldiers stood in clusters on either side. I stopped walking. The doctor's note Kenneth had given me was burning a hole in my purse. I could go; I could get out of here, get back to Seattle and hunker down in my apartment. No one would know, except Kenneth.

As I stood there, a car pulled up near the bus. The back door opened, and a woman fell out, landing hard on the pavement. Then the car drove away, its door still open. A nurse wearing head-to-toe protective gear ran toward the woman, accompanied by a soldier. He was holding what looked like a snare pole used to catch wild animals.

"That is really not necessary!" the nurse snapped at the soldier. He took a step back, but his eyes were glued to the nurse as she helped the woman to her feet. The woman seemed disoriented, unsure of where she was. The nurse led her into the bus.

I couldn't go. Not yet. If I had Gaspereau, I couldn't risk spreading it to the rest of the world. I'm here, I texted Kenneth. Please tell me I don't have to go into that bus.

Stay where you are—I'll come get you, he replied.

I stood rooted to the spot, half expecting one of the soldiers to strong-arm me into the bus if I moved any closer. After a minute, a figure covered in head-to-toe blue protective gear emerged from the hospital and waved at me. I assumed it was Kenneth, but he was unrecognizable under the suit, face mask, and respirator. When I got close enough to hear him, he said in a muffled voice, "It's going to be okay, Clare."

I couldn't answer, so I just followed him inside. The hospital looked different this time. Even though I knew the white walls and linoleum floor were the same, it felt as though I was entering another world. And I didn't know if I would be coming out.

I kept my head lowered as I followed Kenneth down a corridor. No one stopped us; apparently no one wanted to get too close to anyone wearing a hazmat suit.

We entered an examination room, and Kenneth shut the door behind him. I must have been staring, because he said, "The suit's overkill. Especially since Gaspereau's not airborne. But it's protocol now. Don't let it worry you."

I nodded and sat down on the examination table. "Please, can you test me? I need to know." I bit my bottom lip and blinked furiously. "Have you been tested?"

The face mask and respirator bobbed up and down. "We all were. I'm fine." He pulled some swabs and empty vials out of a cupboard.

"Is there really no cure?" I asked. "I mean, if you can test for it, why can't you cure it?"

He stared down at the vial in his hand. "We can identify cancer pretty quickly, too. Maybe whatever the CDC is doing with Wes will result in a treatment. I can only hope. But I'll make sure you know one way or another as soon as possible."

"Have you seen Wes? Do you know where he is?"

He shook his head. "How are you with needles?"

"Fine."

"Then this should be over quickly," he said. He tied a piece of elastic band around my upper arm, swabbed a patch on the crook of my arm, and stuck the needle in me without ceremony. I winced and watched the vial fill with dark red liquid. After a moment, it was over. Kenneth clutched the vial in his hand. "I'll give this to the lab now, and we should have your results within a couple of hours."

"A couple of hours? What about my flight?"

Jodi McIsaac

"That's the best I can do," he said. "And my buddy is fast-tracking you. With the backlog we have on our hands, it would normally take a couple of days, maybe a week. If you're all clear, you can catch another flight tomorrow."

"If there are any seats left." I put my head in my hands. "A couple of hours, and then we'll know if I'm going to turn into a monster or not."

Kenneth placed a gloved hand on my arm. "We'll keep you safe, Clare, no matter what happens."

"What if you can't control it? What if too many people become infected?"

"If everyone follows the right procedures, it won't come to that." His eyes told me he believed what he was saying, but I wasn't that trusting anymore.

"Is that what those soldiers out front are here to do? Make sure everyone follows 'the right procedures'?"

"Partially," he said. "A lot of the nurses and doctors are spooked. They appreciate the extra security. Gaspereau symptoms are so unpredictable. That's why they moved triage to the bus outside. Easier to contain."

"But they'll find a cure soon, right? Then everyone will be okay. They said it's not fatal."

Even behind the suit and the face mask, I could see the sadness in his eyes. At the funeral home he had been warm and comforting, but here . . . he was on the front lines of a losing battle.

"A cure could take months, maybe even years," he said. "We have a long road ahead of us." Then he shook his head. "I'm sorry. I'm not helping things by being maudlin."

"You're just telling the truth. And Kenneth . . . if I have it, can you tell Wes I'm sorry? I . . . I might not be able to do it myself."

He didn't ask what I was sorry for. He just nodded. "I'll let you know as soon as I do," he said.

Then he went out, and I was left to ponder my fate. And the fate of the world.

I paced around the small room. I imagined a world of Terrys and Mr. Sweeneys and Emmas—everyone seeing things that weren't there, hearing voices, believing their loved ones were now their enemies. A world of Weses at his worst.

I sank down in a chair against the wall. If I were infected, would I see Wes again? Would he come and visit me? When I'd visited him, years ago, in this psych hospital, I'd wanted nothing more than to leave. Had he seen it in my eyes? Would he feel the same way?

I tried to think of other things—of Latasha and Amy, of Kenneth and Maisie, of Rob . . . but my mind kept returning to Wes. Had he felt this scared, this trapped, while he was waiting for his results?

For the first time in my life, I saw my brother in a new light. I'd been living in terror of Gaspereau for just over an hour. Did he live with this same fear every day? Was he afraid his schizophrenia could take over—*would* take over—were it not for his daily medication regime? Did he wonder what it might make him do next? Did he second-guess every thought, wondering if it was a creation of his own mind—or a lie told to him by the disease?

I hadn't prayed in years, but I was desperate. "Please don't let me be infected, please don't let me be infected," I muttered, just on the off chance that I had gotten it all wrong—that there was a God after all, and he would choose to answer my prayers. Had Wes prayed this same prayer when he was in the psych hospital for the first time, awaiting diagnosis? How, then, did he still believe in God? What kind of God would let this happen?

And what kind of sister would leave her brother to this fate?

The thought came unbidden into my mind, driving in the truth with the force of a sledgehammer. I knew he'd been right, back in our parents' kitchen. He *had* been the only one to defend me. And I had left him to rot.

***

It had happened ten years ago, but it wasn't the kind of thing a person could forget.

I was as shy and socially awkward as ever, weighed down with the crazy brother and the house full of rules, when I met Myles. He was everything I was not: popular, outgoing, and attractive. He was the mayor's son and the captain of the college track and field team. To me, he seemed perfect. And then he somehow noticed me, sitting beside Latasha in a corner at a house party. We danced, and I felt like I was flying. He asked me out to the theater—*the theater*—that weekend. We went for dinner, saw a show, and drank a bottle of the most excellent wine I'd ever tasted. And then we walked.

We ended up in Cranston Park, a beautiful sprawling park with huge leafy maples and oaks and an expansive, manicured lawn. Flowers grew in orderly groupings beside decorative stones, and a white gazebo stood on the edge of a grove of elm trees, where weddings were often held. In the center of the park, a large wading pool attracted scores of toddlers in the summertime, and a nearby playground rang with the laughter and screams of schoolchildren during the day. It was a delightful place.

We sat for what felt like hours on the swings, just talking, trading stories—his were better—and taking drags off his clove-scented Indonesian cigarillos. He hung upside down from the monkey bars to make me laugh and won me over by singing "I am sixteen, going on seventeen" while dancing around the gazebo. It was the most perfect date I'd ever had.

And then, his cheeks dimpling irresistibly, Myles asked if I wanted to take a swim. It had been a hot day, and the water in the wading pool was warm. We ran and splashed and laughed, and the wine and the cigarillos went to my head and I felt faint with life and love. Then he kissed me, and at first it was so tender, so slow, I felt I might melt into him. He laid me down in the shallow water and put his arm underneath my head to hold it just enough out of the water so I could breathe between kisses.

And then he raped me.

He started out gentle, but the water had cleared my head, and it was only our first date, and I had rules about such things. I said "No," lightly at first, not wanting to offend or upset him after such a perfect evening. But he persisted, and so I said "No" louder and more forcefully. And when I tried to get up, he became angry, ugly, and petulant. He let my head drop so that it cracked against the concrete bottom of the wading pool and I saw stars and struggled to lift my head out of water, gasping for breath. "C'mon, Clare, you owe me this. Stay still— and *quiet*—or I'll hold you under until I'm done," he grunted into my ear, and I panicked and swallowed a mouthful of water. I coughed and choked in his face, but he wasn't holding my head up anymore, and my neck ached with the effort. Finally I took a deep breath and let my head rest on the bottom of the pool to give my muscles a break. I could feel him inside me, and I just prayed that he would hurry up so I could breathe again.

He rolled off me when he was done. I scrambled to my feet, surprised that my legs were still working, and started to run away—not knowing where I was going, just wanting to get away. I chanced a glance behind me as I ran. He was still sitting there in the pool, his pants around his knees, his limp penis lying waterlogged against his leg.

"Call me, or I'll kill you!" he yelled, and I turned my back to him and kept on running.

Everything that happened after that is very vague in my mind. I put those memories behind a wall in my mind, along with all the other things I don't like to think about. I do remember arriving back at home, soaking wet, and ignoring my mother's questions while I locked myself in the bathroom and spent the next hour in the shower, trying to expel all remnants of him from my body.

A few weeks later, once I worked up the nerve, I walked alone into the downtown police station. I made a statement, but the officer gave me a strange look. And then he asked me if I really wanted to lay charges against the mayor's son. Looking me straight in the eye, he threatened to slap me with mischief charges if it turned out I'd made it up. I just shook my head and left.

Then I told my parents, thinking they might help me. But they brushed it off. They told me I was probably exaggerating, and besides, they had always advised me to only date "nice Christian boys." If I'd listened, this never would have happened. And we didn't have the money to get involved in some legal brouhaha. They didn't even ask for his name.

I knew now, in hindsight, that they had been under a lot of stress with Wes, that they probably hadn't been equipped to handle yet another crisis in their family. But at the time, hearing those words, being so casually dismissed by the people who were supposed to love me and take care of me . . . it was more than I could take. I walked out of the house, stumbled down the middle of the road, and finally sat down on the curb outside a three-story yellow Victorian with white window shutters. I made the decision, then and there, to leave Clarkeston as soon as possible, to never look back. To never need anyone again.

But Wes believed me. I didn't tell him the details. No one knew those. But I started to cry when he asked me how it went with "preppy boy," and he gently teased the truth out of me. I begged him not to tell anyone, said I just wanted to forget about it, and he promised, albeit reluctantly.

A few days later, one of my friends told me that the mayor's son had been mugged the night before while leaving a bar. According to the gossip raging around campus, he was fighting for his life in the hospital.

When the police showed up the next day, I didn't have to ask why. Even then, Wes wasn't hard to pick out of a crowd—he already had several tattoos, and his hair was bright blue. True to his promise, he didn't tell them why he'd chosen to beat Myles to a pulp that night. He had looked the police officer straight in the eye and said, "Demons."

"You don't have to say anything until your lawyer arrives," the officer had cautioned him.

"I don't need a lawyer. I have the Lord Jesus Christ on my side. And I tell you, that boy was full of demons."

After almost a year of lawyers and psychiatrists and judges, Wes avoided criminal charges and was sent to Riverside Psychiatric Facility. That whole time, he never spoke a word about what had really happened.

But I never forgot how it felt to be trapped.

***

I stopped pacing the hospital room and sat down again. If I had believed in God, I would have tried bargaining, but I knew it was hopeless. There wasn't anything to do but wait. It was quite possible I wouldn't get a second chance to right all my wrongs; that they would lock me in a room, or keep me strapped down for months or even years . . . And that was assuming a cure would ever be found.

But if I did get a second chance, I knew I had to take it. Wes was the only one who had believed me, the only one who had come to my defense. And I had abandoned him again.

For the first time since I had arrived back home, I let myself cry. I knelt down on the cold, hard floor and wept for my parents, for Wes . . . and for myself. I wept because I had allowed that one horrible night to turn my heart into stone, because I'd shut out the person who needed me most.

I had no idea where Dr. Hansen and his colleagues had taken Wes, when he would be released, or what kinds of tests they planned to do on him. But I'd seen the terror in his eyes as they dragged him away. His voice echoed in the empty room around me as I clutched my face in my hands: *Clare! Help me!*

I will, I promised him. *If I get out of here, I will find you.*

If.

I would not be on that flight even if I could.

The two hours had come and gone, and still Kenneth had not returned. I finally called Rob to explain where I was. He wanted to come see me, but I told him to stay as far away from the hospital as he could. I sent Latasha a text, telling her I wasn't coming home that night after all. I'd explain the rest later. After crying myself dry and evacuating my bowels in the tiny adjoining bathroom at least five times, I lay on the bed, limp with exhaustion.

A knock at the door made me sit bolt upright. A nurse opened the door slowly, but she didn't come inside. "Clare Campbell?"

"Yes," I whispered. Where was Kenneth?

"Dr. Chu asked me to tell you that your results won't be ready until morning."

"Where is he? Is he okay?"

"He's busy with other patients," she said. "He said to apologize and suggest you get some sleep. I've brought you some extra blankets, but I'm afraid you'll have to stay in this room until your results are in. I also have some over-the-counter sleeping pills for you. Dr. Chu thought you might need them."

She set a small plastic bag, a bottle of water, and two blankets down inside the room, then made a hasty exit and closed the door. I padded across the room and examined the two pills in the bag.

"Thanks," I muttered, before tossing them down my throat.

***

I was groggy the next morning when the door opened and Kenneth came in. He no longer wore his hazmat suit, and he looked a little unsteady on his feet.

"Good morning," he said, closing the door behind him.

"Hi," I managed to squeak out, sliding off the bed. I couldn't ask the question, so I just waited.

He responded by pulling me to his chest. "You're fine, Clare," he said. "Your test was negative. Perfectly normal."

I sank to the floor, and he came with me. I sat limply on the linoleum tiles. "You're okay," he said over and over again, his arms still around me.

I'm okay, I repeated to myself, barely able to believe it. "Thank you," I finally managed to say.

"My pleasure," he said. He got to his feet and held out a hand to help me up.

"Have you been working all night?" I asked.

"Yeah. Just finished. Going home to get some sleep now."

"You deserve it. I'm going to find Wes. I should never"—my voice hitched—"have let them take him like that."

"I can come with you to talk to them if you'd like," he said. He grabbed his tablet off the counter and flicked through the screens. "I should be able to find out what room he's in."

I waited, still reveling in the relief of being Gaspereau-free.

Kenneth frowned. "Are you sure he's here? I don't see his name."

"I assumed so," I said with a scowl. "I mean, where else would he be? This is the only hospital in town."

"There's no record of him being here," Kenneth said. "Not since he was discharged into your custody."

"Maybe they just haven't processed him yet?"

He scowled. "Unlikely, but I suppose it's possible in this chaos."

"Maybe . . . he's somewhere else?" Haltingly, I told Kenneth the truth about the armed men, and how they had dragged my brother away.

A muscle under his eye twitched. "I know this is an emergency, but there are still rules. Wes doesn't represent a threat. They should never have taken him without your consent."

"I didn't exactly stand in their way." When he didn't respond, I said, "I'm going to go down to the front desk; maybe they have more up-to-date information."

"Okay. I'll call over to the psych side and check things out there," Kenneth said, but he was scowling. "Dr. Hansen didn't give you any indication of what they were planning to do with your brother?"

"No. I just . . . trusted him," I said, knowing how lame that sounded, how flimsy.

"Text me if you find him." Kenneth fastened a mask on his face and left.

I ran down the stairs. "Hi," I said to the woman at the information desk. "Wes Campbell. What room is he in?"

"Does he have Gaspereau? Because if so, you can't see him," she said.

"No. He came in with Dr. Hansen for some tests."

"Who?"

"Dr. Hansen from the CDC. He was brought here by ambulance yesterday morning."

She checked the computer. "I'm sorry, it looks like Wes was discharged two days ago."

I huffed at her. "Yes, but he was readmitted. Where is Dr. Hansen? He'll know where Wes is."

She scowled as she returned her glance to the screen. "We don't have a Dr. Hansen on staff here," she said after a moment.

"I told you, he's with the CDC," I said, my voice rising. "Where else would he be?"

"I'm not in charge of the CDC," the woman said waspishly.

"I *need* to see my brother," I said, leaning over the desk.

She rolled her chair back. "Ma'am, you *need* to calm down."

A soldier who had been stationed by the front doors walked toward us.

"Okay, okay, I'm calm," I said, raising my hands. "I just have to make a phone call." I went down a hallway and fished Dr. Hansen's card out of my purse. My fingers tightened around my phone as I listened to it ring.

"This is Stuart Hansen," he answered after two rings.

"It's Clare Campbell," I said. "I want to know where my brother is."

"Ah yes, Clare, thank you for calling. Wes is doing just fine."

"I didn't ask if he was fine; I want to know where he is. I'm at the hospital and they told me he's not here."

"Well, I'm afraid I can't disclose his exact location at this time."

My stomach turned. "What are you talking about? I'm his sister! I have a right to know!"

"I understand your concern, Clare. But it's a national security issue at this point. A lot is riding on the results of these tests. I'm just trying to keep your brother safe."

"Safe from what?"

"Clare, I promise I will let you know as soon as I have any information we can share. Remember what we talked about. If I can prove my theory, we'll be one step closer to ending this crisis."

"I don't care about your theory, Doctor. I care about my brother. You don't have his consent, or mine, to do any additional tests on him. I want you to let him go immediately."

There was silence on the other end. Then he spoke. "Please understand, I am not your enemy. I am doing whatever I can to prevent the worst pandemic the world has ever seen. Under the law, your cooperation is appreciated but not required. I believe Wes has a role to play in ending this disease. If I'm right, you'll soon be thanking me. You and everyone else."

Then he hung up.

CHAPTER TEN

"Dammit!" I made another call, this time to Rob. "It's Clare."

"Did you get your results?"

"Yes, I'm fine."

"Thank God. I was so—"

"I'm really worried about Wes," I blurted out. I filled him in on my change of heart and my search for Wes. "They won't tell me where he is, but I know they're not supposed to do anything to him without my consent, right? This Hansen guy is saying it's 'national security' or some bullshit. He claims I don't have a choice."

On the other end, my uncle cursed loudly.

"Can't you do something?" I asked. "What about your friend, the police chief?"

His voice was strained when he answered. "I don't think Jim can help. Governor Preston has declared a state of emergency. The CDC is calling the shots, and the National Guard is here to back them up. They're in charge now, not the police."

A chill ran through my body. "They didn't say anything about this at the announcement."

"I imagine they're downplaying it. People are panicked enough."

"Well, screw that. Who do I talk to at the army? I'll go to the governor's office and tell *them* what happened. They'll have to let him go."

"Hang on a minute. I don't want you getting in trouble. I told you, it's a state of emergency. They can pretty much do whatever they want—the regular rules have gone out the window. That means they can detain anyone they want, as long as they have a good reason. There's nothing voluntary about it."

"That's bullshit. There's got to be some way around it."

"Just wait it out for a bit longer," Rob said. "I'll see what else I can find out from Jim. You don't want to mess with these people. They take this kind of thing *very* seriously."

"So do I," I said as I hung up. I slumped against the concrete wall, thinking about where they might have taken Wes. There were a few medical labs in town; maybe he was in one of those. Or maybe they had a secret laboratory in the basement of a building somewhere. Where would be the most practical place to take someone if you needed to run medical tests on them? Of course, perhaps I was in the right place after all; he could be hidden somewhere in this very hospital. But I would have bet a lot of money that my description was being made known to all the hospital security guards by now if that was the case. Maybe they'd taken him to Atlanta in a military plane. He could be anywhere. *I should never have let this happen.*

My phone buzzed with a text from Kenneth. Any luck?

No. You?

Sorry, no. Looks like he's not here.

Where are you?

In my office. Room 142.

I left the relative calm of the stairwell and made my way to Kenneth's office. He was sitting at his desk, his head in his hands.

I sat in the chair opposite his. "How are you feeling?" I asked, though the answer was evident.

"Exhausted," he muttered. "And . . . overwhelmed. You wouldn't believe what it's been like here over the past couple of weeks. I mean, nothing ever happens. And then we had a patient commit suicide, and now this whole nightmare . . ."

"Wait—you had a patient commit suicide?"

"Yeah. Over in the psych ward. Hung himself."

My conversation with Wes replayed itself in my mind. "What was the patient's name?"

Kenneth frowned slightly. "I don't remember off the top of my head. Why?"

"Was it Winston Ling?"

His frown deepened. "Yes, that sounds right. Did you know him?"

I stood up, still trying to remember what exactly Wes had said. "No, but my brother did."

"Really? I'm sorry to hear that."

A crazy idea started to germinate in my mind. "Wes said this Ling guy was a scientist. He told Wes he used to work in a secret government lab."

Kenneth leaned back in his chair and surveyed me with suspicion. "Okay, but remember that they were both in the psych ward . . ."

"We're looking for Wes, right? What if the secret government lab this guy told Wes about is real, and that's where they've taken him?"

"Clare, I really doubt that."

"You have any better ideas?" I pulled my phone out and googled Dr. Winston Ling. "Ha! See?" I waved the display at him.

"See what?"

"First result. Dr. Winston Ling is—was—a researcher at the Maine Experimental Farm."

"The what?"

"I don't know, but it sounds like it could be a lab. And it's just outside of town. I'm going to go check it out."

"You're not serious."

"Wes was telling the truth about Ling. Maybe the rest isn't so far off either."

"It's a hell of a connection to make."

"What if it's not? If you wanted to hide someone, and you knew of a secret lab nearby, why wouldn't you use it?"

Kenneth put his head back into his hands. "Clare . . . I know you want to find your brother, but why don't you just call the doctor from the CDC and ask where he is?"

"I did," I snapped. "And he told me it's a matter of national security. He wouldn't tell me jack shit."

He looked honestly surprised by my answer. "Really?"

"Yes, really! That's why I think something suspicious is going on. In a state of emergency, the government can do whatever it wants without being held accountable. So they could have him locked up somewhere, and . . . and . . . they could be doing who knows what to him against his will. I'm not going to let that happen."

I had wasted enough time arguing. I turned on my heel and headed back down the corridor. After a second, Kenneth came running after me. "Wait! Where are you going?"

"I told you. To the lab."

"Clare, this is ridiculous. He won't be there."

"I won't know until I look."

"And you think they'll let you in? If it really is some secret government facility, they don't just let members of the public waltz into those places."

I stopped by the front doors and looked him in the eye. "Then I won't waltz."

I turned to go, but he grabbed my arm.

"You always drove me a little crazy, you know that, right?"

"What's that supposed to mean?"

"I'm coming with you."

I shrugged and kept walking, but inside I was more than a little relieved. I had no idea what I'd find there.

Once we got in the car, he asked, "Where is this place?"

"Rural Road Five."

"That's way out there."

"Yep."

"I need to call my mother, let her know I'll be late." He looked tense as he dialed. I listened to him speak in rapid Mandarin. I couldn't understand a word, but he sounded apologetic. Then he switched to English.

"Hi, baby," he said, his tone soft. "Did you have a good night? Uh-huh. No, Daddy worked all night. I haven't even slept yet! I know. Yes, I'll be home today. Soon, I hope. I'm just helping my friend Clare with something. Yes, that's her. Okay, I will. Really? What did Nai Nai tell you? Don't be scared, baby. No, it's going to be okay. I'll be home soon, I promise. I love you. Bye." He hung up. "Maisie says hi."

I smiled. "Hi back. It's great your mom can help look after her."

"God yes. I don't know what I'd do without her. Find a new line of work, probably."

"Is she scared about Gaspereau?"

"Yes." His jaw tightened. "It's more my mother; she's terrified. Maisie picks up on that. I've asked Mom to keep the TV off while Maisie's around, but she wants to know what's going on. And it doesn't help that I've hardly been home this week."

"I'm sorry," I said. "I know you should be with her."

"It's okay. She understands that I'm trying to help people. I think."

"She seems like a wonderful girl."

"She is. She's the best thing that ever happened to me. I never knew the mere existence of another person could make me so happy."

My chest tightened. "That's great."

"So . . . what's your plan?" Kenneth asked as we turned onto a country road riddled with potholes. I slowed down; according to my GPS, we were almost there.

"Well, if he's in there, we'll find whoever is in charge and demand they release him."

"You said yourself they can do whatever they want. What if they still refuse?"

"Then I'll think of something else," I snapped.

His eyes tightened.

"I'm sorry. I know you're just trying to help. I just . . . don't have much of a plan. I'll wing it, I guess." I squeezed his hand, trying to convey my sincerity. "Thank you for coming with me." He didn't speak, but covered my hand with his own for a brief moment before pulling away.

We reached the countryside without incident. The houses and farms were few and far between. Green fields—potatoes, most likely—spread out on either side of the road. "It must be just up here . . ." I said. "There." I pointed to a building set a couple hundred feet off the road and double-checked the GPS.

"It looks like an old factory or something," Kenneth said. It was a rectangular building with faded brown siding. Huge exhaust pipes and fans littered the roof. I turned into the driveway and stopped in front of a small white sign that read "Maine Experimental Farm."

"Well, I guess this is the right place," Kenneth said. "But it looks vacant."

I stepped out. The slam of the car door echoed in the air around us. So much for sneaking in.

A set of glass doors barred the entrance. They were locked, so I pressed my face to the glass and peered inside. It looked like your standard office reception room. On a desk in the corner were a small calendar and a bottle of hand sanitizer. A few plastic chairs were lined up against the wall.

I banged on one of the doors with my fist. "Hello? Is anyone here?"

Kenneth gave me a bemused look, then walked around to the other side of the building. The area around it was rocky and overgrown with weeds, and I had to watch my footing as I walked along the exterior and stretched up onto my tiptoes to peer in the windows.

Then there was a soft click behind me.

"And just what do you think you're doing?" a man's voice growled.

I jumped and turned, my hands halfway up in the air. A security guard in a navy blue rent-a-cop uniform was standing three yards away from me. He was pointing a gun at my face.

"I'm just . . . looking . . . for someone," I stammered.

"No one's supposed to be here," he said, jabbing his gun in my direction.

"Please put that down," I said, my voice a little more steady. "I'm just looking for my brother."

A strange, vacant look passed over the man's face. "I had a brother too, once."

"Please, put the gun down."

He looked as if he was about to comply, but just then Kenneth came running around the corner. "Clare? I thought I heard—" He stopped short. "What's going on? Who are you?"

"I'm the one in charge of this place," the man growled, his whole body rigid, the gun still directed at me.

Kenneth moved slowly toward me. "Listen, please put the gun down. We were just looking around. We'll be on our way."

"I have a higher calling!" the man yelled, and Kenneth stopped in his tracks, his eyes narrowed. He and I exchanged glances.

"Gaspereau," Kenneth whispered, and I nodded.

"What's that you're saying about me?" the security guard asked.

"I'm a doctor," Kenneth said loudly and slowly. "You're sick. We have to get you to the hospital."

The man started to shake. "I know what happens at the hospital. I'm not going anywhere!"

"What is this place?" I asked him. "What's inside there? Is my brother here?"

"No one is here. They all left. No one here but us ghosts." His eyes darted around the yard. The finger on the trigger was twitching.

Kenneth took a step forward. The man bellowed, "Get away from me!" and swung the gun wildly in his direction. His back was now to me. One false move, and Kenneth would be dead. My heart pounded in my ears.

Kenneth put his hands in the air. "No one is going to hurt you."

"I'll shoot you! I will!" As if to prove his point, the man pointed his gun at the sky and fired off a shot.

I grabbed one of the large rocks at my feet and ran at the guard while he still had the gun pointed away from Kenneth. I smashed the rock into the back of his head with as much force as I could muster.

It was enough. He fell heavily to the ground, and the gun scattered across the dirt.

Kenneth rushed toward the guard.

"Stop!" I shouted. "What are you doing? Don't touch him!"

"You might have killed him!"

"He was going to kill us both! And if you touch him, you're as good as dead. Just . . . leave him there. We'll call an ambulance after we leave."

"After we leave? Clare, there's no one here. We need to get out of here right now."

"Not until I'm sure Wes isn't inside," I said grimly.

"And how are you going to get in?" Kenneth asked. Rather than answer him, I picked up another large rock from the ground and hurled it at the door. The glass shattered, and a piercing alarm split the air.

"What are you doing?" he yelled. He tried to grab me, but I twisted away and reached into the broken glass door to open it from the inside.

"I want to get their attention!" I yelled over the noise. "If someone is in here, they'll come out." I half expected to see Dr. Hansen come bowling around the corner, but no one did. I ran through the lobby and down the hall. "Wes? Are you here?"

I threw open doors, still yelling my brother's name. The first three rooms were just offices, filled with desks and piles of paper. Then I came to another door that opened to a staircase.

I ran down the stairs, then stopped because it was pitch-black. I gave my phone a firm shake to toggle on the flashlight and shone it around at the walls, stopping when I found a bank of switches. I hit a few of them, and the space flooded with light.

Stretched out in front of me was a long corridor, with shiny cream walls and fluorescent lights. The alarm was still going off, but the sound was muted down here. I pushed open the first door on my left. Stainless-steel tables and large machines I didn't recognize lined the walls. A row of empty test tubes stood on one of the counters against the wall.

"Wes?" I said tentatively, knowing if he were here, it probably wouldn't be in this room. They said they wanted to do some scans of his brain . . . what if there was an operating room somewhere down here? I shivered. I hurried back out into the hallway and screamed when I nearly collided with Kenneth, who had just run down the stairs.

"Kenneth!" I gasped, clutching my chest.

"Clare, we have to get out of here!"

"Not yet! Help me look!" I said. I ran into the next room, which was very much like the last one except that it had huge glass cabinets under massive ventilation hoods against the walls. "What *is* this place?"

I headed back into the hallway, then stopped when I noticed the small sign mounted beside the door. "Amherst Core."

"Wes mentioned this!" I shouted, pointing. "He said Ling was working on Project Amherst!"

I ran back into the room and started to pull cabinet drawers open haphazardly. At first it just seemed to be a random assortment of instruments and safety equipment, but then my eyes found a file folder. It was empty, but a label in the top corner read "USAMRIID."

"Do you know what this is?" I asked, handing it to Kenneth.

He stared at it as though it might burst into flames. "Clare, we have to leave. I'm not kidding around."

"What is it?"

"United States Army Medical Research Institute of Infectious Diseases."

That's when it all clicked. "Oh my God," I breathed. "That means . . ."

"That means we're somewhere we really shouldn't be." He grabbed my arm and pulled me toward the exit. I let him lead me back up the stairs and out the smashed glass door, my mind racing so fast I hardly noticed where we were going. He yanked open the car's passenger door and pushed me inside, then ran around to the driver's side and got in.

"Give me the keys," he said, holding out his hand.

"What? Oh, here . . ." I fumbled in my pocket until I found them. He backed out of the driveway, his knuckles white on the steering wheel.

"Kenneth . . . do you know what this means?" I said once we were back on the main road.

"That we could be in a lot of trouble?" he asked grimly.

"No . . . Wes was right about Dr. Ling. He *did* work in a secret government lab, on a project called Amherst. What if he was right about the rest of it?"

"What rest of it?"

"He said 'something got out.' Wes thought it was mutants. But what if that something was Gaspereau?"

Kenneth gave me a sidelong look. "I don't know, Clare . . . I admit something strange is going on, but that's a hell of a leap." He sounded less than convinced.

I leaned my head against the window. Now that the adrenaline had worn off, I was starting to wilt, both physically and mentally. A yawn overcame me for a few seconds before I could speak again. "But why have a lab like that in the middle of nowhere?"

"Well, USAMRIID researches cures for infectious diseases, so being isolated is a good thing. But I don't understand the secrecy. Still, there was just that one file; it doesn't mean it's some underground USAMRIID lab."

"Yeah, but Project Amherst . . ."

"Clare. I thought this was all about finding Wes?"

"It is." I watched the fields pass by as we drove back toward town. "I really thought he'd be there. I'm sorry for dragging you with me."

"I offered, remember?"

"We should call an ambulance for that security guard."

"I already did, after you went into the building. I told them he attacked us and smashed the door. They won't know we went inside."

I shivered and crossed my arms.

"We both need sleep," Kenneth said. "And I need to get home to Maisie. But first I need to pick up my car from the hospital. Why don't you drop me off there and then go home and get some rest?"

I hated to admit he was right. Kenneth hadn't slept at all the previous night, and between shock and exhaustion, I was barely lucid. A deep, hopeless sorrow was settling inside me. I wished more than anything that I could turn back time, make the right decision, stand up for Wes when it counted.

Kenneth settled his hand on mine, which was resting in my lap. He squeezed it gently before letting go. "Hey," he said, his voice soft. "We'll find him."

I dropped him off at the hospital, near the staff entrance on the side, then drove slowly through town back to my parents' empty house. Even though I was drained, sleeping didn't seem like an option. I made a sandwich, then settled onto the sofa to get caught up on the news.

Then it hit me. *Latasha*. If anyone could find answers, it was her. My stomach fluttered at the thought. If she got caught, she'd be fired . . . or face jail time . . . or worse. But if she could get away with it . . .

I picked up my phone and dialed.

"Clare!" she exclaimed when she answered. "I was just thinking about you. What's going on? Why aren't you coming home?"

As quickly as I could, I brought her up to speed.

"That's . . . wow," she said after I finished.

"Kenneth thinks I'm crazy, but it makes sense. The scientist, the lab, Gaspereau . . . I mean, doesn't it?" I had the sudden horrifying thought that maybe it *didn't* make sense . . . to anyone but me. But I had tested negative for Gaspereau . . . hadn't I?

"It's weird, but it might just be coincidence."

"Or it might not be. Latasha, do you think you could look into it?"

There was silence on the other end. I held my breath.

"I don't know, Clare. It's not as easy as it sounds. I could land myself in some deep shit."

"I realize that. I wish I didn't have to ask. But this might lead me to Wes. I have no other leads."

I could almost hear her thinking in the background, struggling with the decision. The lump in my throat grew larger with every second of silence.

"Okay," she said finally. "I'll see what I can find. And if you're right . . . well, someone's got to be held accountable. Give me the details again."

I repeated the story and could hear her fingers clacking in the background as she took notes.

"There's only so much I can do," she warned. "But I'll let you know if anything pops up. Just lie low for a bit, will you? You're supposed to be staying away from this disease, not chasing it down."

"Thank you so, so much," I said. "I gotta go; Kenneth's calling."

"Okay. Talk soon."

I switched over to Kenneth's call. "Hello?"

"Hey," he said, his voice low. "I think I found him."

CHAPTER ELEVEN

"What? Where?" I jumped to my feet.

"By the time I got back, the CDC had taken over the entire psych facility and the third floor of the general hospital. They've locked it down. You need to be suited in order to go in; no visitors allowed. The army's enforcing. They've moved inside to help contain the infected patients."

"Contain them?"

"Think about it. With SARS or a flu outbreak, the infected are physically weak. They'll lie on a bed without moving. They won't try to escape, and they're not convinced that someone's out to get them. They won't attack you when you try to draw blood."

"Shit."

"Yeah. The first cases were kept in the psych ward, where there are locks on the doors. Once we ran out of beds there, we started putting patients in rooms on the third floor, but we either had to strap them down or sedate them so they wouldn't escape. The problem is, the sedation isn't working."

"What? Why not?"

"I don't know; it must be related to the prions. But so far, almost everyone with Gaspereau has presented violent symptoms. You saw Emma. Someone's got to be able to contain them. I guess the army drew the short straw. A lot of these kids in uniforms don't look older than eighteen, and they seem pretty freaked out by their assignment."

"I don't blame them."

"Apparently they're rigging up the college dorm to serve as a field hospital, but unless those doors lock from the outside, there's going to be the same problem."

"Have any of the soldiers been infected?"

"Not that I know of. They all have good respirators and protective equipment, but whether they know how to use it is another question. An armed soldier with Gaspereau . . . Jesus."

The carnage that would result from such a scenario wasn't hard to imagine. What if one of them went on a shooting rampage in the hospital? I pressed the heel of my hand into my forehead. This couldn't be happening. But it was, and we were right in the middle of it.

"Listen, Clare, I'd bet anything Wes is on the third floor somewhere. You said they wanted to study his brain, right?"

"That's what Dr. Hansen said."

"There are a lot of ways to do that fairly noninvasively—an MRI or a CAT scan, for example. But a colleague of mine says he got called into that wing to do a lumbar puncture."

"A what?"

"It's sometimes called a spinal tap—you extract a small amount of cerebrospinal fluid from the spine. It's a relatively safe procedure," he hurried to add.

"On Wes?"

"He didn't know who it was; the patient was fully covered, and they just referred to him as John Doe."

"Oh my God, he was dead?"

"No," Kenneth said quickly. "He wasn't dead; they just didn't want anyone to know his identity. Given what you've told me, I think it must be him."

"Why would they want his cerebrospinal fluid?"

"I don't know, exactly. Likely to compare it to a similar sample from someone who has tested positive for Gaspereau. CSF can be used for a number of different tests."

"Is he okay?"

"There's no reason to assume he's not. He's probably in recovery now. But they might have more tests planned for him, and some of them might not be as relatively risk free."

"Well, they can stop now, because he's coming home with me."

"Clare, you can't just walk in there and take him home."

"Why the hell not?"

"Because this place is crawling with soldiers, that's why. And there's no way you'll be able to get into the isolation floor."

I was silent, not wanting to ask.

He exhaled loudly. "There's something else," he said.

"What?"

"You said Dr. Hansen gave you the cold shoulder. That didn't make sense to me. So I took a chance and called the CDC director."

"You did? What did he say?"

"It took me a while to get through to him. But I dropped some names and said I had some important info about Gaspereau."

"Did you tell him about the lab?"

"No. But I asked about Dr. Hansen and Wes. He didn't have a clue what I was talking about."

"But if they think Wes can help find a cure . . ."

"Exactly. He couldn't even remember who Stuart Hansen was at first. I checked him out and he *is* an epidemiologist with the CDC, so he was telling the truth about that, but . . ."

"What the hell is he doing, then?"

"He might be doing exactly what he said: looking for a treatment. But it doesn't seem to be as . . . official as you were led to believe."

"Shit. We have to get him out of there. You're sure that's where he is?"

"Sure? No. But it's our best guess."

I was buoyed by the fact that he'd said "our." But this was my brother, my responsibility.

"I know what you're thinking," he said.

"I'm not going to ask you to do anything that could endanger your career, Kenneth. I'll get him myself."

"It won't work."

"I have to try."

"Have you considered talking to your lawyer? He can probably mount a constitutional challenge or something. You can get him out through official channels, particularly if this Hansen guy's operating off the books."

"Yeah, and how long will that take? Months? Years? No, thanks. I'm not waiting around."

"Listen, Clare, I don't agree with their tactics any more than you do. But this thing scares the shit out of me. If Hansen really believes studying Wes will help them . . ." He seemed unwilling to finish the sentence.

"I get it," I said. "I really do. I, of all people, have a reason to stop this thing. *Someone with Gaspereau killed my parents.* Do you know what it was like, those hours I spent in isolation, not knowing if I was going to turn into this raging monster? Knowing there is no cure? *I get it.* I don't want anyone else to get infected. But it can't be on Wes's shoulders. He's already gone through more than enough. And I owe him one. They're not even giving him a choice."

"I think we know what his choice would be."

"Exactly. It's not like Wes is the only person with schizophrenia in the world, or even in this town. Surely Hansen can do his tests on someone who is willing. That's all I ask."

"Something tells me this has to do with more than his schizophrenia. But I don't know what." He paused, then said, "Fine."

"Fine what?"

"I'll help you. I'll get him out."

I sat back down on the sofa. "Kenneth . . . *thank you.*"

"Meet me in the staff parking lot. And you're going to stay outside while I get him."

"No way!" I protested. "I'm coming in with you."

"Clare, they know what you look like, and they know you want him back."

"They know what you look like, too."

"Yes, but I'm supposed to be there. Doctor, remember? No one will question my presence in that ward, whereas I doubt you could get in the front door. You can be the getaway driver."

I huffed at this demotion, but he had a point. "Okay," I said. "And thanks again. I couldn't do this without you."

"No, you couldn't."

I slapped on a medical mask and jumped into the car. A few minutes later I pulled into the staff lot, which was on the far side of the hospital, away from the triage bus and main doors. A convoy of military vehicles was pulling out as I entered.

Kenneth waved me down and got in the passenger side.

"Where are they going?" I asked, nodding at the retreating army trucks.

"The college dorm, I imagine." He slipped his staff parking pass over the rearview mirror. "Just in case anyone asks questions."

"What's the plan?"

"There isn't much of one," he admitted. "First, I need to get to him. Once I know what state he's in and how much security they have on him, I'll figure out how to get him out."

"And me?"

"You wait in the car. Give me fifteen minutes—if I'm lucky. It might be more. Then drive around to the morgue entrance in the back."

"The morgue?" I asked, alarmed.

"Trust me." He gave me a nervous smile, then got out and went into the hospital. I checked the time: 2:13 p.m.

I stared at the concrete walls of the building, wishing I could see through them and know what Kenneth was doing. If he lost his job or went to jail over this, I'd never be able to forgive myself. And then there was Latasha . . .

But I'd also never be able to forgive myself for leaving Wes inside those doors. It looked like a lose-lose situation—unless Kenneth got Wes out and the CDC left him alone. Fat chance of that happening.

I have to get Wes out of Clarkeston, whether he wants to go or not. We were both clean; we wouldn't risk spreading the disease to Seattle. Kenneth would write us notes attesting to this. I'd had more than enough of this town—and I didn't think Dr. Hansen and his cronies would appreciate my busting their guinea pig out of the hospital. It was time to get as far away from this train wreck as possible.

Finally, the fifteen minutes were up, so I drove around to the back of the hospital. I'd never been to the morgue entrance, so wasn't exactly sure where it was. There were another parking lot, a couple of service bays, and a number of unmarked doors. I started to panic that I wouldn't be in the right place when Kenneth needed me.

A small sign on one of the doors caught my eye. I got out of the car and ran up to read it. "Clarkeston Morgue. Ring for Assistance." An arrow pointed toward a round doorbell on the side of the wall. I pulled the car up close and waited.

Another ten minutes passed.

My nerves were starting to reach the breaking point. I turned on the radio to see what station Kenneth had been listening to. Country. Ew. I checked over my shoulder every thirty seconds, terrified a soldier or police officer would appear and demand to know what I was doing there, then arrest me for loitering or some other trumped-up charge. I thought about calling Rob to see if he'd found out anything new, but he'd told me to lie low. The less he knew about what I was up to, the better.

The song on the radio ended, and the DJ's booming voice interrupted my thoughts.

"We've got some breaking news for our listeners. Governor Angela Preston is holding a press conference momentarily with an update on the Gaspereau crisis. We'll be bringing this to you live when—okay, it appears we're going live now. Here is Governor Angela Preston."

The governor's voice came over the air. "Our health officials have been working tirelessly since the discovery of the Gaspereau prion disease, and I would like to thank them for their commitment and dedication. Our police forces and state troopers have also been doing their best to maintain safety and security of the public in this difficult time. They, too, deserve our thanks.

"As you know, I have declared a state of emergency so that we can deal with this crisis as quickly and efficiently as possible. We are grateful for the support of the Centers for Disease Control and Prevention as well as our National Guard.

"Despite the best efforts of everyone involved, a treatment for Gaspereau has yet to be found, and the infection rate is showing no signs of slowing down. In order to prevent the spread of this disease to other parts of the state and country, I am quarantining the town of Clarkeston, effective immediately. All travel into and out of the region is prohibited. All flights have been canceled, and as of this time, all roads out of the area have been closed.

"It is imperative that no one leave the area until we know we have contained this disease. I realize this will be inconvenient for some, but our priority must be the health and safety of the public.

"I must remind you again, there is no reason to panic. Supplies will be brought into Clarkeston; there is no need for hoarding. Stay home if you can and avoid contact with others. We *are* going to beat this thing."

The DJ's voice came back on, less confident than before. "And there you have it. That was Governor Angela Preston, speaking to the media, declaring Clarkeston under a state of quarantine. We'll be following this story closely and will update our listeners as more information comes in."

Another country song came on, and I slammed my fist on the dial, shutting the radio off.

"Fuck!" I screamed, banging my head on the steering wheel. If only we'd left when we had the chance.

A knock at the passenger window made me jump. A young man in a blue shirt emblazoned with "ParkLine" in white letters was peering in at me, a mask affixed around his mouth and nose. I made sure my own mask was fastened tight and rolled down the window a crack. "What?" I snapped.

"Ma'am, are you okay?"

"I'm fine," I said, reining myself in. "I just . . . found out about the quarantine."

"They've quarantined us?" His eyes went wide.

I nodded. "The whole town. The governor just announced it."

"Shit," he said.

I nodded again and made to roll up my window.

"Wait," he said. "I came over to tell you that this isn't a parking zone. Are you waiting for someone?"

"Oh yeah, I'm just waiting for my friend. He's a doctor here."

"Is this his car?" the attendant asked, eyeing the parking decal dangling off the rearview mirror.

"Yes. He asked me to pick him up."

"Staff parking is over there," he said, pointing back the way I had come. "That's probably where he'll be expecting you."

"Oh!" I exclaimed, sounding clueless. "This is the first time I've picked him up. I wasn't sure where to go."

"No problem. And don't worry too much about the quarantine. We're all in this together."

I forced a smile—not that he could see it behind my mask. He stepped back, pointing again in the direction I was clearly expected to head. I didn't have much choice but to put the car in reverse and turn around. I watched the attendant in the mirror as I slowly drove away. Finally he headed back to a small booth I hadn't noticed before in the corner of the lot. Dammit. If—*when*—Kenneth came out with Wes, we'd have a witness.

I wanted to text Kenneth, but what if his phone buzzed while he was sneaking Wes out of there? I pulled into a parking space in the staff lot and pressed my knuckles to my forehead. I had to get back to the morgue entrance, and that meant I needed to get rid of the parking lot attendant—now.

I peered out the window, looking for security cameras. I didn't see any but pulled my hoodie up over my head just in case. Then I rummaged through the glove compartment and found what I needed—a Swiss Army knife.

There was no way this plan would work.

I walked a few cars over, gave one last furtive glance around, and stabbed the knife into one of the rear tires of a shiny black Lexus.

It was harder than I thought it would be, and I had to give the knife a good tug to get it back out. But then the air escaped with a hiss. I did the same with the other rear tire.

I sprinted back to my car and drove to the attendant's booth near the morgue entrance.

"Excuse me," I said, rolling down my window. He looked down at me. "My friend called and said he had to work late, so I'm going to come back later. But when I was in the staff lot, I noticed a car with two flat back tires. I'm pretty sure they were slashed. I thought someone should check it out, make sure there's not a vandal working his way around the parked cars. Or, you know . . . someone who's sick."

"Really?" the attendant said, glancing around at the cars near us.

"Yeah, it looked pretty bad," I said with a worried nod.

"Okay," the boy said as he climbed down from his booth, looking like he wanted to be anywhere else. "I'll get one of the security guys. We're supposed to let them know about anything unusual."

I drove slowly around the lot, waiting for him to round the corner to the staff lot, then raced back to the morgue entrance. It had been almost half an hour at this point. I was about to head into the morgue myself to look for him when the door opened. Someone in a blue protective suit was backing out, pulling a gurney with a body bag on it. My heart forgot to beat for a few seconds, but then the suited figure turned and waved at me. I jumped out of the car.

"Is he okay?" I asked, as Kenneth unzipped the body bag.

"Get in the backseat, quickly," Kenneth said to Wes, who looked barely conscious. I helped him off the gurney and into the car, where he collapsed onto the seat. "He'll be okay," Kenneth told me. Then his eyes tightened. "Where the hell were you? I looked out the door a few minutes ago and you weren't here. Do you know how dangerous this is?"

I glared at him. "I've been waiting for you. I had to get rid of a parking attendant who was wondering why I was lurking around the morgue. And yes, I know perfectly well how dangerous this is."

"Sorry," he muttered. "I'm on edge. They were keeping Wes sedated. He'll come out of it in a bit. Made my job easier, for sure."

"What did you do?"

"Turns out people tend to stay away from you when you tell them you're carting around a Gaspereau-infected body with several open wounds. I kept my face covered as much as possible—not hard with this getup—so I don't think anyone knew who I was. But I'd better get back in there and give myself an alibi. You just get Wes out of here."

"I'm going to kiss you so hard the next time I see you," I said without thinking. My hands flew up to cover my mouth. "I'm so sorry. I didn't mean . . ."

"Forget it," he said. I wished I could see his expression better. But he didn't sound angry. "You'd better hurry."

"Kenneth, I just heard it on the radio. They're totally quarantining the town. No one can leave."

A heartbeat of silence passed between us.

"I'm not surprised, but I'm sorry for your sake. I know you wanted to get Wes out of here."

"Yeah. Well . . . I'll think of something. Thanks again for your help. I owe you."

Our eyes lingered on each other. I was the first to look away.

"I'd better get back inside," he said. "Good luck." Then he wheeled the empty gurney into the morgue without looking back.

I drove away from the hospital as fast as I could. How long would it be before they discovered Wes was missing? Would they think he had walked off by himself? Would they send people to look for him, or would they just replace him with some other person with schizophrenia?

"Clare?" Wes groaned from the backseat.

"Hey there, big brother. How are you feeling?"

"Gross. Where are we going?"

"Somewhere safe."

"Are you working with them?"

"What? No! Of course not."

"Yeah, right."

"Wes, I'm serious!" I tilted the rearview mirror so I could see him better. "I came back for you. I should have done more to keep them from taking you in the first place. I'm sorry."

He didn't say anything, just stared out the window.

"Hey, listen." I softened my tone. "You have to stay with me, okay? I'll stand up for you. If you go off on your own, they'll find you."

"Do you know what they did to me?"

I wasn't sure how he was going to react, but lying wasn't the way to regain his trust. "I don't know all of it, but I think they extracted some cerebrospinal fluid."

"What the hell is that?"

"I'm not sure, to be honest, but it has something to do with the brain."

"How do you know?"

"Kenneth told me. He's the one who got you out of the hospital."

"Did he, now? And since when do we trust Kenneth?"

"I do."

"Bully for you. I don't trust anyone."

"You can trust me."

"Says the girl who skips town whenever shit hits the fan."

I pressed my lips together. "I'm here now, aren't I?"

"Want to know what I think?"

"Sure."

"I think they want to study me. They know I'm one of God's chosen warriors. They think it's something in my brain, but it's not. It's something in my spirit. And they can't cut that out of me."

I knew it would make things worse, but I couldn't help it. "When was the last time you took your medication?" I asked.

"This has nothing to do with my schizophrenia!" he shouted, lunging forward between the two front seats and making me swerve into the other lane.

"Hey!" I said sharply. "Are you trying to get us killed? Sit down and buckle the hell up."

He slumped into the backseat, but he didn't buckle up. The anger rolled off him in waves. What was I supposed to say? "Yes, you're a spiritual warrior chosen by God to rid the earth of demons?" I didn't even believe in God, let alone demons and angels. Bad things happened to good people all the time, and there was no rhyme or reason to it, no battle for souls going on behind the scenes.

In my opinion, if there was a God, he was an asshole. If God had the power to create the world, but he chose to ignore the cries of little girls being raped, mothers who sent their kids to school and picked them up in body bags, and little boys forced to kill their own families as child soldiers, then he wasn't the kind of God I wanted to know. And if he wasn't all-powerful, what was the point?

But I knew better than to tell Wes any of that. The last thing I needed was for him to decide I was under a demonic influence that needed eradicating.

"Where are we going?" he asked again.

"Mom and Dad's first," I said. "I need to get my things." I kicked myself for not bringing everything with me. "Then we're getting out of here." An idea started to crystalize in my mind. The quarantine had been declared only minutes ago. Surely they didn't have every road blocked off already. It was now or never.

"You ever heard of a FEMA camp?" he asked.

"Um . . . no. FEMA like Federal Emergency Management Agency?"

"Yeah. They've got these concentration camps set up in old military bases and shit. When the world starts ending, that's where they'll round everybody up."

"Why?"

"Well, not everybody, probably just the people they want to keep an eye on. They've got a list."

"Okay . . . so?"

"I'm on the list."

I actually snorted at this. "How could you possibly know that? I'm assuming that if this list actually exists, it's top secret."

He glared at me from the backseat. "I can see the future, okay? I know this is going to happen. And it's going to be soon."

The hair on my arms rose. Normally I would have brushed this off as one of my brother's many delusions. And it wasn't like I believed he could tell the future. But the idea of the end of the world coming soon was suddenly not such an outlandish idea.

"Hey," I said. "You don't need to worry about that. We're going to find a way out of town, then we'll drive down to Bangor and get on the next flight. You can come back with me to Seattle for a bit."

"Whoa, no way. I hate flying," he said.

"Whatever. We flew lots as kids."

"Why not fly out of here?"

"They've canceled all flights and quarantined the town. But they probably haven't had enough time to block off every single road out of Clarkeston. We'll take one of the dirt roads by our old home in the country."

"I'm not doing it. I don't trust you."

Ouch. "You want to stay here and go back to the hospital? Come on. You've never seen my place in Seattle. You'll like it there."

"You don't want me on a plane, Clare," he said ominously.

"I'm trying to help you! You'll be right beside me. It will be fine."

"No, it won't."

I couldn't tell if it was a promise or a threat.

CHAPTER TWELVE

Nine years ago, Wes and I sat across from each other, a small square table between us, as nurses and orderlies bustled around, going about their business while keeping a close eye on the visitation room. He'd only been in the psych hospital for a month.

"So, listen, I'm, um . . . moving," I said.

"Oh yeah?" he said. "New apartment?"

"No . . . well, yes. But I'm moving to London. England."

He scowled at me, as though he wasn't sure he had heard me right. "What do you mean?"

I laughed nervously. "I mean I'm moving to London. In a couple of days. I came to say good-bye."

He stared at me, dumbfounded, for a moment. "Do Mom and Dad know?"

"Not yet."

"What about your friends?"

"I'm going to tell them all soon. I wanted to tell you first."

His face hardened. "You can't."

"Why not?"

"Because I need you here!" he said. A couple of nurses looked in our direction.

"You'll be fine," I whispered, hoping that would coax him to keep his voice down. "You have really good care here, and Mom and Dad will visit lots, I'm sure."

"Are you fucking kidding me? After what I did for you? I kept it a secret because I promised you I would. And look where it's gotten me! If you're going to take off, the least you could do is tell them the truth, and maybe they'll let me out of here earlier. They'll know I'm not crazy."

But you are *crazy. You need this place.*

"It wouldn't change anything," I said. "It doesn't matter why you did it—or even what you did. You're not here because you beat up Myles; you're here because you're sick and you need help."

"So that's it? You're just going to leave me?"

"It's not like you'll be alone. Like I said, Mom and Dad will visit you lots. I bet Uncle Rob will, too. I'll call and send postcards. I might not be gone that long." This wasn't true. I didn't ever want to come back.

His voice changed. It was no longer defiant. He was begging now. "Clare, please. You don't know what it's like in here. If you don't want to tell them what happened, the least you could do is stay."

"What, in here?" I asked, alarmed at the thought.

"Hell no. I wouldn't wish that on anyone. Here in Clarkeston, where you can visit me . . . and I can call you if I need you."

"You can still call me if you need me," I said, tracing the grain of the wooden table with my eyes.

"What good will it do if you're in fucking London?" he said, slamming his hand down on the table.

"I'm sorry," I said. I pushed back my chair and stood up. "I love you. This is just something I have to do. For myself."

"You bitch!" he screamed, his chair clattering to the floor as he jumped to his feet. "This is the thanks I get for protecting you?"

"Wes, calm down," I urged. A couple of orderlies were making their way toward us. "I'll come back and visit, I promise. I just don't know when. Don't . . . let's not say good-bye like this."

"How dare you!" he yelled, and lunged toward me. The orderlies were close enough to grab him by now, one on each arm.

I put my hands out. "It's okay. Let him go." I wanted to calm him down, give him one last hug before I left. But as I got close enough to touch him, he bared his teeth and snarled at me.

"Ma'am, you should go," one of the orderlies said.

"But . . . it's the last time I'll see him . . . for a while."

"Go!" Wes snarled. "Go on, get out of here. Go enjoy your precious life."

"I love you. I do. Please believe me. I just . . . have to take care of myself now."

He snarled again. I walked away without looking back.

***

I pulled into the driveway of our parents' home, glancing behind to make sure we hadn't been followed. I considered asking Wes to stay in the car, but figured it would be safer if he was inside with me.

"Grab a suitcase from the storage room and put some stuff in it," I told him. "Your things are still upstairs. And change out of that, obviously." He was still wearing a hospital gown, which was open at the back.

While he was doing that, I went into my dad's office and locked the door. I filled a backpack with the gold and silver coins, the hockey cards, and a roll of bills I found stuffed in the back of the safe. I didn't need the money, but I figured it might help me get Wes set up in Seattle—and maybe pay off whatever debts my parents had incurred.

When I came up from the basement, he was sitting in the living room, his face in his hands. Tears squeezed between his fingers. A suitcase was splayed at his feet. I moved toward him, but he growled at me like a wounded animal. I backed away before moving gingerly forward again, this time toward the chair on the other side of the room.

"I'm sorry," I said fervently. "I was wrong. I know you hate doctors; I should never have let them take you. It's just that they said you could help find a cure for Gaspereau, and—"

"Don't make excuses for them," he snarled. "Or for yourself. All you are is selfish."

I winced, hearing my mother's words in his mouth. How many times had she called me selfish for wanting to come and go as I pleased, for wanting to throw off the shadow of my brother and live my own life? I understood now that her words had come out of a place of anger, frustration, and helplessness as she watched her family fall apart—but the wounded young girl inside me had never forgotten.

"I want to help you," I said, pushing down my anger, trying to be the grown-up. "But we need to get out of here. You say you don't like flying—fine. But if you stay here, they might come for you. And you can be as pissed off at me as you like, but if they come back here with the National Guard, I'm not going to be able to stop them. So it's your choice. Let's get out of here while we still can. Come stay with me, at least until this all passes over."

"And will you still skip town if I decide to stay?" he asked.

At this, my stomach rolled. "No," I said through gritted teeth. "If you stay . . . I will stay. I won't leave you." Panic whirled in my head, and my heart strained against my rib cage.

"Are you okay?" Wes asked, pulling me back into the present moment. His fists were still clenched, but his eyes had widened in concern.

"I'm fine," I said, straightening up. *Breathe. Control.*

"Well, I'll go, then," he said.

I stopped breathing. "What?"

He stood up, hauling the suitcase with him. "Let's go. Let's see if we can beat these motherfuckers."

I glanced at him uncertainly but decided not to question him on his change of heart. That conversation could happen when we were safely thirty thousand feet in the air—or better yet, after we'd landed.

He threw our bags into the backseat of the car while I locked up. A pang of regret made me hesitate. Should I call Kenneth and tell him what we were doing, insist that he and Maisie come with us? But he'd made his decision. And it was better if he didn't know. Plausible deniability.

Sirens screamed in the air as I drove away. I sped up and turned onto a seldom-used side road.

"Do you think they'll come after us?" Wes asked, glancing behind us.

I tried to quell my own paranoia. "I don't know," I answered, hoping I was right about the back roads. "Normally, they can't force you to stay in the hospital against your wishes. But I don't know what they'll do. It's different now; the government has more powers."

My cell phone rang, and I fished around for it in my bag. It was Dr. Hansen. *Shit.* I considered letting it ring, but there was no way they could know I had Wes—and I might find out more information about what they had done to him. "Hello?"

"Ms. Campbell, it's Stuart Hansen. Is Wes with you?"

"No, of course not. You wouldn't even tell me where he is," I retorted.

"I need you to be honest with me, Clare. This is a very serious matter."

"I don't know what you're talking about. You came and took him. Are you telling me you've lost him?"

There was silence on the end of the phone. "He is no longer in our care," he said eventually.

"Is that what you're calling it now? Care?"

"You don't seem too worried to hear that your brother is missing. Did he contact you?"

"I've spent most of my life not knowing where Wes is. He can take care of himself. And no, he hasn't contacted me. He hates cell phones, computers, and anything that's not a carrier pigeon." I shot an apologetic look at Wes.

"Where are you now?"

"I don't think that's any of your business. You abducted my brother, Dr. Hansen. And now it seems he's escaped, and I'm glad. I'm the last person who would help you find him."

"It was hardly an abduction, Miss Campbell. You were right there beside me."

I didn't respond. I felt sick.

"Look at the big picture," he continued. "You know I believe your brother can help us cure Gaspereau. A lot is at stake here."

I hesitated. What if Dr. Hansen was telling the truth? What was I doing? "You said it was just a theory."

He sounded frustrated when he answered. "The more I study your brother, the more I'm certain he is the key. You *must* bring him back, Clare."

I'd heard enough. I'd made my decision. "Listen, Doctor, do your experiments on someone else. You might be with the CDC, but I get the feeling your bosses don't know what you're up to. I don't know what you want with my brother, but until you can give me something more substantial than a bunch of vague statements that may or may not be true, I'm not letting you near him—if he does get in touch with me." I winced, hoping I hadn't given too much away.

There was another pause. "We're all taking risks here. But we have a chance to end this thing. That, to me, is worth taking a few risks."

"Look, there are plenty of people with schizophrenia. I'm sure some of them would be happy to help you. Wes does not want to be involved;

he made that pretty clear. Go find someone else." Why was he so fixated on Wes?

"You're right, Clare. There *are* others who might be able to help us study the similarities between the effects of Gaspereau and schizophrenia. But I have reason to believe your brother's case is . . . special. The way his brain works is unique."

"How?" I demanded. So Kenneth was right: something else was going on.

"If you and Wes would just come in, I'd be happy to sit down and explain it to you. Show you, even."

"Nice try," I snapped. "Look, I really hope you find a cure for this thing. I do. It's a bitch. But Wes's role in your research is done. Understand?"

"I'm afraid it's not that simple, Ms. Campbell," Dr. Hansen said. "We'll be in touch." Then the line went dead.

"Bastard," I said, throwing my phone back into my purse.

"What was that all about?" Wes asked.

"Well, they know you've left the hospital, and they want to know where you are."

"Why? What do they want?"

"More research, it sounds like." I didn't tell him what Dr. Hansen had said about him being special; Wes had enough delusions of grandeur as it was. "But it doesn't matter. If you don't want to volunteer to help them, I'm sure as hell not going to make you."

"As if you could."

I kept driving, my hands tight and sweaty on the steering wheel. We were just outside town. Growing up, we had often taken the back roads to my grandparents' home about an hour away, much to my father's delight and my mother's irritation. Dad had loved showing us the fields where he'd worked as a young man, the old logging roads he'd driven with his first truck. Surely they wouldn't have blocked all of them . . .

"You know, I don't even know how to use a carrier pigeon," Wes said suddenly.

I couldn't help it; I burst out laughing. Wes mimed tying a letter to a pigeon's leg. "Ow!" he said in a mock tone. "It poked me with its beak! How do you get these things to stay still?"

Our laughter died as we turned a corner on the dirt road I'd hoped would be our salvation. A military jeep sat in the middle of road about a hundred yards away. A soldier was leaning against it, smoking. On the road beside him were several barriers that had yet to be erected.

"Shit," I said, slowing the car.

"Should we turn around?" Wes asked nervously.

"He's seen us now anyway," I said. The soldier had stamped out his cigarette and was standing straight, his eyes on our car. "Just . . . stay quiet," I said.

I rolled down my window as we approached the jeep. The soldier gripped his weapon nervously.

"Hey there," I said, as casually as I could muster.

"The road is blocked, ma'am," he said.

"So I see. We need to get to Bangor for my cancer treatment. I just came from the hospital; my brother and I both tested negative for Gaspereau, so my doctor said it would be okay for us to leave town. If I miss a treatment . . . well, I've only got so long to live as it is. I'd like to have as much time as possible."

I didn't dare look at Wes, but I hoped he was keeping a straight face.

"I'm sorry, but I'm not supposed to let anyone leave."

"I understand about the quarantine, but we haven't been exposed to anyone who has it, and like I said, we both got tested just in case. We haven't been in contact with anyone else since we got our results. The quarantine is supposed to keep people from spreading Gaspereau, right? Not to keep people from getting cancer treatments."

The young man looked uncertain. "My mom died of cancer two years ago. I'm sorry."

"Thank you." I nodded gravely. "And I really appreciate what you're doing to protect our country. All I'm asking for is a little grace . . . for whatever time I have left." Was I laying it on too thick? But then the soldier stepped back and moved the metal barriers off the road. He returned to my window.

"I hope your treatments go well, ma'am. Good luck."

Trying to not let my astonishment show on my face, I nodded and drove slowly forward, past the jeep. I wanted to slam my foot to the floor and get out of there as fast as possible, but I forced myself to drive at a normal, nonpanicked speed.

Finally, once the barrier was out of sight, I risked a glance at Wes.

"You should be an actor," he said. "That was fucking awesome!"

"I can't believe it worked," I gasped. "We got out. We might even be able to get a flight to Seattle tonight."

I was calculating the distance to Bangor in my head when I glanced in the rearview mirror and my heart plummeted.

"Shit!" I cried. The jeep had followed us. A cloud of dust billowed in its wake as it closed the gap between us.

CHAPTER THIRTEEN

For a moment, I considered attempting to outrun it. But a Honda Civic was no match for an army jeep on dirt roads.

Maybe he's not after us; maybe he's just getting out of Clarkeston, too. But that hope was dashed when a red light flashed in his window and he called through a megaphone, "Stop the car!"

"Should we make a run for it?" Wes asked, reaching for his door handle.

"No!" I said. "If we run, he'll assume we're infected. He'll chase us. He might even shoot us." I slowed the car to a stop and put on my most innocent expression. The jeep passed us and then turned, blocking the road. The soldier got out.

"Is there a problem?" I asked, rolling my window down again.

"I'm sorry, ma'am, but I can't let you go. I called it in to my supervisor and he reamed me out big-time. He says there are no exceptions."

"I see . . ." It wasn't hard to look crestfallen at this turn of events. I leaned out the window and looked up at the young man. "Listen, between you and me, what if you just tell your supervisor that you sent me back. I'll continue quietly on my way, and no one will get in trouble."

He shook his head firmly. "Can't do that, ma'am. I shouldn't have let you through the first time. I'm going to have to ask you to turn your car around."

I glanced at the road ahead. There was no way for me to get around his jeep without ending up in the ditch. And I didn't want to do something that would get us arrested—or back in Dr. Hansen's custody.

"Fine," I croaked out, my throat tight. The soldier stepped back, and I executed an awkward three-point turn. The jeep followed us until it reached the roadblock site, where it stopped. But I could see him in my rearview mirror, watching us.

"It was a good try," Wes said after a while. I couldn't speak. My cheeks burned with disappointment and frustration.

"Do you think they're after me?" he asked.

I almost said, "You tell me. You're the paranoid one," but caught myself. This wasn't paranoia; it was reality. The CDC was in charge of Clarkeston now, and if they were looking for Wes, they would make damn sure he didn't leave. "I doubt they would set up a roadblock just to find you." I tried to sound reassuring. "They're keeping people with Gaspereau from leaving, remember?"

"Where are we going now?" he asked.

Good question. If they were looking for Wes, they'd be watching Rob. Going back to our parents' house was out of the question, too.

"We'll stay with Kenneth tonight, if he'll let us." I pulled over and sent Kenneth a text, then waited for a response. When my message alert went off, I read his response and sighed in relief.

"What's he say?"

"He just got sent home for some rest. He says it's fine."

"Where does he live?"

I raised my eyebrows as I looked at the address on my screen. "Fourteen Garden Way." That was one street I knew how to get to. It was the street that ran beside the river, and it was home to several turn-of-the century houses I'd always envied.

Wes was tapping his steel-toed boot against the underside of the dashboard. His hands were shaking.

"Are you okay?" I asked.

"I need a smoke. They took mine."

I released a sigh of exasperation. *Stupid habit.* But I didn't want him any edgier than usual. "Can it wait?" I asked.

He shrugged.

I kept driving.

"Are you and Kenneth, like, a thing?" he asked.

"No," I said with a pang in my chest. "I mean, we used to be really close friends, but no." What if we were, though? I pushed the thought aside and tried to ignore the bump in my heart rate as we drove toward his house.

I kept seeing flashing lights in my rearview mirror, but it always turned out to be another car's turn signal or the low-slung sun glinting off a window. Soon the houses were getting bigger and the lawns more opulent. I had no idea which one was number 14, so I slowed down and peered at the numbers: 10 . . . 12 . . . . "This must be it," I said, pointing at the next house.

I steered the car into the half-circle driveway. Kenneth lived in a white two-story Victorian complete with upper balcony, wrap-around veranda, and wood lace trim around the eaves. Bright red, purple, and yellow pansies grew in window boxes, and huge red rhododendrons beckoned from the front lawn.

"Fancy place," Wes said.

I got the suitcases out of the back and pulled them up the driveway. There didn't seem to be a doorbell, so I grabbed the brass knocker on the door, which was shaped like two cupids' heads kissing. I grabbed one of the heads and banged it against the other. A second later, someone fumbled at the door, as if they were trying to open it but couldn't quite manage it.

"Maisie!" came Kenneth's voice from inside the house. "Wait for me, baby." A moment later the door opened.

"Hey, Clare," Kenneth said, his face softening.

"I'm sorry to show up like this. Can we come in?" I said quickly, glancing at Wes, who was standing on the front step.

"Of course," he said, opening the door wider.

Maisie's eyes grew big as she took in Wes's hair, tattoos, and piercings.

"Thanks." I closed the door behind us and fastened the deadbolt.

"What happened?" Kenneth said. His eyes were scanning Wes, who had squatted down awkwardly next to the little girl.

"Hi! I'm Wes!" he said, holding out a hand. Maisie stared at it.

"My dad says I'm not supposed to touch anyone," she said. "Not even him."

Wes withdrew his hand and stood up. "You've got a good dad, then. He's careful."

"I like the stamps on your face," she said.

Wes laughed. "Thanks! Maybe you can get some when you're older."

Maisie looked up at her dad. "Can I?"

"We'll see," he said, still looking worried. "What happened? Everything okay?" he asked me.

"I'm not sure." We followed him and Maisie through a wainscoted hallway to the living room, which was lined with dark bookshelves.

"Have a seat," he said. "I'll get us some drinks." He headed back down the hallway.

I sank down into a tall wingback chair and watched Kenneth's daughter, who was doing the same with me. "How old are you?" I asked, though I already knew the answer.

She held up a hand, her fingers splayed out. "Five," she said.

"Are you going to kindergarten in September?" I asked.

She shook her head, sending her hair flying. "I already did kindergarten. But Daddy says I might go right into second grade."

"Maisie is a bit of a prodigy," Kenneth said, coming back into the room carrying a platter loaded with three bottles of beer, a pink plastic cup with a bendy straw, and a bowl of nacho chips. "She taught herself to read when she was three. I'm trying to figure out what to do with this little genius. Skipping a grade is only one option." He smiled proudly down at his daughter and handed her the pink cup, then passed beers to Wes and me. "I don't know if you've eaten yet, but I've got a lasagna in the oven."

"Awesome," Wes said, giving Kenneth the thumbs-up. "Is it okay if we take these off for a bit?" He pointed to his mask.

"Of course," Kenneth said. "But I don't want Maisie getting too close to anyone . . . just in case."

"Are you sure it's okay if we crash here tonight?" I asked. The last thing I wanted to do was put them in danger . . . but we had nowhere else to go. And I had to admit I felt safe with Kenneth. Or maybe it was just that I felt less alone.

"Of course," he said. "What are old friends for?"

"Sleepover!" Maisie cried, jumping up from her seat on the floor and bouncing onto the sofa where Wes sat. He drew back in surprise as Maisie did a happy dance beside him.

"Maisie, time to get ready for bed," Kenneth said. She stuck out her bottom lip but then bounced off the sofa and headed up the stairs. "I'll be right back," he told us.

I watched him follow the still-giggling girl out of the room, an ache growing in my chest.

"You gonna have kids?" Wes asked, apparently reading my expression.

"What? Oh, I don't know. I doubt it."

"How come? Too much work?"

"No, I'm just . . . getting old," I said, hoping he would drop it.

"Never too old for a miracle," he said, and I forced my mouth into a smile. Miracles were for other, more naive people. I pulled my phone out of my purse as a distraction and saw a text from Latasha.

Hey, I miss you. And our gaming nights! Let's meet online in that game we played last week.

I frowned at the tiny screen. Did she really think I was in the mood to game right now? Unless . . .

Sounds fun, I wrote back. How about now?

I dashed back out into the hallway so I could get my laptop from my bag and nearly ran into Kenneth as he was coming down the stairs.

"Sorry," I said, stepping back. "Is she asleep?"

"She's going to read in bed for a while. It's a bit early for bedtime, but I wanted us to be able to chat without her listening. What's going on? Where did you go after you left the hospital?" His hand rested on my arm, just above the elbow. I felt an insane desire to step into him, to wrap my arms around his waist and hold him like an anchor in an angry sea.

I took a step back.

"We tried to leave Clarkeston, get down to Boston. Obviously, it didn't work." I filled him in on the call from Dr. Hansen and the road-block. "I'm sorry I didn't tell you. I actually didn't know what I was going to do until we left . . . and I didn't want you to worry."

"It's okay," he said, though he looked slightly dejected. "I'm glad you felt safe coming to me."

"Honestly, I think I might be going a little crazy myself," I said, running a hand through my hair. "Am I totally overreacting? Give me your professional opinion," I added with a smile, hoping to lighten the mood.

His face was serious. "I don't think you're going crazy. Gaspereau has everyone on edge."

"Something's not adding up," I said. "Hansen seems totally focused on Wes. He said his brain is 'unique.'"

Kenneth's eyes narrowed. "What does he mean by that? He didn't say anything else?"

I shook my head.

The buzzer on the oven sounded. Kenneth went into the kitchen, and I found Wes watching TV in the living room. On the screen, a line of riot police advanced toward a crowd outside a grocery store.

"Where is that?" I asked.

"It's here," Kenneth said, coming back into the room. "The whole town has gone insane." Seeing the expression on my face, he hurried to add, "Not with Gaspereau, though I'd wager quite a few of the people out there are infected . . . or soon will be. People lose their minds in a crisis."

"Jesus . . ." I said softly as I watched the chaos unfolding. "I had no idea it had gotten this bad."

"You've been rather busy the past couple of days," Kenneth said wryly. "But people are terrified; they're not acting rationally. News about the quarantine seems to have made it worse." He walked over to the television and turned it off. "Come have some dinner. Let's pretend everything is normal for a little while."

We sat down at a round table in the corner of the kitchen, but instead of eating I opened my laptop. "Can I get your Wi-Fi password?"

"Sure. It's 'fluffybunnies.'"

I raised an eyebrow.

"Maisie picked it," he said with a wry smile.

"What are you doing?" Wes asked, watching my computer screen warily.

Kenneth glanced over my shoulder. "You're playing video games? Is this your idea of normal?"

"It's Latasha," I said. "I know I shouldn't have, but I asked her to help me find out where they were holding Wes. I forgot to text her after we got him. But I got a weird message from her saying she'd meet me online. Maybe she found something."

"Is this your friend who works for the NSA?" Wes asked.

"Mm-hm," I said. "So she can be a little sneaky." That was an understatement.

I waited for the game to load and took a bite of lasagna, hoping it would quell the nausea in my stomach.

Despite his misgivings about computers, Wes watched the screen with interest as I moved my avatar through the world. Kenneth's eyes were trained on the game, too. Latasha wasn't online. I texted her, I'm here. No answer, so I headed to the next town in the game universe, where I knew there was a mailbox. Maybe she'd left a message. There had to be some reason she'd wanted me to log on, and I doubted it was just to have some down time.

Kenneth and Wes ate their lasagna while mine cooled on a plate beside me. After a few minutes, Kenneth gave up interest in the game and began washing dishes, but Wes's eyes stayed fixated on the screen.

"Remember when we used to play games as kids?" I asked.

"Yeah. What was it called? That one we played all the time?"

"Phantasy Star II. It was awesome. You always figured out the maps and secrets before me, so that made it easier." I smiled at the memory. Most of my good memories of when things were normal, of when we were just your average brother and sister, had been eclipsed by everything that had come after.

"Yeah, well, I had help from Mom. She was better than I was!"

"She was not."

"She was! We used to play while you were at Scouts."

"I have a hard time believing that."

"It's true." He looked more closely at the screen. "What exactly are you doing?"

"I'm looking for the mailbox. Sometimes it moves around a bit." I played for a few more minutes, fighting some mutated wolves along the way, and then spotted it: a treasure chest sitting under a tree in the middle of a field. I went over to it and typed in the Open command. A window popped up, asking me for the password.

"Password?" I muttered. "I've never had to use a password."

Kenneth returned to the table and squinted at the screen. "It says you can click for a hint," he said, pointing. I clicked, and a question popped up on the screen. **Where do you want to live?**

I frowned at the screen. Why was Latasha being so cagey? I checked my phone—still no response from her. "Where do I want to live?" I asked out loud.

"Well, we know it's not here," Kenneth said wryly.

I shot him a look and typed in **Seattle.**

Password incorrect.

"Um . . . New York City?" I said, typing it in. I had often dreamed of living in New York—the New York of the movies, anyway. I'd imagined myself sitting in some artsy loft apartment with brick walls, writing the Great American Novel on my laptop and drinking red wine out of long-stemmed glasses.

Password incorrect.

"Oh, come on! There are a hundred places I want to live!" I tried Dublin, London, Edinburgh, Montreal, Vancouver, Los Angeles, San Diego, Bangkok, and Tuscany, but none of them were correct.

And then it hit me.

"Ohhhhh," I breathed. "Of course."

"What?" Kenneth and Wes asked at the same time.

"It's not serious," I said, staring down at the keyboard. "It's just something Latasha and I joked about once." I typed in **Albany.**

"Albany, New York?" Kenneth asked.

"Australia," I said.

"Why would you want to live there?"

I couldn't think of a convincing lie, so I told the truth. "It's as far away from here as you can get."

Neither Kenneth nor Wes said anything. I clicked "Enter."

The treasure box opened, and a screen popped up with a short message from Latasha. It read This explains a lot. Be careful.

"What explains a lot?" Kenneth said from over my shoulder.

"There's a file," I said, pointing to a tiny paper-clip icon beside her message. I clicked on it, and a document opened up on my screen. No one spoke.

Across the first page was a gray watermark that read "CLASSIFIED." The letterhead read "Department of Defense."

"That looks like something we shouldn't be seeing," Kenneth said.

Wes's breathing grew ragged.

"Are you okay?" I asked him.

"I need a smoke," he said.

"Hang on," Kenneth said. He got up and left the room, then came back a moment later. He handed Wes a nicotine patch. "That's the best I can do right now. We can make a smoke run later."

"You're a doctor," I pointed out. "Why do you have patches?"

"My ex decided to quit during our divorce. Not a good combination. I found some of her patches in my things after we moved."

We turned our attention back to the document on the screen as Wes slapped the patch on his chest. "This is so fucked up," he muttered. "I gotta get outta here."

"You'll do no such thing," I said sharply.

He stood up.

"Hey. Where do you think you're going?"

"I just need some space," he said. "I get fidgety."

My father had once told me that Wes needed massive amounts of sleep and hated crowds. Did Kenneth and I count as a crowd?

"You know, I've got some books upstairs in the library if you want to check them out," Kenneth said.

"You have a library in here? That's cool, man."

"C'mon, I'll show you." Kenneth led Wes up the staircase.

I watched them go, then moved my computer to the living room. I sat cross-legged on the sofa and scrolled through the document.

I hardly noticed Kenneth coming back down the stairs.

"Maisie's asleep and Wes is reading. He's in the guest room with a stack of books." He sat next to me. "So . . . what is it?"

A growing sense of dread spread through my stomach. For the simple crime of accessing this document, let alone sending it to someone outside of the NSA, Latasha could go to prison for treason. She had taken an enormous risk, which meant that she was very, very serious.

"It's from the Department of Defense. According to this, there was a breach at a government facility outside Clarkeston that was working on a biological weapons project called Project Amherst, and the project has been shut down," I said slowly. "That has to be the lab we visited. I thought they were finding a cure for something like Ebola! Not *developing* biological weapons! Why would they test something like that on U.S. soil, especially where there are people around? Are they crazy?"

"They used to do it all the time, back during the Cold War," Kenneth said, a look of deep concentration on his face. "I remember reading an article about some of the experiments they did—light bulbs filled with pathogens placed on the rails of the New York City subway, for example. And they would burst balloons filled with who knows what over major cities to track how the pathogens spread."

I drew back. "Are you serious?"

He nodded. "But it supposedly ended in the seventies. The U.S. and most other major countries signed a treaty to not use or test biological weapons anymore. Russia signed the treaty, too, but apparently there was still evidence of their program in the mid-nineties; some of the scientists working on it defected to the U.S."

"So if Russia didn't stop, chances are the U.S. didn't stop either," I said. "They just pretended they did."

"I don't know," Kenneth said. "It would be a hell of a job to move something like that underground. And we don't know for sure that's what this report is even referring to. But Project Amherst . . . that's too much of a coincidence to ignore."

"Damn right it is."

"Why would Latasha send this to you?"

Why indeed? I shook my head. "I don't know. I told her about the lab and asked her to look into it, but that's because I wanted to find Wes. She must have found this instead. But it's more proof that something screwy is going on. It says right here that there was a breach. Kenneth . . . I think they were developing Gaspereau as a biological weapon."

I got up and paced the room. "Do you have a flash drive?" He nodded and retrieved one from his office.

"Why else would they shut the project down, if not because of a breach?" I said as I downloaded the document onto the flash drive.

"I don't know, but does it matter? Let's say all of this is true. What—if anything—are we supposed to do about it? It doesn't change anything. It doesn't make Gaspereau go away."

"Maybe not. But it sure explains a hell of a lot. If the government created the pathogen that causes Gaspereau, then they'll be desperate to find a cure before anyone can point a finger at them. Hence the quarantine and the National Guard. And if they think Wes can help them develop a cure . . ."

"Then they'll stop at nothing to find him," Kenneth finished for me.

"Maybe Hansen isn't such a lone ranger after all." I cast a nervous glance up the stairs. I stood. "We should go."

"Go where? If they're looking for Wes, there won't be an easy way out."

"I don't know where!" I burst out. "I just need to get him out of here."

Kenneth regarded me silently for a moment and then said, "Stay the night. We're all exhausted, and we're not going to make good decisions. Get some sleep, recharge, and we'll figure out a plan in the morning before I have to go back in to work. Keep in mind that the safest place for you might be right here."

"I don't want to wait until morning. I want to get out of here now! I hate this place!"

"There are worse places to be stuck, you know." He sounded wounded.

"I doubt that," I muttered.

"Christ, Clare. Do you even know what you sound like? You've hated Clarkeston ever since I met you. Maybe it's not the big city, but it's your home. You belong here."

"Screw you," I shot back. "You think that because we had a one-night stand almost a decade ago, you have some special insight into my life? You don't know anything about me."

"I don't think *you* know much about you either," he said, his eyes flashing. "I don't get it. What exactly are you running from, Clare? Parents who loved you? A brother who's different? Life in a small town? Why are you always so desperate to get away?"

"Don't be so self-righteous," I spat. "The only reason *you* moved back to this hellhole is because your wife left you."

He gave me a single furious look before stalking over to the tall windows lining the far wall. He rested his hands against the wide windowsill and leaned his forehead against the glass. The window fogged up from his breath.

Shame crowded out my anger. As I watched him against the window, I regretted more than my harsh words. What was I doing? Kenneth had only ever been good to me. And yet I was still pushing him away.

"Kenneth, I—"

"Stop."

"What?"

"Just . . . stop. You're right; that's why I moved back. And you're right—I don't know you, not anymore. But I can't help it. A part of me is glad you can't leave. I want you to stay. I want you to *want* to stay."

I closed my eyes. When I opened them again, he was watching me. He didn't move, just stood there. Waited.

I stared at the pattern in the carpet. I couldn't do it. I couldn't push him away, not this time. Something wonderful was standing right in front of me, and for once in my life I wasn't going to let fear chase me from it.

"I *don't* want to stay," I said. "And maybe I don't have a good excuse. I don't know what it is about this place, other than I have a lot of bad memories and not very many good ones. Being here is toxic for me." His face twisted with pain, so I rushed on. "But that doesn't mean I don't want *you*. I do."

I'd taken the plunge; now I held my breath. His face softened, but his eyebrows lifted in skepticism. Still he said nothing, so I continued.

"In the hospital, after I said I was sorry, you asked me which part I regretted," I said, moving closer. "The truth is . . . I regretted leaving you. Not giving us a chance. That's it. I know things have changed and we're different people now. But I'm willing to give us a chance."

His eyes stayed trained on me, as though he had no idea whether I was going to hit him or kiss him.

I kissed him. At first, his lips didn't move, but then his arms tightened around me and he crushed his lips against mine. His touch and his smell and his taste swirled around me.

His lips found my neck, right above the collarbone. I moaned and pressed myself into him, threading my fingers through his hair. His hands slid down my back and scooped me up, and my legs wrapped around his waist. In two strides, he had me pressed against the wall.

His hands were frantic, as though he wanted to touch all of me at once. I pulled him closer to me with my legs and felt him stiffen in response. His hand slid inside my shirt and cupped my breast. A whimper of pleasure floated from my lips.

"Wait," I murmured, remembering. "What about Wes and Maisie?"

"Right. There's a lock on the bedroom door." He buried his face in my neck and said, "God, you feel so good." He let me down, and we ran up the stairs to his bedroom.

"Hang on," he said, as I moved to pull him down onto the bed. He left the room for a moment, and I quickly did a mental inventory. When was the last time I'd showered? Shaved?

He crept back into the room and closed the door. "They're both asleep." He came toward me, a shy smile spreading across his face. He lowered himself on top of me, taking his weight on his arms. For what seemed like a long while, I just drank him in—the flecks of light in his dark eyes, the faint scar on his chin, the way his shoulder muscles moved when he shifted position.

"I've missed you," I whispered.

"I've missed you, too," he said. Then his eyes sparkled. He lowered himself so his head was hovering over my thighs, and nibbled at them through my jeans. He came up a few inches and lifted my shirt so he could kiss my stomach, just below my waistband. I squirmed pleasantly and let out a soft groan.

Wordlessly, he slid my jeans off. I sat up and tugged my shirt over my head, then started to take off my bra.

"Let me do that," he said. He scooted closer to me and gathered me in his arms. He kissed my collarbone, then the tops of my breasts, while behind me his hands were busy with the clasp. "Victory," he murmured as the bra fell open and he slid the straps down my arms. Then his mouth closed around one of my nipples, and I was done with foreplay.

"You don't get to stay clothed," I said with a wink, pushing him down on the bed and straddling him as I undid his belt. I removed pants, boxers, and socks in one fell swoop, then climbed on top of him, pausing just long enough for him to slip on a condom. My hands dug into his chest as he entered me, and we both held still for a beat, savoring the moment. Then, eyes locked, our hips began to move in the dance we'd only just begun.

With every thrust he held me closer, his hands locked firmly on my hips. Finally, I felt him spasm under me and cry out, his neck arched and his fingers gripping me even tighter.

I smiled at him and slid off, preparing to curl up beside him.

"Oh, no, you don't," he said, flipping me onto my back. Then he kissed his way down my body, stopping between my legs. I moaned and squirmed and begged him not to stop. He didn't, not until my whole body convulsed and I fell back onto the pillows.

"That was . . ." I started, but couldn't find the words.

"Even better than last time?" he offered.

"Mm-hm. You've learned some new tricks."

"So have you. You're a lot more . . . aggressive, maybe? In a good way. A *very* good way."

"Call it a boost in confidence," I said, leaning my head on his chest.

"Hang on," he said, getting up and disappearing into the en-suite bathroom. He returned a moment later with a warm washcloth, which he handed to me. We cleaned each other up and then crawled under the covers, our skin still pressed against each other.

"Kenneth?" I asked, after a few blissful moments of silence.

"Mmm?"

"There's something I haven't told you. About why I left." Part of me didn't want to say anything, didn't want to ruin the moment. But he deserved the truth.

He rolled over and propped himself up on his elbow, studying me. "What is it?"

"Do you remember Myles Davidson?"

He frowned. "Yeah. The mayor's kid, right?"

"Right. Before I . . . before you and I slept together, I went out with him. Once."

"I remember that, vaguely," he said, his forehead wrinkling. "You were excited about the date. I was jealous, but then nothing really came of it."

Haltingly, I told him what had happened, including the response from the police, my parents—and Wes.

His expression darkened as I spoke. "I'm so sorry that happened to you," he said when I paused.

"Thanks. Me too. But the reason I'm telling you is because I want you to know *that* was why I left . . . It wasn't because of what happened between us. I just . . . couldn't handle it all. I thought the only way I could get over it would be to leave. Start fresh somewhere else."

I wanted him to wrap his arms around me, but he sat up and drew his knees to his chest, his eyes fixed on the other side of the room. "Why didn't you tell me?"

"I don't know."

"Did you tell Latasha?"

"No."

"Can I ask you something else?"

"Of course."

"Why . . . why did you sleep with me, back then, if you didn't feel the same way I did? I've never understood it. Was it . . . a rebound thing? A reaction to what had happened to you?" His voice ached.

"No. I don't know. Maybe."

"I loved you."

"I know. And I think . . . I was starting to love you, too. It scared me. I was overwhelmed by everything. It's not an excuse for what I did. It just seemed easier to leave than to sort it all out."

He nodded slowly but still didn't meet my eyes. "I understand. It makes . . . much more sense now."

"Are you still angry?"

"God no, especially after what you've just told me. I *was* angry, for too long. I guess I'd convinced myself that you felt the same way I did. Then to find out it hadn't really meant anything to you . . . It was a hard pill to swallow."

"It *did* mean something to me. I just didn't know what to do about it. I was afraid of everything back then."

He turned to me, cupped my cheek with his hand, then let his fingers trail down my lips and over my neck. "Thank you for telling me. I know how hard it must have been. And Clare . . . it wasn't your fault. Any of it."

"I treated you like shit."

"It wasn't your fault," he repeated.

We lay back down on the bed, arms and legs tangled like our messy lives. "You don't seem afraid now," he said.

I let out a short laugh. "I am. I'm terrified. But I'm braver now. I think."

He kissed my forehead. "You've always been brave." We fell silent, and a few minutes later Kenneth was asleep beside me. I slipped out of bed and pulled on his robe, then tiptoed down the hall to check on Wes. He was asleep on top of the covers, his boots still on his feet. He was snoring softly. I stood and watched him for a moment. His face took on an almost cherubic look in his sleep. I bent down and kissed his head, wrinkling my nose slightly—a shower was in order. But then I untied his black boots and tugged them off as gently as I could and found a spare blanket in the closet that I spread over him.

Wouldn't it be odd if the four of us lived together? Kenneth and me, Wes, and Maisie. What a strange family we would make.

I crawled back into bed beside Kenneth. My body was exhausted—from lack of sleep and the evening's exertions. But my sex-induced high was wearing off, and my mind was churning like a river in spring. I tried to puzzle it all out—Latasha's secret document, the dead scientist in the psychiatric hospital, Dr. Hansen's theory, and the nightmare of Gaspereau.

I thought back to the roadblock we'd come up against. I'd spoken to Dr. Hansen only minutes before. Could the whole quarantine have been meant for Wes and me, to keep us in town? I shook my head in the darkness. *Don't be paranoid.* But so many things didn't add up. If the army had created Gaspereau, why would they need Wes to help them study it? Wouldn't they already know all about it? Why would they need to compare it with schizophrenia? How long would they keep coming after my brother? And if they did, how would I keep them from taking him again? I checked my phone; still nothing from Latasha. Worry gnawed at my insides. Where was she? What was happening on her side of the world?

I finally drifted off to sleep, only to be startled awake several hours later by flashing lights outside the window. I slipped out of bed and peeked through the blinds. Police cars surrounded the house.

CHAPTER FOURTEEN

"Kenneth!" I whispered frantically, shaking him awake.

"Hmm?" he said, grinning at me sleepily. "Ready for round two?"

"The police are here!" I hissed.

He bolted upright in bed and pulled on a pair of pajama pants, then his robe, which I'd slung across the back of a chair.

"I'll deal with them," he said. "You go wake Wes up, but make sure he stays quiet. And don't leave the guest room." He hesitated. "Hopefully Maisie won't wake up. I don't want to scare her."

"What are you going to do?"

"Convince them you're not here, hopefully."

A loud knock boomed from the cupid door knocker below.

"But our bags! They're right by the door!" I said with a jolt of panic.

He grimaced. "Don't worry. Just go wake Wes up, and stay quiet."

I ran across the hallway to Wes's room and closed the door. As gently as I could, I shook his shoulder. "Huh? Whassaap?" he mumbled, his eyes looking blearier and more bloodshot than normal. I put a finger to my lips.

"Shhhhh. You have to stay quiet," I whispered. "The police are here. Kenneth is downstairs talking to them."

"Timezit?"

"Three in the morning."

There was another knock, and Wes swung his feet around and sat up on the bed. The stairs creaked as Kenneth walked down them, apparently taking his time. I opened the door of the guest room a crack and sat on the floor so I could hear what they were saying.

Fear pricked at my spine when the front door opened. Had Kenneth managed to move the bags? "Can I help you?" he asked.

"Kenneth Chu?" a man's voice came from the doorstep.

"That's me," Kenneth said with a yawn. "Is everything okay, officer?"

"We're looking for two individuals, Wes and Clare Campbell. We have reason to believe you might know where we can find them. Here are their pictures."

There was silence for a few moments. Then Kenneth spoke. "Sorry," he said. "I don't know where they are. Why are you looking for them?"

"I can't disclose that," the officer said. "You don't have any idea of their whereabouts?"

"No," Kenneth said. "I saw Clare at her parents' wake the other day, but not since then. What's this all about?"

"When you saw Clare, did she indicate any plans, say where she was staying?"

"I assume she's staying at her parents' house. They were recently murdered. I'm sure you heard."

"She's not there. Where do you think she might have gone?"

"I told you, I have no idea."

"Are you going somewhere?" the officer asked. "Looks like you're packed."

"I was going to take my daughter to stay with her mother in Boston. That is, until the quarantine was declared. I haven't had a chance to unpack yet."

"I see. Well, we'd like to search the house, if you don't mind stepping aside."

"I do mind, actually. It's the middle of the night. My daughter's asleep, and I just came off a very long shift at the hospital. I told you I don't know where they are. They're certainly not here, if that's what you're insinuating. I don't want my daughter to be woken up by police officers tearing our home apart for no good reason."

"It can't wait," the officer said. "Our orders are to search until we find them."

"And who exactly is giving you these orders?"

"I'm not at liberty to say. You understand that we are in a state of emergency, Doctor?"

"And even during a state of emergency, you can't enter private property without a warrant." There was a pause, then Kenneth continued. "Officer Jackson. You must be Katelynn and Andrew's father, right?"

"Yeah," the officer said, sounding confused. "How do you know . . . ?"

"I'm your children's physician. How's Katelynn's new puffer working out?"

"Uh . . . fine. Sorry I didn't recognize you; her mother takes her to all her appointments. Listen, Dr. Chu, my superior insists we check this place out as soon as possible. But I'll see if I can delay it until morning so you and your daughter can get some rest."

"I'd appreciate that," Kenneth said. He closed the door and bolted it, and then there was the slow creak of stairs as he climbed toward us. I was amazed at how calm he'd been, but when he reached us, he was shaking.

"Wait," he mouthed, putting a finger to his lips as he entered the room. I sat back on the bed and took Wes's hand. I wished I knew what my brother was thinking. He'd sat perfectly still throughout Kenneth's exchange with the police officer. Even now, he was like a statue. His pale blue eyes stared straight ahead.

Kenneth brushed aside the curtains and looked down at the street below. Then he turned back to us. "They're watching the house. A couple of cars left—to get a warrant, no doubt. But you won't be able to just walk out the front door."

"What are we going to do?" I asked. "How'd they find us here?"

He shrugged. "It's no secret that we know each other. A dozen people probably saw us together at the hospital."

"My parents' car is parked right outside. Do you think they noticed?"

"They didn't say anything, but they could be running the plates as we speak."

"I'm sorry," I said. "I didn't mean to bring this down on you."

"How you doing, Wes?" Kenneth asked, watching my brother closely. I put my arm around Wes's shoulders and squeezed.

"I knew this would happen," Wes muttered. "They've always been after me. But I'll go down fighting."

Kenneth squatted and looked into Wes's eyes. "Hang in there," he said, putting his hand on Wes's shoulder. "You have to take care of your sister. You can't do anything stupid. And you can't let *her* do anything stupid. She needs you."

I opened my mouth to say I was perfectly capable of taking care of myself, but Kenneth shot me a warning glance. "Clare, come help me with the luggage downstairs, please. Wes, can you stay here?"

Wes nodded mutely and lay back down on the bed, his arms folded across his chest, as though he were laid out in a coffin. He stared, unblinking, at the ceiling. A chill ran down my spine.

"Is he okay?" I whispered to Kenneth once he had closed the door. He held out a hand to stop me as he headed down the stairs.

"I don't really need help with the luggage, but I do need to talk to you. You shouldn't come downstairs; they might be watching the windows. Go back into my room. I'll be right there."

I did as he asked, peeking in on Maisie as I passed her room. She was sound asleep, her black hair spread out on her pink pillowcase, her rosy lips puckered and slightly open. I'd always dreamed of having a little girl, one with long, dark curls and a wild imagination. But I was afraid I would lose the genetic lottery, that my child would be more like Wes than she was like me. I didn't think I had it in me to go through what my parents had gone through. It was too great a chance to take.

A couple of minutes later, Kenneth joined me in his room. I'd left the lights off and was sitting on the floor by the far wall, away from the windows. He set the bags down inside the door and squatted beside me. I leaned against him, letting him support me. "Do you think they'll really come back with a warrant?" I asked.

"I think that depends on how many strings your friend Stuart Hansen can pull. I'm pretty sure I saw him in one of those cars outside the house."

"We're trapped, aren't we? They're going to take him back."

"There might be a way I can get you both out of here," Kenneth said. "But then you'd be on your own. I have to stay with Maisie; I can't come with you."

"Of course not. But how? You said they're watching the house."

He went to the closet and grabbed two large backpacks, which he tossed to me. "Put your things in these. They saw the other bags, so you'll have to leave them here." He paused. "You asked if Wes is okay. He isn't. He needs his medication or things might start to go downhill very quickly. If he gets to the point of full-blown paranoia, it might be very dangerous for you. Do you know what he's taking?"

I shook my head. I'd never made it to see the pharmacist, and the family meeting had been canceled. I had no idea.

"I'll go get him," Kenneth said, leaving the room. He returned with Wes a moment later. Wes looked alert and on guard—and more than slightly twitchy.

"Do you know what your medication is called, Wes?" Kenneth asked him, taking a prescription pad out of the drawer of his desk.

Wes gave him a name, and Kenneth scribbled on the pad, then ripped off the top sheet and handed it to me. "I don't know how serious they are; they might have sent an alert to all the pharmacies in town to keep an eye out for Wes. But I don't like your chances without it. Get the meds, and then get out of here."

"You still haven't told us how we're going to do that," I said.

"I'm going to drive you out," he said.

"What?"

"I think it should work," he said. "I'm a doctor, remember? I'm on call. It's totally normal for me to leave in the middle of the night."

"But what about Maisie?" I asked. The last thing I wanted to do was put his daughter in danger.

"I'll take her to my mother's."

"And then what?" I asked, confused.

"And then you and Wes will take my car, and I'll lie low at my mom's."

"And you'll use her car?"

"That's right. The town is falling apart, in case you haven't noticed. The cops have better things to do than follow me around once they realize you're not here. Just hide out for a bit. You should be able to come back once the heat dies down."

I glanced at Wes, who was looking at Kenneth with a kind of respect. "Cool plan, man," he said. "It's like a movie or something."

"Or something," I muttered. "I don't know, Kenneth. You could get into a lot of trouble."

"Come on," he said, ignoring me. He pulled on a white lab coat from his closet. "I've closed all the blinds, but don't get too close to the windows, just in case."

Walking as silently as we could, we followed him down the stairs and toward the attached garage at the back of the house. Inside the garage was a set of golf clubs, a stack of winter tires, a couple of bikes, and a Volkswagen Passat.

He lifted up the trunk of the sedan. "Let's get you situated, then I'll go wake up Maisie. It's not going to be comfortable. But it won't be for too long."

I climbed in first and pressed myself as far toward the back as I could get, folding my legs against my chest.

"Do you know where you'll go?" he asked.

I'd been thinking about this, and only one option had come to mind. "Our old place in the country," I said.

"You don't think they'll look for you there?"

I shook my head. "Why would they? It doesn't belong to us anymore—not the house, anyway. Other people live there now. But there are plenty of places to hide out. We still own some of the adjacent property and outbuildings. My dad and Rob keep saying maybe they'll build another house on the property someday."

He looked doubtful, but then he reached for his wallet. "It's all I've got; I don't carry a lot of cash. And don't forget about the prescription." He handed me a few bills, which I stuffed into my jeans pocket in my cramped position.

"Thanks. I'll pay you back soon. For everything."

He leaned into the trunk and kissed me, and I wished that he could crawl in next to me. Instead, he helped Wes climb into the trunk and then stuffed one of our backpacks in with us, tossing the other one onto the backseat of the car. He gave me a long look before he turned to Wes and said, "Hey. Look after her."

"I will," Wes said, and then Kenneth closed the trunk.

Fortunately, I was the opposite of claustrophobic. All my life, I'd sought out small, confined spaces in which I could be alone: a reading tent I'd made behind a dresser in the spare room; a small closet I'd discovered in the apartment Latasha and I rented during college.

After a minute the car door opened again and I heard Maisie's sleepy question, "Where are we going?"

"To Nai Nai's, baby," Kenneth said. "Daddy has to go back to work." When the engine started, my chest tightened and my head swam. Those other spaces had also been easy to escape when I was ready, and I hadn't been running from the police at the time.

"You okay?" I whispered to Wes as the garage door lifted and we slowly rolled out. He grunted in response. I closed my eyes, pretended I was back in my reading closet, and started to count my breaths. Then the car stopped. We must have only gone a few feet. I fumbled around in the dark until I found Wes's arm, and squeezed it. All they'd need to do was open the trunk, and Wes would be back in the lab.

The trunk was hot and stuffy. A trickle of sweat ran down the side of my face and pooled in my ear. I longed to reach up and wipe it away, but I didn't dare move.

A woman asked, "Where you headed, Doctor?"

"To the hospital," Kenneth answered calmly. "I've been called in."

"You're taking your daughter with you?"

"I'm dropping her off at my mother's house."

"Wait here, please," the officer said, and her voice grew quiet. There was static and the sound of other voices, and then her voice became clear again. "You're good to go, Doctor. Good luck. And stay safe."

"Thank you," Kenneth said, and then we drove away. Wes exhaled loudly, but neither of us said a word, still afraid of being overheard. After only a couple of minutes, the car stopped again. Kenneth's door opened and closed, and soft voices floated into the air as he took Maisie inside. Then a rush of fresh air filled the trunk, and I squinted against the glare of a streetlight.

"Hurry," Kenneth said, helping Wes out of the trunk. Then he extended his hand to me. We hadn't been in there for very long, but the stress, combined with my awkward position, seemed to have fused my joints together. I winced as I straightened out my legs and clambered out of the trunk.

We were in a back lane, tucked into a gravel driveway surrounded by trees. Kenneth opened the front door of his car, and I climbed into the driver's seat. Wes was already seated on the passenger side.

"There's a phone charger in the glove box. Keep your phone on and I'll let you know of any developments on this end. And . . . be safe." Giving me a worried look and a forced smile, Kenneth walked down the lane, heading back toward his mother's house.

"Are you okay?" I asked Wes.

"No," he said dully.

I clenched the steering wheel as I drove, sticking to back lanes and sleepy residential streets. Sirens wailed in the distance and I tensed, but then we drove by the source of the trouble: someone's house was on fire. A cop car passed us at top speed, lights flaring. I quickly turned onto an intersecting road, and Wes grabbed the dashboard to steady himself.

"Seat belt," I said from behind gritted teeth. I wanted to floor it, but I knew getting pulled over for speeding would be a bad idea—if the police even cared about things like that anymore.

"Are there any twenty-four-hour pharmacies in town?" I asked. I dreaded going somewhere we might be recognized, but we needed to get his medicine.

Wes shook his head. He was sweating, but his skin was pale under the tattoos.

"We'll have to wait until morning, then. But at least we can get you some smokes," I said. We drove for a few more minutes, and then I pulled up to a corner store. The neon "Open" sign was off, but the lights were on inside and someone was moving around. "Put the seat back and lie down," I told him. He obliged silently, which made me even more nervous. There was often a calm before Wes's storms.

I walked up to the door and looked inside. Someone was definitely in there, but when I tried the door, it was locked. I rapped on the window. "Hello? Are you open?" The figure moved out from behind one of the shelves and headed toward the door. I hesitated, my hand still on the handle. This didn't look like the owner. She looked about my age and was wearing yoga pants and a hoodie. Her blonde bob looked wet, and both of her hands were clutching a tote bag. A bag of Doritos stuck out of the top. Through the glass I could hear a child crying somewhere in the back of the store.

As the woman came toward me, she stumbled. I instinctively looked down at her feet and cried out. She had tripped over a body. An elderly man lay sprawled near the cash register. The side of his skull had been smashed in.

The woman reached the door and started fumbling with the dead-bolt as I started in horror. Then she raised her head and looked right at me. There was no flicker of reason in her eyes. They were manic, terri-fied. I sprinted back to the car and yanked the door open.

"What happened?" Wes asked as I fought to get the key in the igni-tion. The engine finally started and I tore out onto the street, unable to hide the terror on my face.

"There was an infected woman in there . . . with a child . . . I think she had killed someone . . ." I stammered.

"Hey. Hey, it's going to be okay. You're safe with me," Wes said.

But I shook my head, my chin trembling. "We're not safe anywhere." I tried to block the scene out of my mind as I kept driving.

"So," Wes said after a couple of minutes had passed. "I guess you didn't get the smokes?"

"Jesus Christ, no," I said. "You'll have to wait until morning."

"Whatever. It's kind of cool, isn't it? We're heading to our old home. Just you and me."

"Yeah," I said. "Cool."

My parents hadn't lived in the country house for some two dozen years, but it was where I'd spent the first eight years of my life. I still thought of it as home, partly because it was the one place from my childhood unmarred by memories of drugs and abuse and illness. My parents had sold it when I was in the third grade, but I'd always had this crazy dream of going back and buying it someday. It wasn't that I wanted to live in it; I just didn't like the idea of other people living in it. As though their lives would somehow tarnish my good memories.

But maybe those memories were embellished. Maybe they were just ordinary, and they only looked bright and shiny compared to everything that had come after. The house was inside the quarantine zone, so there was no reason we would encounter any roadblocks en route. As I'd told Kenneth, there were probably other people living in it now. It may have even changed hands several times since we'd sold it. But there was one building in particular that I hoped would give us refuge.

We drove past the graveyard where my grandparents and cousin were buried—and where my parents' remains would be interred once all of this was over. I'd always hated graveyards, even in the middle of the day, but Wes was drawn to them like a vampire to blood. I averted my eyes, setting them on the welcome sight ahead: an old farmhouse, all white siding and black gables, sitting on a small rise off the side of the road.

It was a quintessential turn-of-the-century farm home. My mother had been born here, and my grandparents had sold it to her and my dad for a penny as a wedding gift. When I was young I had imagined it as Green Gables and myself as Anne Shirley.

I slowed down, watching for any sign that we were expected. There were no lights on in the main house, no cars parked outside. My hands relaxed on the wheel. Barely visible in the dark behind the old house, sitting just on the edge of the forty acres of forest my family had once owned, was our destination: the hen pen.

The hen pen, as we affectionately called it, used to be just that: a barn where my grandfather kept hens. Either he or his father had built it; I could never remember which of them. After we stopped using it for hens, it was converted to a storage barn by my grandparents, my aunt and uncle, and my parents. It was four stories tall, and though it shared the same white-painted siding as the main house, it was in much poorer repair. I assumed my uncle and my parents had continued to use it after my grandparents died a few years ago, but I couldn't be sure. The paint was peeling on almost every board, and the roof was sagging in more than one spot.

It was also the place where Tracey had died. I glanced at the tattoo on Wes's neck. Would coming back here set him off?

I turned onto the long gravel driveway and pulled up on the far side of the hen pen, out of view of the house. Directly in front of us was a corrugated metal door large enough to drive a tractor through. I hoped it wasn't too rusted over to open; the sooner we could get this car out of sight, the better. Beside me, Wes was vigorously rubbing his temples. "We're here," I said, poking him gently with my elbow.

"Yeah," he said, but he didn't stop rubbing.

I turned off the headlights, hoping the light of the moon would be enough. I jogged over to a small door near the corner of the building. The knob looked rather new. It didn't turn. I gestured to Wes to join me, hoping his penchant for destruction would actually come in handy this time.

"It's locked. Can you kick it in?" I asked him.

"Fuck yeah," he answered. "Get back."

I took the requisite few steps back and glanced down at the road, watching for cars. Would the noise of the door breaking down alert the occupants of the house only a few hundred yards away? I prayed that it was as empty as it looked. I couldn't see my uncle's old house across the tracks from here. Were its owners at home? Had the police warned them to be on the lookout?

I needn't have worried—about that, at least. The sound created when Wes's boot connected with the door was more of a smoosh than a resounding crack. The door had rotted, and his leg went right through the middle. "Fuuuck!" he cried out, his leg still halfway through the splintered door.

"Shhhhh!" I ran over to him and helped him pull his leg out. His heavy black pants had protected his skin from the sharp splinters. I cautiously reached through the hole he'd made and felt around until I located the doorknob, then unlocked it. The hinges creaked loudly as I pushed the door open, and I winced. How much more noise would the corrugated door make when we opened it? A small bit of moonlight followed us, and I could make out vague shapes within but nothing else.

"Did you bring a flashlight?" Wes asked.

"I didn't bring anything!" I said in frustration. "Go look in the glove box." I could use my phone as a last resort, but I wanted to save the battery. Kenneth seemed like the kind of guy who would have a safety kit in his vehicle, though I knew there wasn't one in the trunk. If anything had been in there, I'd still have the imprint on my face.

I felt my way around the inside walls, struggling to remember where the pulley was that lifted the door. I'd played here as a kid—much more than my parents would ever have allowed had they known—but I'd only been back a couple of times since our move into town. Many, many years had passed since then. This place felt both familiar and foreign.

Something hit me on the shoulder, and I barely managed to stifle a scream. "Found one," Wes said with a grin. Then he switched it on and held the beam under his chin. "Boo!"

I snatched it from him. "Stop that." I shone the flashlight around us. It was just as I remembered it, though there seemed to be more cobwebs this time. A small dark shape darted across my beam of light. More rats, too. Great.

"There it is," I said, pointing the flashlight at a length of rope hanging from the ceiling, a wooden handle on its end. There was also a light bulb hanging from a cord, a thin metal chain beside it. I gave Wes the flashlight and pulled on the rope. The corrugated door lifted off the ground with a loud screech of protest that arrested me.

"Keep going," Wes said, and, cringing, I pulled again. As soon as the door was open enough to let the car through, I ran back out and drove it inside, cutting the engine as soon as possible. When I got out, Wes was once again holding the flashlight under his face.

"I am the demon slayer!" he said in a gravelly voice.

"Uh-huh," I said, relieved to have gotten this far undetected. "Look, I don't know about you, but I'm exhausted. Let's get a few more hours of sleep. I'll go get your medication in the morning."

That consideration worried me more than I was willing to admit; if these CDC guys were serious, they'd flag Wes at every pharmacy in the area. Or wait for him to self-destruct, in which case he'd probably lead them right to us.

Wes didn't move. He was pointing the flashlight at the floor, at a spot near the rustic elevator platform. "That's where she died," he said. His hand caressed his throat.

"Hey," I said. "Come on. Let's get some sleep. We can pay our respects to Tracey in the morning."

"She knows we're here."

His words made me shiver.

"I gotta take a piss," Wes said, stepping outside. I hung back uncertainly, not wanting to watch my brother relieve himself but also not wanting to let him out of my sight. I compromised by hovering near the door and watching his dark form out of the corner of my eye.

"Come. Sleep," I said when he had finished, opening the passenger door and beckoning him inside. He sat down and reclined the seat.

"I'm hungry," he said.

"I'll get some food in the morning."

"Maybe we could cook up some of those rats."

"That's disgusting."

"Good source of protein," he said, then laughed as though he'd told a hilarious joke.

"You're so weird," I said with a slight smile.

He grinned over at me and tapped the side of his head. "Not just weird. Crazy." Then he laughed again.

"Hey, Wes," I said, my mind returning to the bigger picture now that we were once again safe, however temporary that state might be. "Remember when we were talking on the phone before . . . before I came home, and you told me about that scientist who committed suicide?"

"Yeah. What about him? He hasn't been talking to you from the dead, has he?"

"Um, no. But I'm interested in his story. You said he was working on something called Project Amherst?"

"Yeah."

"Do you know where?"

"Some secret lab, he said."

"Why was he in the facility with you, do you know?"

"A lot of the people in there were geniuses," he said. "They knew things, y'know? I bet most of them were in there because someone wanted to keep them quiet."

"Do you think that's why this guy was in there?"

"Maybe. Wouldn't surprise me. He knew a lot of fucked-up shit."

"Oh yeah? Like what?"

"Well, like I told you. He said there was this government project . . . something to do with mutants, I think . . ."

"Mutants? Not . . . biological weapons?"

He frowned. "Nope. Didn't say anything about that, though it wouldn't surprise me. Whatever it was, it got all fucked up."

"Fucked up how?"

"He didn't give me details—probably afraid of being knocked off and shit. I wonder if that's what really happened to him."

"You really think he was killed?"

"Dunno. Maybe he was just a mad scientist." At this he laughed again.

"You've got the giggles tonight."

"Well, it *is* kind of funny, you have to admit. Mom and Dad are dead, and the two of us are on the run from the feds, sleeping in your ex-boyfriend's car in the hen pen."

"Wes, this isn't funny at all," I said, sitting up slightly.

He shrugged. "Everything's funny if you look at it the right way."

We sat in silence for several moments. I closed my eyes and willed my brain to stop churning, knowing even as I did it that it was an exercise in futility.

"Why did you ask me about that scientist?" Wes asked suddenly.

"Just . . . curious," I answered, staring into the darkness. "I was wondering: if something like that *did* happen, how far would they go to cover it up?"

***

Sleep eventually found us both. I awoke a couple of hours later, stiff and disoriented. The dim morning light forced its way through cracks in the walls and through the hole Wes had made in the door. He was still asleep in the seat beside me. I climbed out and stretched.

My head ached, and I longed for a coffee. I peeked outside to make sure the coast was clear, then squatted against the wall of the hen pen that bordered the woods and relieved myself. That done, I went back to the car and checked my phone. There were a few work emails, which I ignored. It seemed strange that the world outside Clarkeston continued to go about its business. There were several messages from Rob, wondering where I was and if I was okay. I ignored these as well, certain that Dr. Hansen and the CDC were leaning on him. I hoped they believed him when he told them he didn't know where we were. I checked my texts—still nothing from Latasha.

You okay? I texted her. It was a rhetorical question. Obviously she wasn't okay; otherwise she never would have gone this long without responding. My mind raced with possibilities: Had her bosses at the NSA found out she'd sent me that document? Was she currently in a cell somewhere, being interrogated?

A horrible possibility occurred to me then. If Latasha had been caught, then Wes and I were no longer being hunted by just Dr. Hansen. The NSA would also be looking for us, and they wouldn't be so easy to evade.

CHAPTER FIFTEEN

I dropped my phone as though it were on fire, then picked it up again and held down the power button until it turned off. *Shit.* Could they still track my cell if it was off? I had no idea how these things worked in real life. I'd left my laptop at Kenneth's, so I could only hope he had hidden it along with the other things I'd left.

Oh, Latasha, what have I gotten you into?

"Morning," Wes croaked from beside me.

"Hey."

"What time is it?"

"About six. The pharmacies should be open in a couple of hours."

"How long are we going to stay here?"

"Until it's safe to go back to Kenneth's . . . or longer. It might be better to stay here until they lift the quarantine—or until they stop searching for you. I wish I knew why they wanted you so much."

And I hope they find a cure soon. What if they didn't, and the infection spread to the rest of the world? Were these . . . the end times? I shook my head vigorously to clear that thought. This wasn't some zombie movie or horror novel. They would find a cure. They had to.

"I told you why, but you refuse to believe me," he said.

"You're right; I don't think it's because you're God's warrior. It probably has something to do with that cerebrospinal test." I was too worried about Latasha to indulge his delusions. But there was nothing I could do . . . and I might get her into even more trouble if I continued to try and contact her. I had to focus on Wes.

"Want to explore?" I asked, hoping this would distract him. "When was the last time you were in here?"

"I broke in a few years ago," he said. "Wanted to pay my respects to Tracey, y'know? Must be why they got the new lock." He snorted. "Like that could stop me."

"Hey, look at this," I said, pulling a tarp onto the floor. "Mom and Dad's old dirt bikes!"

"Cool," Wes said, coming over to take a look. Dirt bikes in the summer, snowmobiles in the winter; that had been my parents' motto. I remembered sitting in front of my mom on the bike, putting along in the driveway. Sometimes she would even bring me down the road to the store to get ice cream. In the winter, we would take the snowmobiles out into the "back forty," as my dad called the nearby woods. I'd loved it—the warm snowmobile beneath me and my mother's arms around me, stopping to build a fire and melt snow in an old tin can for hot chocolate, roasting hot dogs on a stick before heading back home to a warm bath.

"I thought they sold these years ago," I said.

"Maybe they still work."

"Don't even think about it." I threw the tarp back on the bikes. Beside them was an old sofa I vaguely remembered from my grandmother's house. It might make for a more comfortable bed than the car, if I wasn't so worried about what else might be living in it. There was also an old ride-on lawn mower and a few rusted pieces of farm equipment.

"Do you think our tree fort is still up?" Wes asked.

"Good question. I imagine it's overgrown by now. Want to see if the elevator still works?" Riding on the elevator had been the highlight of my visits to the hen pen as a child—until Tracey had fallen from it. It was ancient, and I was amazed it hadn't crashed yet. It was a bit generous to call it an elevator; it was more like a platform, about five feet by five feet. There were no walls, only a pulley system that required a fair amount of manual effort. Now that I'd suggested the idea, I was already having second thoughts. The two of us dead at the bottom of an abandoned elevator shaft would be a fine conclusion to this ordeal. But Wes was already standing on the platform, gripping the rope that would start the pulleys and send us up to the next floor.

"You comin'?" he asked.

Feigning confidence, I stepped onto the platform beside him. "You remember how to work this thing?"

He gave the rope a tug. I didn't really expect anything to happen, but the elevator jolted to life and began a halting ascent.

"Wheee!" he said, grinning at me. "Want me to make it swing?" He stopped pulling, and the elevator stopped, too. We were hovering several feet off the ground. Wes shifted his weight back and forth to make the platform sway in place.

"Stop it!" I said, grabbing one of the support ropes as my stomach lurched.

"What's the matter? You used to love this when we were kids."

"I hated it, but I was too afraid to say so. Seriously, stop."

He rolled his eyes dramatically, but he stopped. "Party pooper," he said. I grabbed the rope from him and hauled it down, setting the elevator back in motion. As soon as it met the second floor, I jumped off. This floor was mostly empty, and apparently it had been for a long time. Little puffs of dust rose up behind each of our footsteps. There were a few boxes stacked against the far wall and a random assortment of garden tools. The only thing that looked of interest was an old chest under a heavy orange blanket. I pulled the blanket off, coughing at the dust storm it created. The wooden chest looked handmade—my grandfather had been a master woodworker—but I didn't recognize it. Maybe it was Rob's. I ran my hand over the scrollwork that decorated the top.

"It's my sword," Wes said from behind me. He was squatted down beside a pile of boxes filled with old photo albums.

"What?" Had he found an old sword in one of the boxes?

"That's why they're looking for me. I'm sure of it."

"I don't think a sword has anything to do with Gaspereau," I said testily. "Besides, where did you get a sword?"

"It's a spiritual sword," he said, his blue eyes intent on me. "God gave it to me."

"Mm-hm," I said, already tuning him out. I lifted the lid on the chest and almost dropped it in surprise. So that's where Dad's hunting rifles had gone. I reached to the bottom and found boxes of ammunition. There was also another surprise: a handgun. *Well, this might come in handy if the world goes to shit.*

"What's in there?" Wes asked.

"Just old quilts." I closed the lid and threw the orange blanket back on top. "Sorry, you were saying you have a sword?"

"Yeah. Want to hear how I got it?"

"Sure." There was little else to do while we waited for the pharmacy to open.

"I was at this party. Everyone was drunk and stoned and stuff. It was pretty wild. I'd had a few drinks, but no drugs—I don't do that shit anymore. Anyway, I was just hanging out, having a beer, when I looked across the room and saw one of my friends sucking the blood of an angel."

"I'm sorry, he was what?"

"I know, crazy, right? I could see this angel lying across his lap, and my friend was chewing on the side of its neck. The angel was kind of twitching, and then it turned its head and looked right at me. Right into my fucking eyes! My friend kept feasting, but then he looked up at me, too, and there was blood running all down his mouth and he had little bits of flesh stuck in his teeth."

"That's . . . disgusting," I said.

"No shit! The thing is, I was the only one who could see it. I mean, if anyone else had seen this guy feasting on an angel, they would have freaked out. Everyone would have run out of the house screaming. So I just stood up, acting calm as could be, and walked toward him. I knew I was seeing him in the spiritual realm. I was seeing what no one else could, but it was completely real. And then this sword appeared in my hands, and I knew what I had to do." He mimed holding a sword out in front of him, then slashed it through the air and screamed, "Raaargh! I cut off my friend's head. Blood splattered everywhere. It was awesome. Then the angel got up and started healing right in front of me. It kind of nodded at me, y'know? Then it disappeared."

"Wes . . . please tell me you didn't really cut off anyone's head," I said, pinching the bridge of my nose.

"Not in the physical world. This was all in a different realm. But then shit got real in the house and everyone was staring at me like 'what the fuck is he doing?' so I thought I should leave. I grabbed my sword and got the hell out of there. And I still have it."

"Have what?"

"The sword. You can't see it, but it appears to me whenever I need it." He snorted. "They probably think they'll be able to use it."

"Wes, like I said, I'm not saying I doubt you have this spiritual sword, I'm just saying I doubt the CDC is interested in it."

"They're probably a front organization, anyway," Wes said. "I bet they're all Masons or something."

"Let's go to the next floor," I said, scrambling to my feet. I took charge of the elevator this time, but the third floor was disappointingly empty, save for an exceptional collection of cobwebs. This was as far as the elevator reached, but there was a small staircase leading to the attic level.

"After you," Wes said with a gallant bow. There was no handrail, so I placed a hand on the grimy wall to steady myself, mindful of how far I was off the ground and thinking of the rotten wood in the door downstairs. I didn't completely trust these stairs to hold our weight.

There was a curve in the stairs, then a wooden door at the top. I turned the knob and pushed the door open. My first impression was that this floor was much brighter than the others; a small window at either end let in the morning sun. I stepped inside. Something crunched under my feet. I yelped.

Covering the floor in front of me were dozens and dozens of bird skeletons. All the flesh and feathers were long gone—eaten by the rats, no doubt. Only the inedible parts remained: beaks, skulls, and bones. The light shone in through a broken window panel. Apparently the birds had been able to get in, but not out. My whole body shuddered. I tried to back up, but Wes was behind me.

I was wholly unprepared for what came next. He pushed me aside and rushed into the center of the room, wailing in utter despair. I stared at him, my shock at the grisly sight forgotten. He was picking up the bird skeletons and crushing them against his chest, all the while sobbing, "No, no, no."

"Wes, put them down. They're just birds," I said. I took a few steps toward him, cringing at the crunching beneath my feet.

"What are you talking about?" he wailed. "These are Tracey's children!"

"Wes, no, please," I begged. I put my hand on his arm. I needed to tether him to reality. "We need to go downstairs now. They're just birds. They must have gotten trapped in here, that's all." He ignored me, caressing a tiny skull he held in his hands. "Wes!" I raised my voice. "Let's go." I tugged on his arm, but he jerked it away violently.

"What's wrong with you? Look at their faces! They look just like her!" he bellowed. I took a step back. Sad Wes was one thing; angry Wes was an entirely different matter.

"We should just leave them here," I said, trying another tack. "They're safe here. But I'm scared, Wes. I want to leave."

"I bet you do," he said, all reason gone from his eyes. He picked up another skeleton and cradled it in one of his arms, then advanced on me. "Did you kill them?"

"What? No!" I said, edging toward the door.

"Tell the truth!" His hand flew through the air. The beak still clutched in his fist seared across my cheek.

I cried out and lost my balance, falling with a sickening crunch amidst the skeletons. I scrambled to my feet as fast as I could. My best defense at this point was to run. Eventually, he would calm down, and there would be apologies, as there always were. But he dropped the skull and grabbed my arm before I had fully gotten to my feet.

"Did you kill Mom and Dad, too?" he snarled, giving me a vigorous shake. His eyes were bloodshot. I started to cry now, from a potent mix of pain and fear. I wanted to wrap my arms around him and hold him close until the episode passed, but I knew he would only throw me off. Or worse, think I was attacking him.

"No," I sobbed. "I swear it. Please, you're hurting me. Let me go."

"I don't believe you!" he raged. "Why else would you have come here? What did you do to them?"

I didn't know if he was talking about our parents now or the so-called children that littered the floor around us. "I came back for *you*!" I said. "To keep you safe!"

"You fucking liar! You don't care about me! You only care about yourself!" He accentuated this last statement with a shove that sent me crashing down the short flight of stairs. Then he hurled bird skeletons at me, all the while ranting about my conspiracy to murder our entire family.

I forced myself to my feet, crying out at the new pain in my tailbone, where I'd landed. I hobbled down the rest of the stairs, moving toward the elevator. He wasn't following me; perhaps he didn't want to leave the skeletons behind. I hesitated for only a moment before I pulled the rope.

As the elevator went down, I yelled up, "Stay here, Wes! Don't leave. I'll come back, I promise."

CHAPTER SIXTEEN

I stopped on the second floor and limped to the wooden chest. I didn't know what I was going to do with it, but I knew I'd feel better with some firepower in my hands. I was shaking so badly I could barely load the handgun. It had been years since I'd fired one. I hoped my father's lessons would come back to me if I needed them. I could hear Wes keening above, and prayed again that the farmhouse was vacant. But I had to leave and get his medication.

I was about to open the corrugated metal door and take the car, but then I stopped. A set of keys hung on a rusty nail beside the door. I took them off and examined them.

"I hope this works," I muttered, grabbing my backpack out of Kenneth's car. I caught a glimpse of myself in the side mirror and winced. There were bits of bone in my hair, and I had a long red gash across one cheek. I pawed around in the glove box for a first-aid kit, but there were only napkins, so I pressed one to my face and mentally added bandages to my list of needed supplies. Then I uncovered the dirt bikes. If I could take one of them, I wouldn't have to worry about

Kenneth's car being recognized. After the second try, I found the right key, and turned it into the ignition of my mother's bike.

Nothing. I swore and tried again. Nothing. Then I tried my father's, with the same result.

"Shit!" I ran back to the pulley and opened the large door. I'd have to risk the car. I backed out and then closed the door again, hoping Wes would stay inside.

From what I could remember, the closest drugstore was in a little strip mall about twenty minutes toward town. If everything went well, I could return to Wes within the hour.

The sun was rising in the sky when I pulled into the strip mall, and my stomach gave a loud growl. There was a Circle K, a pharmacy, a nail salon, a pet store, and a cell-phone shop. Already people were running back and forth between the Circle K, the pharmacy, and their cars, carrying armloads of goods or pushing full carts. But at least there were no riot police—yet. I kept my head down and hoped I wouldn't run into anyone I knew.

I went to the cell shop first. I made sure my mask was on tight and pushed the door open. The only employee was a young man in his twenties wearing a camouflage mask over his nose and mouth. I kept my distance, and he made no move to come out from behind the counter. His eyes flickered to the gash on my cheek, then away.

"I need a phone," I said. "A burner, if you've got one."

"'Kay," he said. He reached behind the counter and pulled out a plain black phone in plastic packaging.

"Can you activate it?"

He grunted and tore open the package. A minute later he slid it toward me. I paid him with Kenneth's cash and left the store. My shoulders relaxed slightly. The prospect of being disconnected from the world had put me even more on edge.

Back in the car, I plugged the phone into the charger and texted Kenneth, grateful I still had the business card he'd given me at the hospital. New phone. Everything okay? I risked sending the same text to Latasha, so she'd be able to get a hold of me . . . if she could. I wished to God I knew what was going on with her.

I held the phone in my hand, waiting for it to vibrate with a response. People ran through the lot around me, clutching bags of supplies. The fear on their faces was very familiar by now.

You could just drive away . . . find somewhere to hide out until this is over . . . leave Wes to battle his ghosts in the hen pen. The thought only lasted a second, but it was plenty long enough for me to be ashamed of myself. No matter how much I wished it, there was no more running now.

I struggled to remember Amy's phone number, cursing myself for not writing it down before shutting off my old phone. I dialed what I hoped was her number and held my breath.

"Hello?"

"Amy? It's Clare."

"Clare! Thank God. Are you okay? I've been watching the news. I can't believe it."

"I'm okay, yeah. But do you know where Latasha is? She's not responding to my texts."

"That's odd; mine neither," Amy said. "We were supposed to meet for lunch, but she didn't show up. I called her work number and her cell—no answer. So I popped by your place and she wasn't there either. I was wondering if she was sick or something. Have you been in touch with her?"

"Not since yesterday."

"Weird. I hope she's all right. Are you still in Clarkeston?"

I hesitated. "I'm okay," I said again. "Listen, if Latasha gets in touch with you, tell her to text me at this number. It's important."

"Are you in trouble? Can I help?"

"No. I just . . . want to talk to her, that's all."

"Okay . . . well, take care. I hope you can come home soon."

"So do I."

I hung up and stared out the window for a minute, not sure if that call had been a good idea. Would they think to trace Amy's phone? I shook my head; I was being paranoid again. I had to keep moving.

Inside the convenience store, almost every shelf was empty, and one of the display cases was bent. Garbage littered the floor. A woman in a light-blue cardigan was scooping the few remaining bags of chips and boxes of crackers into a basket, which she drew closer to her body when she saw me come in. A small Asian man was sitting on a high stool behind the counter, a shotgun across his lap.

"Leave bag here," he said, gesturing for me to put my backpack on the counter.

I reluctantly complied. "You don't have much left," I said.

He raised an eyebrow. "Quarantine," he answered. "Everyone panic. Deliveries are delayed."

He pointed at the TV hanging from the ceiling in the corner. I stood and watched it, mesmerized. Just as in the newscast I'd seen at Kenneth's house last night, the scene was one of chaos. Frantic shoppers in masks were dumping armloads of groceries into carts behind the newscaster. The picture changed to a man pushing a wheelbarrow of firewood down the middle of the street, and then to lines more than fifty cars long at the gas station. Then the mayor appeared on the screen, behind a podium at Town Hall. He looked slightly shell-shocked, his coiffed gray curls frizzy and his cheeks sagging.

"Can you turn it up?" I asked.

The store owner snatched up the remote and switched on the volume.

". . . came as a surprise to us, but our emergency preparedness initiative is well equipped to ensure the safety of our citizens during this time," the mayor said. "However, I cannot express strongly enough that there is no need for panic. Rioting and looting will be dealt with using the full force of the law. I urge each citizen to purchase only enough supplies for themselves and any elderly or shut-in neighbors and relatives. We are arranging for deliveries of food and essential supplies to be brought into Clarkeston. There is no need to panic," he reiterated, though it looked like he was on the edge of panic himself.

I bought three packs of cigarettes for Wes and then headed to the drugstore.

Taped to the front doors were two signs:

WE DO NOT HAVE ANY MEDICATIONS
EFFECTIVE AGAINST GASPEREAU

MASKS AND GLOVES SOLD OUT

I feigned confidence as I stepped inside. It was busier here than in the other two shops—almost every aisle was jammed with people loading their baskets with protein bars, painkillers, and toilet paper from the already combed-over shelves. I headed straight for the pharmacist's counter in the back. The same sign that was on the door had been taped to the counter, surrounded by several hand-drawn stars in black marker.

There was a long line in front of me. No one spoke much as we waited for our turns; we all just fidgeted nervously and avoided making eye contact with each other. Two pharmacists with tight mouths and bloodshot eyes worked feverishly behind the counter.

I checked the news on my new phone. There was no mention of Wes or me, which was a good sign. I hoped Dr. Hansen's interest in my brother wouldn't grow into a full-fledged manhunt.

Finally I reached the front of the line. I handed the pharmacist the prescription from Kenneth and held my breath as she typed the info into the computer. She looked down at the prescription, then at me.

"This for you?" she asked.

"No," I said. "It's for a family member."

"Insurance?"

Shit. I had no idea how my parents' insurance policy worked, or even which company it was with.

"Um . . . it should be covered. It's my parents' policy." I could only assume they had one, and hadn't been paying for Wes's treatment out of their pocket. Yet the police officer had said they were in debt . . .

"I'll need the policy number."

"Uh . . . my parents died a few days ago," I said. "But my brother still needs his medication. Isn't there some kind of . . . compassion clause?"

The pharmacist looked at me without pity. "I'm sorry, but unless you have insurance, you'll have to pay the full price."

"How much?"

"For this?" She typed some more on her computer. "This is a month's worth of antipsychotics. It'll cost you eight hundred and eighty dollars." She looked at me suspiciously while my mouth hung open. "It won't work on Gaspereau, you know," she said.

"Eight hundred and eighty dollars? Are you serious?" After buying the phone and Wes's cigarettes, I only had about a hundred dollars left from the cash Kenneth had given me. I'd brought the gold from my dad's safe, but I'd need to go to a bank to exchange that . . . and I had already left Wes alone for too long. I could put it on my credit card, but if they were tracking me, it would lead them closer to our location. My own insurance didn't cover dependents—something I supposed I would have to change if we made it out of here alive and uninfected.

"Fine. I'll pay for it," I said. "How long until it's ready?"

She raised an eyebrow at me. "Half an hour."

I nodded and then went to hunt for supplies. After grabbing a shopping basket, I loaded it up with bottles of water and one of the last remaining boxes of tissues. There were a few loaves of gluten-free bread left in the food aisle—apparently things weren't that desperate yet. There were still several boxes of bandages. I added a tube of antibiotic ointment and briefly considered sleeping pills, but decided against it. We would need to be completely alert if we had to make another escape in the middle of the night.

The aisles were a mess, as though shoppers had dumped the contents of the shelves onto the floor in their haste to get what they needed and get away. A couple of harried employees scrambled around, struggling to keep things in order. I guarded my basket of treasures, including a bag of beef jerky and a loaf of gluten-free bread, and headed toward the checkout.

Someone jostled me from behind, and I dropped the phone. I bent to retrieve it and at the same time took off my backpack. I held it in front of me, against my chest, knowing the handgun was on top. Was I that desperate? My heart drummed. I'd pay for the supplies and take them out to the car, then come back and . . . and what? Rob the pharmacy at gunpoint? If I wanted to avoid attention, that wouldn't be the way to do it.

I paid, left the store, and threw my bags into the backseat of the car. Then I took the gun out of the backpack with trembling fingers and slipped it into my waistband, under my hoodie. How many other people were packing heat in Clarkeston? And how many of them were infected?

I set my jaw and went back inside. Wes needed those meds, but I had no idea how to get them without giving us away. I'd have to take a chance on using my credit card. Maybe we could get away before they traced it.

I joined the line at the pick-up counter. In an aisle behind me, two men were having an argument. One of them, sporting a red plaid jacket and a Budweiser hat, was shouting about a drug he'd read about on the Internet. It was supposed to make you immune to Gaspereau, he said. He looked like he hadn't shaved in a few days. He wasn't wearing a mask.

"I'll prove it!" he said, marching toward the pharmacist's counter. He tried to cut to the front of the line, but the other customers jostled him back.

"There's no cure, man," someone said. "No vaccine, either. You're just fooling yourself."

"I lost my kid in Iraq, and I'll be damned if I'm going to lose anyone else to this son of a bitch!" he said.

Finally, it was my turn at the counter. I gave the pharmacist my credit card. She kept the white paper bag clutched in her hand while she ran the card through.

The argument continued behind me. "It doesn't work. You're just deluding yourself!" someone told the man in the Bud cap.

"Declined," the pharmacist said, snapping me back to attention.

"What? That's impossible." I leaned over the counter to look at her screen. She turned it away from me.

"There's a drug?" a woman's voice called out from the back of the line. "Why aren't they giving it to us?"

"That's what it says. Declined." The pharmacist's tone brooked no argument. "Do you want to pay another way?"

Someone shoved me aside. "If you don't have the money, let someone else go!"

"Hey!" I elbowed my way back in front of the counter. "I have the money! Run my card again."

"Ma'am, it doesn't work," the pharmacist said. "Next!"

"No, you have to try again!" I gripped the counter with my hands. Then someone behind me shouted, "What the fuck are you doing?"

The man in the Budweiser cap was shoving his way to the front again. He came to a stop right behind me, pinning me to the counter.

"Why aren't you giving out Zorifan?" he yelled. "You want us to all get sick? Big Pharma holding it back?"

"Sir, despite what you may have heard, Zorifan is *not* effective against Gaspereau." The two pharmacists exchanged glances. One of them picked up a phone receiver.

"You're keeping it for yourself, aren't you?" he ranted. "Or are they waiting until we're willing to pay whatever they ask for it?"

People were starting to back away from him now. Someone muttered, "Maybe he's infected. Doesn't seem right in the head."

"Sir, you need to leave *now*," the pharmacist said.

"I'm not leaving until I get my hands on some Zorifan!" He reached into his jacket and pulled out a gun, pointing it over my shoulder at the pharmacist.

I dove to the floor. Screams filled the air around me. Some customers dropped to the ground; others ran. I didn't dare stand but started crawling frantically along the counter.

A burly man crept closer to the gunman, his hands outstretched. "Hey, buddy, we're all freaked out. This isn't helping. Just put the gun—"

A bullet in the stomach silenced him. His body crashed to the floor in front of me. He clutched at his stomach, his mouth moving soundlessly as blood puddled on the floor.

"Give me the Zorifan and no one else will get hurt!" Seconds later, the gunman fired behind the counter. There was a yell, but I couldn't tell—had he shot one of the pharmacists? I twisted around and wrenched the gun out of my waistband. His back was to me. My hands were shaking too much; I couldn't hold the gun still. I aimed low, but then raised my hands. If I missed . . .

I trained my eyes on him and took the shot.

He crumpled, his hip shattered.

More screams. The pharmacists abandoned the counter and ran out through a back door. I sprang to my feet and kicked the gunman's weapon out of reach, then sprinted behind the counter. The white bag with Wes's medication lay on top of the keyboard. I grabbed it and bolted out of the store. Someone would have called the police by now. I had to get out of there, and fast.

The parking lot was chaos as people threw their supplies into their cars and tried to escape from the single exit. Most decided to hell with it and just drove over the curb. I pulled the car around and followed their example.

After driving like the devil was on my heels for ten minutes, I pulled over to the side of the road and threw up. The green grass, now soiled, seemed like something from another world. How could something as ordinary as green grass still exist when I had just shot a man?

You did what you had to do. You didn't kill him. You probably saved the pharmacists' lives. Now get a grip. I panted by the side of the road for a few more minutes before deeming myself fit to drive.

Soon, I was back at the hen pen. "Hello?" I said as I eased the door open. The inside of the building seemed darker than it had been this morning, and I waited for my eyes to adjust. "Hello?" I called out again. I clutched my backpack to my chest and stepped onto the elevator. The second floor was empty except for the boxes and the chest of guns. The lid was open.

Shit! I ran toward it—had I left it open, or had Wes found the guns? I hadn't counted them earlier, so I couldn't tell if any were missing.

"Wes?" I called out. I ran back to the elevator. A lone rat greeted me on the third floor. I sprinted up the stairs to the attic level, then stopped. If Wes was still having an episode and he was armed, bursting into the room and surprising him was the worst thing I could do.

"Wes, I'm back!" I called, wanting to give him as much advance notice of my arrival as possible. I even knocked on the door before gently pushing it open.

It was empty, save for the skeletons of the dead birds, arranged on the floor to spell out the words "I'M SORRY."

CHAPTER SEVENTEEN

I stepped into the center of the skeleton-filled room. "Wes?" I cried. "Where are you?"

No, no, no. This isn't happening.

"Wes!" I screamed, running back down to the third floor. There weren't that many places to hide—and why would he hide from me, anyway? Had he been found? Had they taken him? I checked the second floor, but he wasn't there. I took the elevator to the bottom and stood in the center of the room. What should I do? Should I wait in the hope that he'd come back? Or should I go looking for him? If he left on his own, he couldn't have gotten too far—all the vehicles were still here. But if they took him, how would I find him again?

I'd wait. He'd left me the message with the skeletons; he must have known I'd come back. I sat down on the old sofa and pulled the gun out of my backpack, unloaded it, and set it on the floor. I didn't want to ever use it again, even as an empty threat.

Had the man I'd shot in the drugstore been infected, or had he just gone a little nuts from fear and panic? Could anyone even tell the difference anymore?

I opened the car and grabbed one of the packs of cigarettes I'd bought for Wes. Off went the plastic wrapping. I pulled one out and lit it, using a pack of matches from the convenience store, then returned to the sofa to smoke it slowly. As much as I derided Wes's habit, I still kept an emergency pack in my freezer for times of high stress. If this didn't qualify, I didn't know what would.

So this is it. It's the end of the world, and I'm alone. I could have done so much differently. If I'd never told Wes about the rape, he wouldn't have attacked Myles and ended up in the psych hospital. Maybe I would have stayed in Clarkeston and married Kenneth, and Maisie would be our child. Maybe . . .

I banged my head against the back of the sofa. Too late for regrets. But I couldn't escape the truth that inched chillingly closer every day. What if they never found a cure? Gaspereau would burn through Clarkeston, eventually infecting everyone. How soon until it spread to the rest of the world, quarantine or not? I shuddered and took another drag on the cigarette.

A rifle shot shattered the silence.

I jumped to my feet, then stood perfectly still, trying to gauge which direction the shot had come from. The woods. I picked up the handgun from the floor and reloaded it—perhaps I'd need it after all— and peered through the hole Wes had made in the door. There were no police cars, no army jeeps, not even a farm truck in view, so I stepped out and ran toward the woods. Once I reached the cover of the trees, I ran parallel to the tree line until I came to the old snowmobile trail. I didn't know whether to call out for Wes or not—or even if he was the one who'd made the shot. I stopped, panting, and realized I had no idea where I was going. How would I find him in the trees?

"Wes?" I called out tentatively. I ran again, heading deeper into the woods. "Wes, are you there?"

Another shot came from my left, almost deafening me. I dove to the ground and put my hands over my head. "Wes? Stop shooting, for

Christ's sake!" A rustling in the leaves told me someone was running toward me. Wes burst out onto the path, holding one of our father's hunting rifles. His eyes were wild and shining.

"Did you see it?" he asked.

"See what?" I moaned. I knew how my mother must have felt the day she found me playing by myself on the banks of the swollen spring river when I was five. She'd hugged me so hard I'd thought she might never let go, and then spanked me so hard I couldn't sit down for the rest of the day.

"That deer! I've been hunting," he said.

I uncovered my head and got gingerly to my feet. Wes was standing tall, his chest stuck out proudly.

"Can I . . . ?" I asked, holding my hands out for the gun.

"You want to try? Sure!"

I took it from him. "No, Wes, I don't want to try. Do you know how scared I was when I came back and you weren't there? And then heard gunshots? What were you thinking?" At least he wasn't cradling bird skulls anymore.

"I didn't know where you went," he said defensively. "I thought I'd get us some food!"

"Okay," I said, breathing heavily through my nose. "We can talk about it back in the hen pen. But please . . . no guns." He eyed the handgun I'd dropped on the ground while diving for cover.

"What's that, then?"

"Protection." I picked it up and stuffed it in my waistband. "In case you were in trouble."

He started to speak, but I held out my hand. "Stop." Something was in the bushes a few feet in front of us—Wes's elusive deer? Someone with Gaspereau? "Who's there? Come out slowly; I'm armed." I raised Wes's rifle in front of me.

"I don't think anyone's there," Wes said. Before I could stop him, he grabbed the gun from my waistband. "But just in case—here you go, sucker!" He shot several rounds into the bushes, laughing. Then a man's voice cried out.

"Wes, stop!" I shouted, dropping my rifle and grabbing his arm. "Someone's out there!"

"Then they're dead," he said with a shrug.

"Not quite," said a voice. A figure stepped out from behind a thick tree trunk.

"Kenneth!" I cried, running toward him. "Oh my God, he could have killed you! Are you okay?" Both Kenneth and Wes looked ashen.

"Oh . . . sorry, man. I didn't actually think anyone was there," Wes said, dropping the gun.

"Well, I was," Kenneth said with a grimace. He was gripping his arm, and blood stained his fingers.

"He hit you!"

"Just a graze," Kenneth said. "I'll be fine."

I rounded on Wes, but Kenneth put his hand on my arm. "It's okay, Clare."

"It is *not* okay," I said. "Let's get you inside."

The three of us crept back into the hen pen. A car—Kenneth's mother's, I assumed—was parked outside. With his uninjured arm, he opened the trunk and took out a first-aid kit.

"What are you doing here?" I asked once we were back inside with the doors closed.

"I came to check on you. I tried your cell and there was no answer. I found my car, but you guys weren't here, obviously. I thought I'd check the woods. I was beginning to think I'd gotten myself lost when I heard the shots."

"You and who knows who else," I muttered. "But how did you know where this place was?"

"You showed me once, remember? Back in the day. We drove out here."

"Good memory."

"Did you get Wes's medication?" he asked. He opened the first-aid kit and started to dress his wound.

I wanted to tell him the whole story. I wanted him to comfort me, to tell me it was okay, that I'd done the right thing. But I couldn't bear to say the words. I had shot a man who was possibly sick. He would never understand.

"I got it," I answered. "But he hasn't taken it yet." I retrieved a bottle of water from the car and handed it to Wes, along with one of his pills.

He looked like he wanted to refuse, but thankfully he didn't. I relaxed fractionally when he swallowed the pill. "You take these every day?" I asked, examining the label.

"Yeah," he said. "They make me tired, though."

I was about to say "Better tired than delusional" but changed my mind. "I'm going to talk to Kenneth for a bit. Want to crawl into the car and have a nap while the meds kick in?"

He nodded and climbed into the backseat. I motioned for Kenneth to follow me to the elevator, which he eyed with suspicion.

"It's fine," I said, and he stepped up beside me, still carrying the first-aid kit.

"Clare . . ." he began, but I interrupted him.

"Wait until we're out of earshot," I whispered. I pulled the rope until we reached the third floor. "Are you sure you're okay?"

"I'll be fine. It's just a scratch. And speaking of which . . . how did you get that?" He pointed at my cheek, which was still stinging.

"You won't believe it," I said. He took some antiseptic wipes out of the first-aid kit and dabbed at my cheek, then covered it with a square bandage.

I told him about Wes's breakdown in the attic. "I'm so glad you gave us that prescription. But God, what a nightmare getting it . . ."

A question flickered across his face.

"It was just really chaotic," I said.

"I bet. There are a lot of very scared, very confused, and very angry people out there. They think the government should have a better grasp on things. And it's happened so fast . . . The rate of infection isn't helping things, either."

I frowned. "How bad is it?"

Kenneth went over to one of the tiny windows and wiped away some of the grime. A faint ray of light shone through it. "Infectious diseases have what's called a basic reproductive rate—the average number of people one person will infect. It's called the R-nought rate. The flu is between two and three, and you've seen how fast that can spread in a school or workplace. Gaspereau is seven."

"That's bad."

"It's all bad, Clare. They've been trying to keep it quiet to avoid a panic, but it's getting out of hand. We're not going to be able to stop it."

He looked out the window again, and a chill crept into my bones. There was something about the way he said, "*We're* not going to be able to stop it . . ."

"Why are you here, Kenneth?" I asked warily.

He turned around slowly. There were no apologies, no weak lies. "I came to explain to you what is *really* going on."

"And how do you know what is really going on?" I asked. "Or should I say '*How long* have you known?'"

"Only for a few hours. Since you left. I swear it, Clare, I was in the dark just as much as you were. But they came back with a warrant . . . and the CDC—"

"Dr. Hansen, you mean?" I snapped.

"Just hear me out. I want what's best for you and Wes; I really do. But a lot of lives are being destroyed, and there is no end in sight. Please . . . just listen to me and I'll explain what he wants with Wes. Then you can decide what to do."

"I've already decided what to do," I said. "But tell me why they want him so much."

Kenneth took a deep breath and motioned to the dusty floor. "Should we sit?"

"I'll stand."

A flicker of annoyance crossed his face. "You know a little bit about how Gaspereau works, right? It's not a virus or a bacterium. It's more like mad cow disease—it's caused by infectious particles called prions, which are misfolded proteins. These rogue prions attack healthy proteins and cause them to misfold, and so on and so on. Because they're attacking the brain, they cause delusions and massive behavioral changes—all the things we've seen in the victims so far. The difference is that mad cow can only be spread through contact with infected brain tissue. Gaspereau is spread through contact with infected droplets— from a sneeze or a cough, for example—or contaminated surfaces. Just like the flu."

"Which is what makes it spread so fast," I interjected. "I know all this; I saw the press conference."

"Just bear with me. As long as the people who are infected are still living, they can spread the disease to others. So far no one has died from it, except those who have killed themselves or tried to fly out of a window or something. I told you, sedatives don't work. It's spreading beyond our ability to contain the infected. There are too many of them now."

Images from every zombie movie I'd ever seen swam through my head. I pictured dozens, maybe hundreds of people swarming in the psych ward where Wes had been kept—all of them angry and convinced that the horrors in their heads were real. They stampeded down the hall, cutting down doctors and nurses, and burst out of the hospital in droves, ready to vent their rage on the world.

I sat on the floor and brought my knees up to my chin. "Where does Wes fit in?"

"It's his brain," Kenneth said, sitting down in front of me and crossing his legs. "They noticed an abnormality in the first round of tests they did before releasing him from the hospital. They weren't supposed to release him; it was a misunderstanding in the chaos."

Was he telling the truth or just speaking from Dr. Hansen's playbook? "Why did Dr. Hansen tell you all this?"

"I'm a doctor. And things have changed," Kenneth said softly. "They've run out of options. They realized that they've been . . . going about this the wrong way. Trying to force you into helping them. That's why they sent me—someone you can trust. Someone who will tell you the truth."

"Who are *they*? Just Dr. Hansen?"

"It *was* just him at first. But he's shown the results to his superiors at the CDC. They think we have to try."

"Did you lead them here?" My eyes darted to the window.

"No. I volunteered to come and find you, and answer all of your questions. At least, as much as I can. It turns out that Wes was exposed to Gaspereau in the psych hospital. They didn't tell me how, but I suspect it was that scientist you spoke of."

"Dr. Ling," I breathed. "Patient Zero."

"Yes. I suspect he was the source. And he infected a lot of other people before he killed himself."

"Oh my God. And Wes . . . ?"

"Is perfectly fine. That's the mystery. Or was. They knew he'd been infected with Gaspereau, and yet the prions weren't showing up in his system. That's why they needed to test his cerebrospinal fluid. They ran a whole gamut of tests—they even introduced infected cells to the spinal fluid, to see how his body would respond. It stayed perfectly healthy."

"Why?" Torn between anger and relief, I strained to keep track of what Kenneth was saying.

"It's due to a mutation in his brain cells. They not only protect healthy cells from unhealthy prions, they actually unfold the prions and make them healthy again. They fight back."

I stared at him in disbelief for a long moment, while he waited for me to say something. Silence pressed in on us in the empty room. Finally Kenneth spoke again. "Clare, *Wes* is the cure for Gaspereau. He's the antidote."

"How is that possible?" I whispered.

"Like I told you before, we don't understand a whole lot about human mutation. Somehow, Wes's brain cells have mutated in this way, but we don't know why—not yet. What we do know is that it works—at least in the lab. Dr. Hansen believes these cells will cure the infected."

A cure for Gaspereau. Wes would love this; he'd always thought he was special. "Are there others with this same mutation? These special cells?"

"Not as far as they know."

"So what do they need? More cerebrospinal fluid?" If Kenneth was right, surely Wes would be willing to undergo one more procedure.

Kenneth rubbed his forehead with the palm of his hand, making the front of his hair stick up. When he looked back up, his eyes were wet. "I wish it were that easy," he whispered.

A stone seemed to lodge in my throat. "What are you talking about? Why isn't it?"

"They haven't been able to replicate these special cells. And there aren't enough of them in the CSF. It seems the highest concentration of them are in a certain area of his brain. His hippocampus, to be exact. And they would . . . need to harvest them. All of them. It's the only way they can halt the spread of Gaspereau in time."

"They want to harvest . . . his brain?"

"Parts of it. Just the two hippocampi. He would live; that's almost certain. But . . . it would drastically change him. There's so much about the brain we still don't understand. But we know the hippocampus plays a major role in memory, especially in creating new memories. He would possibly lose that ability."

A wave of nausea swept through me, replacing the lightness that had filled my chest at the prospect of discovering a cure.

"I don't know exactly how it would play out," Kenneth continued. "It's still rather unpredictable. But there's a very good chance he would come out of the operation quite . . . impaired."

"And that's the only way?" I choked. "There's absolutely nothing else they can do?"

"Hopefully they will eventually be able to make a synthetic version," Kenneth said softly. "But right now . . . there just isn't time. Not if we want to contain the outbreak before it's too late."

I gripped my head in my hands to keep the room from spinning, to keep the whole world from spinning. A fleeting image flashed through my mind, of a game show host surrounded by blinking white lights. "Behind door number one is your brother on an operating table, left to live life as a vegetable and not remember anything or anyone! Behind door number two, the whole world goes stark raving mad! It's all up to you! Step right up and make your choice. Time is running out!"

"No, no, no," I moaned. "This isn't happening. There has *got* to be another way."

"I'm so sorry," Kenneth said. He looked so pathetic, sitting cross-legged in the dust. But I couldn't find it in myself to feel sorry for him. He wasn't being asked to make this decision. He wouldn't have to live with it for the rest of his life.

"Latasha. I need to talk to Latasha," I said, getting up and grabbing my new phone.

"Why?"

"Because . . . this can't be right! You saw what she sent me! Gaspereau came out of a government lab! It's a biological weapon. Why would they create a weapon without making an antidote?" Hysteria threatened to finish off my already frayed nerves. I took several deep breaths, but that only made me light-headed. "But she's gone. Something's wrong; I know it. I think they caught her."

"Who caught her?"

"I don't know—the NSA, USAMRIID, the CDC, the same people who are hunting us! She's not responding to any of my messages. It's not like her."

"Maybe she's just lying low," Kenneth said, his calmness infuriating. "And you don't know for sure that Gaspereau was meant as a weapon. All we know is that there was a breach and then Gaspereau showed up. It looks suspicious, sure, but you don't have any proof."

"What about that classified document? What about what Wes said? What about Dr. Ling and Project Amherst or whatever the hell it's called?"

"Clare . . . I know you're upset, but this isn't about how Gaspereau started. It's about stopping it."

I stalked over to the far wall and rested my head against the peeling paint. "I need more information," I said. "They can't possibly expect me to make this decision."

"You're the only one who can, Clare. Wes is unique. It's your call."

"What would you do?" I asked, gazing up at him through a haze of tears.

He looked away, his face tight. "I know it's a lot to ask . . . but try to see the big picture. There are a lot of people suffering. Families being destroyed. If you have the power to stop it, to cure this disease . . . that's what I would do."

The silence sat heavy between us. Of course I wanted to help; what sane person wouldn't? But it was at too steep a cost. For me, there was really only one choice. The world would have to wait for another savior.

"You said yourself, they're not going to die, right? The people who are infected?" I asked, hating the sound of my own voice. It was a horrible thing to say. "So there's time for some other cure to be discovered."

Kenneth still wasn't looking at me. "It's not fatal. You're right. And thank God for that. But some things . . . some things are worse than death, Clare. The victims of Gaspereau, they lose all empathy, all compassion. They lose the ability to relate to the people who love them. At first, we thought it was the same as a severe case of mental illness. But it's worse—much worse. It's as if they stop being human."

His shoulders twitched, and he buried his face in his hands.

"Kenneth, I'm sorry. I know you think I should do the right thing. But there *is* no right thing here. And I can't—I won't—hand over my own brother to be sacrificed. I just can't."

He lifted his head, revealing cheeks stained with tears. "Just think about it a little longer," he pleaded. "Please, Clare." His voice broke. What had he seen—or what had they told him—to make him this insistent? But I'd seen it myself. I knew what the stakes were. Could I really stand by while the whole world burned?

"Think about it," he said again. "This could be Wes's chance to do something really meaningful with his life."

Hadn't I said something similar to Wes just a couple of days ago? My cheeks burned at the memory.

But we were both wrong; the decision wasn't mine to make. My resolve strengthened. "His life *is* meaningful, just as it is," I said. "But you're right. It's *his* life. This is his decision. And whatever he chooses, I'll support him."

Kenneth nodded slowly, as though in a daze. "I understand why you would want to ask him. I wouldn't want to make a decision like this, either. But you're his legal guardian. We know that he has an irrational fear of doctors. I don't really think he's capable of choosing."

"He *is* capable," I said. "He's capable of protecting the people he loves. And he is capable of choosing his own fate." I held out my hand to Kenneth, who was still sitting on the floor. "Help me explain it to him. I don't know if I would get the details right on my own. But he deserves to know the truth."

Kenneth accepted my hand and rose shakily to his feet. His eyes were sad and guarded. "Okay. I'll help you."

I wrapped my arms around his waist, and he rested his chin on the top of my head.

We went back down to the first floor, where Wes was sleeping in the car. "Listen," I said to Kenneth. "Don't make him feel guilty if he doesn't want to do it. It's his life, remember. We're just going to present him with the scenario and let him decide." I knocked on the window to wake Wes up.

"Whasss?" he said groggily, opening the door.

"Kenneth has some information we need to talk with you about."

He climbed out of the car and sat on the hood, the chains that dangled from his belt clanging against the metal. Kenneth and I sat down on the sofa, facing Wes. Haltingly, I explained how fast Gaspereau was spreading, with Kenneth jumping in here and there to elaborate or correct something I'd gotten wrong.

"So it's like, the end of the world?" Wes asked, his face intense.

"I don't know if it's gotten to that point yet," I said, but then caught Kenneth's eye. "But yeah, it looks pretty bad."

"And they still haven't found a cure?" Wes asked.

"Well, that's what we wanted to talk to you about." I explained what the doctors had discovered. "So you see, there *is* a cure. It's . . . these special cells in your brain."

"Ha! I told you so," he said.

"You told me what?"

"That I'm a warrior."

Kenneth nodded, a little too eagerly. "That's right. And as a warrior, you could save a lot of people. You'd be a hero."

I glared at him. I didn't need him feeding into Wes's delusions in an attempt to sway his decision.

"They used the cells from your cerebrospinal fluid to do some tests in the lab," I continued. "They're pretty confident that it could work."

Wes opened his mouth to respond, but I rushed on. "The problem is that they need more of them. They can't just take a few and then be done with it. They would need to . . . cut out parts of your brain."

Wes stared at me as though I had just suggested we conduct a child sacrifice. His nostrils flared, his eyes doubled in size, and his lips drew back over his teeth as he recoiled from me.

"Hell no!" he said. He scrambled off the roof of the car, away from us. "Are you crazy?"

I stood up and held out my hands. "No one's making you do anything. I'm just . . . explaining the facts. That's all. It's your decision. It wouldn't be fatal—you'd live. But . . . the parts they need are the parts that control memory. Honestly, they don't really know what would happen. But you might forget everything . . . or wake up a totally different person. I don't know."

"I don't care if everyone fucking goes to hell," he said angrily. "No one's getting near my brain."

"Like I said, you don't have to do anything you don't want to do . . . but I know that you do care about what happens to other people."

"So this is my choice?"

"Yes," I said firmly. "It's your choice. That is . . . if they catch us, I don't think they'll give you a choice, even if it's illegal. But until then, I won't be the one to turn you in. I won't. No matter what the stakes are."

His eyes met mine, and there was perfect clarity in them. He nodded. I knew then that I was finally forgiven.

"Yeah," he said. "I do care—about you. About Mom and Dad. But everyone else thinks I'm a freak. They can't see what I see. They just want to lock people like me away. Why should I give my life for them?"

"Wes, you wouldn't be giving your life—" Kenneth said from the sofa.

"Shut up," I snapped. I grabbed both of Wes's hands and held them in my own. "Then we'll keep running. So they don't find you. They'll figure out another way in time."

I turned back to Kenneth. "Tell them you couldn't find us. No, you've been gone too long; they'll know you're lying. Tell them you delivered your message but we got away." I spied a coil of rope hanging from a nail in the wall. "We'll make it look like we tied you up or something but you got free after we left."

"Clare . . . I can't." Kenneth's face shone with sweat despite the coolness of the hen pen.

"Why not? You came to deliver a message, and you've done that. They should leave you alone."

"It's not that. You can't . . . you can't leave. They know you're here."

CHAPTER EIGHTEEN

He may as well have picked up the gun and shot me in the gut.

"What are you talking about?" I demanded. "You said you weren't followed."

"I needed for you to believe that. Otherwise you wouldn't have listened to me." Kenneth looked positively wretched as he spoke, his head in his hands.

"You . . . you brought them here? All along, you knew they were just going to come in here and take him anyway."

"I wanted it to be your choice! Or his choice," Kenneth said. "It's just Dr. Hansen and a couple of officers. They're a mile down the road. Consider it an escort. But if you run, it could get much worse. You don't want the United States government after you, Clare."

"You fucker . . ." Wes began, advancing on Kenneth.

I threw out an arm to stop him. "Explain," I said, angry tears pressing against my eyes. "Why? Why would you do this to me? To us?"

"I wouldn't have, Clare, if I'd had any other choice," he said, his voice breaking. "I didn't want to tell you this. But it's Maisie. She's been infected."

"What? How?" I had seen his lively, clever girl just hours ago. It didn't seem possible.

"I don't know; I have no idea how she could have been exposed. But when we went back to the house, they were waiting for us. They made us take tests. I was still negative. So was my mother. But Maisie tested positive."

"Oh my God, Kenneth." The anger at his betrayal still pulsed through me, but now I knew what madness had brought him here. "Why didn't you tell me?"

"How could I? How could I ask you to choose between your brother and my daughter? I didn't want to put you in that position. I thought that maybe setting the stage in global terms would be enough to convince you."

"Is all that a lie, too?" I asked softly. "About how bad it is?"

"No," he said, shaking his head. "It's all true. It's just . . . hitting close to home now. When they told me that Wes could really cure her, I didn't believe them at first. I thought it was a trap. But they showed me the results of the tests. It all checks out. And think about it: why else would they want him so desperately?"

"He's standing right here, you know," I reminded him. "You can talk to him directly."

Kenneth rubbed his face as though clearing cobwebs. "I know. I'm sorry," he said to Wes. "And I know it's an impossible thing to ask. But here I am, asking it." He slid off the sofa and onto his knees. "Please," he said, looking up at Wes with desperate, bloodshot eyes. "It's my little girl."

The two men stared at each other for a long moment. Then Wes said, "I'm sorry. I like Maisie. She's a cool kid. But I'm not gonna do it." Then, before Kenneth had a chance to respond, Wes picked up a shovel leaning against the wall and swung it at Kenneth's head. It connected with a solid thump.

"Oh my God, Wes!" I screamed. I ran to Kenneth, who was lying prostrate on the floor. I grabbed his wrist frantically and felt for a pulse. Then I sagged over his body. "He's alive," I breathed.

"Of course he's alive," Wes said. "You think I've never hit anyone before? I hit him with the flat of the blade."

"It's a shovel, you idiot, not a sword!" I said. "You almost killed him—again!"

"Whatever." He shrugged. "Now we can get out of here."

"What are you talking about? He said they know we're here! They're probably waiting to ambush us as soon as we leave."

"Then I guess we'll go down in a blaze of glory."

"We are *not* going down in a blaze of glory." I kept my fingers on Kenneth's wrist and closed my eyes, thinking hard.

We had to get out of here; that was certain. But how? And where could we possibly hide, here in our hometown, where so many people knew us? How long until the CDC was splashing our faces across every news site, TV station, and newspaper? How long until the NSA discovered just who Latasha had been communicating with? Even if I cut and dyed Wes's hair and took out his piercings, there wasn't anything I could do to hide the tattoos all over his face and neck. He would be recognized anywhere.

"I think we should go to Canada," I said suddenly.

Wes wrinkled his nose. "Canada? Why?"

"We can claim asylum. I used to volunteer at a transition house for refugees. They'd come to the States and then they'd try to get into Canada, where there was a better chance they'd be accepted."

"Yeah, but we're Americans, not refugees."

"What they want to do to you is illegal. Government agents want to forcibly confine and experiment on you. At the very least, they'll have to consider our case, and that can take years. By then, they'll have found another cure, and we'll be able to come home."

"Yeah, maybe the government will have to pay us off, too!" Wes said, his eyes shining.

"Don't get your hopes up. We have to get to the border first. And we already failed once."

Wes shoved his hands into his pockets, making the chains on his pants clink together. He frowned. "I've got some buddies on the Mistigouche reservation. It's on the border."

"You think they'd help us? What if they turn you in?"

Wes snorted. "They won't. Tony's awesome. My friends are a little less dickish than yours."

I bit my tongue. Kenneth stirred beside me. His eyelids fluttered open, then closed again. "Thank God. I think he'll be okay," I said.

"We should go before he wakes up," Wes said, eyeing Kenneth nervously. "If we go through the woods, we should be able to lose the pigs."

"Don't call them that," I said, but he ignored me. I grabbed some of the supplies I'd bought that morning and stuffed them into my backpack, including the gun. Then I put some of the food in Wes's bag—if we got separated, at least he'd be able to eat. I held his medication in my hand, wondering if I should split it between the two of us.

"I'll take that," he said. He snatched it out of my hand and shoved it into his bag.

Was I doing the right thing? How could I leave Kenneth lying unconscious on the floor, knowing his only child was probably all alone in an isolation room somewhere? She had to be terrified. But the thought of them dragging Wes away to a gruesome fate was just as terrifying.

"Do you think they're watching the door?" Wes asked.

"You can't see it from the road," I said hesitantly. "And he said they're about a mile away. Probably didn't want to risk tipping us off by getting too close."

"All right, let's run for it."

"Wait! Take off your chains. They make too much noise."

Wes unfastened the various chains that hung from his pockets and belt. He smirked at me. "Should I tie your lover boy up with them?"

"No!" I said. "Let's get out of here."

I pushed the door open, just enough for us to squeeze through. I peeked out, and my heart nearly stopped. Coming up the long driveway were three police cars.

"Now! Run!" I said. We ran around the corner of the barn, the open door blocking us from their view. From there we sprinted into the cover of the woods.

"Go, go!" I urged Wes, but he was already huffing and puffing, his years of smoking and sedentary living catching up to him.

"I . . . can't . . ." he gasped, stopping to rest. The hen pen was still in sight through the trees. If they came into the woods now, they'd hear us running.

"I have an idea," I said.

He nodded, still struggling for breath.

"The old fort. Is it still there?" I craned my neck back and looked up in the branches around us. Another world ago, our father had built it for us way up high in the branches of a huge spruce tree. One of his logging buddies had lopped off some of the upper branches to make room for the rudimentary fort. The lower branches were still there, so when you were in the tree fort, it was as if you were separated from the world. And when you were on the ground, it was almost impossible to see. It used to drive our mother crazy—she could never find it as easily as the rest of us could, and she hated heights, so as long as we stayed quiet, we could hide up there for hours.

"It was a bit closer to the house," I said. "C'mon."

We moved through the woods as quietly as we could, keeping an eye on the tree line, which was uncomfortably close.

"There," Wes whispered with a nudge to my side.

I looked up and nodded. If you knew what you were looking for, you could just make out a small glimpse of planks through the dense spruce needles. Dad had nailed a few leftover blocks of wood to the tree trunk to make the climbing easier.

"You first," I mouthed.

For all his inability to run more than fifty feet, Wes was still a capable climber. He scaled the tree trunk as easily as he had when we were kids, and in moments I could hear his boots clomping on the wooden floor above. Casting one last glance around me, I grabbed onto one of the handholds and hoisted myself up—as unsure and awkward as ever.

When I reached the top Wes was sitting in the corner, grinning. It was much as we had last seen it, except the floor was now carpeted in needles. The four walls still seemed sturdy enough. A large open window was situated at the end pointing toward the house, with a smaller window on the other side. There was no roof but the sky.

I edged further into the fort, testing each step before planting my full weight. A bird had built a nest in one of the corners, but it was empty.

I crouched down beside Wes, who was stretched out on the floor, his head and feet just inches from the walls. It had seemed so much larger when we were kids; a castle of our own. Now, it was a few wooden planks placed precariously high in a tree. "Wake me if I need to shoot someone," he said, moving his pack under his head.

I looked in my backpack to make sure the gun was still there. It was.

I rested my head against the wall. A car door slammed down below, and my head jerked up. Wes opened his eyes and gave me a questioning look, but I shook my head and he closed them again. Staying as close to the floor as I could, I crept over to the window facing the edge of the woods. I couldn't see anything through the foliage except a few slashes of white barn. Then I heard Kenneth's voice drifting toward us.

"It was an hour ago," he said to someone. They must have been standing outside the hen pen. "Maybe more. She said he didn't have his medication; it wasn't his fault."

The other voice was sterner. "Did they tell you where they were going?"

"You think they'd trust me with that information?" Kenneth asked. "But my money would be on their old house, just over there."

I frowned. Did he actually think that was true . . . or was he trying to help us by sending them in the wrong direction or making them think we had a head start? I remembered how his eyes had fluttered open while Wes and I were discussing what to do. How much, if anything, had Kenneth heard?

More voices spoke now, and then engines started. I held my breath as more car doors slammed and the sound of the engines grew closer. But then they faded as they continued on the gravel road toward the house. I felt sorry for the people who lived there now, if they were actually home, but at least Dr. Hansen and the others didn't seem to be planning a search of the woods just yet. I turned back to tell Wes we should keep going, but he was fast asleep.

A breeze drifted through the windows, and I snuggled closer to him. I rested my head on his arm, which was flung out to the side. He smelled awful—but I was sure I didn't smell like a rose either. The afternoon sun streamed like ribbons through the branches above us, making me feel warm and dozy. I fantasized about a warm shower, a soft pillow . . .

It was dusk when I woke up, needing to pee. "Oh!" I gasped when I realized I'd fallen asleep. Wes was still conked out beside me. I listened for the sound of voices or cars or even dogs that might have been sent to sniff us out, but heard only the hum of crickets. Hoping it was safe—and not able to hold it any longer—I made use of the hole in the floor by the tree trunk. That done, I sat down beside Wes.

The moon was visible against the darkening sky, just above the neighboring treetops. It was almost full, the smiling face beaming down on the world, oblivious to our pain. It was an odd thought, that the stars and the moon would continue to exist just as they always had, whether or not the world descended into horror, whether or not anyone bothered to look up at them in admiration anymore.

At the height of Wes's illness, before he was on any medication, I used to escape out my bedroom window and sit on the dormer above the garage on moonlit nights like this one. I'd tell the moon all my troubles, about the boys I liked and the fight I'd just had with my mom, about Wes's latest meltdown. And the moon would listen without judging or giving patronizing advice. He'd just smile, and I would feel better.

"What do we do?" I whispered to my old confidant. Wes's suggestion that we attempt to escape to Canada through the reservation was a long shot. I didn't see how his friends could help us—they'd just as likely turn him in if they knew the truth. But . . . if we convinced them that the government was hunting us, without saying anything about the cure, maybe they *would* help. The Mistigouche reservation was part of the quarantine zone, so there shouldn't be anything to keep us from getting in. And it might be our only hope to leave the country undetected.

I had no idea who Wes's so-called "friends" were, but now that Kenneth had switched sides and Latasha had gone AWOL, I was running out of people to trust.

"Wake up," I said, shaking Wes gently.

"Are they gone?" he whispered.

"I think so. I've been thinking about what you said. About your friends on the reservation. Do you really think they'll help us?"

"Yeah." He rubbed his eyes and stretched, yawning widely. "Tony will, anyway. He hates the feds. Let's go see him in the morning."

"I think we should go now," I said. "If we wait until daylight, it'll be harder to get there unseen."

"What time is it?" he asked.

"Just after eight. Do you have Tony's phone number?" He shook his head. "Will he shoot us if we show up unexpected?" I asked pointedly. I'd known enough of Wes's friends to recognize this as a distinct possibility.

"Dunno. How we gonna get there?"

Good question. Driving would be faster—and I still had Kenneth's car keys. But they'd probably be keeping an eye out for Kenneth's car . . . and starting it would make too much noise. If the cops had gone to visit the main house, anyone who was in there would be on high alert now.

"We'll have to walk," I said. "It shouldn't take more than a couple of hours."

I hoisted my backpack onto my shoulders and climbed slowly down the tree. Going down was easier than going up. When my feet hit the ground, I froze, listening. There was still no sign of anyone nearby. Had they searched the woods while we were asleep?

"It's okay," I whispered up into the tree. A few seconds later he was beside me—having chosen, of course, to jump the last several feet. I led the way toward the road, keeping out of sight of the house and listening for any movement around us. I gripped the handle of the gun but kept the safety on. The last thing I needed to do was shoot a squirrel and wake up everyone within a mile.

"How are you feeling?" I asked. "It's going to be a long walk."

"I'm good," he said. He slung an arm around my shoulders and gave me a kiss on the cheek. "Some adventure, huh?"

I rolled my eyes. "Sure is."

We walked in silence for several minutes, with only the chirping of the crickets to keep us company. I averted my eyes as we passed the cemetery. Wes nudged me. "Sure you don't want to take a shortcut?" he said, and the moonlight reflected off his teeth when he grinned.

"Ha-ha, very funny. No."

"You gonna come back when they bury Mom and Dad?" he asked. It was strange that he still believed life would return to normal after all of this—that someday I would go back to Seattle and he would stay here, and we'd have a proper funeral and burial for our parents.

"Um . . . if I can, yeah."

"It's going to be weird with them gone," he said.

It's already weird. We continued in silence for at least another mile. Then he said, "I'm sorry, you know."

"What for?"

He laughed, the wild laugh that always made me feel slightly uncomfortable. "For this!" he said, spinning around, his arms held out wide. "For being a fuck-up! For being sick in the head! For making you and Mom and Dad suffer. You think I don't have compassion, but I do. For the people who count."

"Shhh. It's not your fault," I said.

"I know. But I'm glad I'm the way I am, y'know? God made me this way for a reason. He has a purpose for me." I opened my mouth, but he cut me off. "And it's not to be a guinea pig in some government lab. I know that's what you were thinking."

"The Lord works in mysterious ways," I said.

"Not with me. He tells me his plans."

"Oh yeah? Can you fill me in on them?"

"I've told you this before. My calling is to rid the world of demons. It's why I was created. If I were to let them have a go at my brain, it would be like saying, 'Fuck you, God!' I would be turning my back on his purpose for my life."

The sight of headlights far down the road interrupted his sermon.

"Quick!" I said, pulling him into the cemetery. We each crouched behind a tombstone as we waited for the car to pass. It seemed to slow down as it got closer, but maybe that was just my paranoia at work. There was no danger of me moving; I was paralyzed with fright, both from the risk of being caught and from the fact that I was in the middle of a graveyard after dark. Some childhood fears never died.

"Did I ever tell you about the hooker who was stoned out of her mind and screwed herself on the pointy bits of the fence around the old cemetery downtown?" Wes whispered as we watched the taillights grow dimmer. "She died of internal bleeding."

I made a face. "Eww, that's horrible. And probably not even true."

"Need some help?" He held out a hand to me, and I stiffly got to my feet.

I didn't look back as we continued down the road. We kept our eyes peeled for headlights and took back lanes whenever possible.

A couple of hours later, we were on the road leading to the Indian reservation. The sky was full dark now, and both Wes and I were more shambling than walking.

I froze and grabbed Wes's arm. Someone stood ahead of us on the path. But it was too late to run. The man pointed a flashlight at us and shouted, "Stop right there!" A click of cold metal punctuated his command. The moonlight glinted off the barrel of his gun just before his light shone full in my face and I could see nothing at all.

CHAPTER NINETEEN

"Get behind me," I said to Wes, releasing the safety on my handgun. With my free hand I blocked the light from my eyes. "What do you want?" I said loudly.

"Put the gun down," the voice said. "I don't want to shoot you, but I will."

I hesitated. Could we make a run for it? My hand tightened on the grip. "Just let us through."

"I said, put the fucking gun down!"

Wes shifted behind me. "Rick?" he said. He took a step forward, his arms in the air.

The man whipped the beam of light away from me and onto Wes's face.

"Jesus fucking Christ. What in God's name are you doing here, Wes?" Then he pointed the beam at me again. "Tell her she still needs to drop her gun."

"Do it, Clare," Wes said.

"That's *Clare*?" Rick said. "Your sister? What the fuck?"

"We need your help, man," Wes said. "That's why we came."

I put the safety back on and slipped the gun into my bag, watching this exchange warily.

"Well, shit. I'm not supposed to let anyone other than our own onto our land," Rick said. "We've got our own perimeter set up to keep out all those crazy people."

"C'mon, man. For old times' sake?"

Rick hesitated, but finally lowered his rifle and nodded. "I can't leave my post unguarded, but I'll get someone to replace me." He spoke into a black radio, then turned back toward us.

"So what the hell's going on? You're not in trouble again, are you?"

Wes grinned sheepishly. "Hell yeah. But it's not my fault."

"It never is," Rick said. Then he nodded to me. "Hey. I'm Rick. I'd shake your hand, but . . ."

"It's okay," I said.

"Sorry for almost shooting you."

"Um . . . likewise, I guess?"

"I'm assuming you've got a story to tell—everyone does these days—but it should wait. The fewer people who know you're here, the better—for my ass and yours. Go wait in the truck until my buddy arrives." He shone his flashlight at a dark pickup parked on the side of the road.

I glanced at Wes. "You sure it's okay?"

He scowled at me. "Of course it's okay. These are my people."

We climbed into the back of the four-seater and waited. A minute later another truck drove up, and Rick exchanged words with the driver. Once the other man had taken up his post in the middle of the road, Rick climbed into the front seat.

"You guys okay?" he asked, looking at us in the rearview mirror.

"Yeah, man, we're cool," Wes answered. I stayed silent.

The houses on the reservation were simple one-story structures, with gravel driveways leading from the paved main road. Weeds grew in some yards; flowers in others. The pickup truck seemed to be the vehicle of choice. The reservation area itself was huge, but there were only a couple dozen houses here close to town, plus a gas station and convenience store. The kids all went to the local public school and more or less blended in with the rest of us. Every year on Christmas Eve, our parents would take Wes and me for a drive through the reservation to look at the Christmas lights, which covered nearly every single house around the holidays. The chief's house was always the most spectacular, with a blinking Santa and all eight reindeer on his roof, plus an army of snowmen on the lawn. My mother loved it. *Had loved it.*

Rick pulled into the driveway of a blue clapboard house. We got out and silently followed him inside. Once he'd closed the door behind us, he turned to face Wes, a grin spreading across his face.

"Good to see you again, man!" he said, and the two of them hugged and pounded each other's backs.

"I didn't know this was your place. Nice digs," Wes said.

"Thanks," Rick answered, as he stripped off the mask he'd been wearing. "Your sister nearly gave me a heart attack out there. Good thing I was on patrol and not one of the other guys. They would have blown your heads off."

Now that we were inside, I had my first good look at Rick. He had a lean, athletic build and a long white scar against the brown skin of his shoulder. "You guys clean?" he asked, still holding the mask.

"Yes," I said. "We've both been tested."

"Want a beer or something?"

"Nah, man, my stomach don't feel so good," Wes answered, and I shook my head.

"Coffee?" he offered.

"Hell yeah," Wes said, and I added, "Please." Rick led us into the living room, which opened up into the kitchen.

"Have a seat. You both look like shit, by the way."

"We've been livin' rough, man. Crazy shit goin' on in town."

He handed us each a mug of hot coffee, and I clutched mine as though he had given me the Holy Grail. After savoring the first sip, I gave Wes a meaningful glance. "So, do we need to talk to Tony, or . . . ?"

"Nah, Ricky's all right," he said. "Didn't know you were still here. Haven't seen you in a while."

"Still kickin', man. Still kickin'. Want me to call Tony over?"

"For sure," Wes said.

Rick pulled out his cell. "Tony? It's Rick. Yeah, I know. But guess who's in my house? Guess. Okay, fine. It's Wes. Yeah, that Wes. No, not yet. Wanna come over? Yeah, okay." He put the phone back in his pocket and said, "He's coming over."

"Can I use your bathroom?" I asked.

"Just down the hall on the left," he said, pointing.

I escaped into the sanctuary of the bathroom with my pack, happy to have a door to close behind me. I didn't look as bad as I'd imagined—Kenneth had managed to clean off most of the blood back in the hen pen, and my hair looked lank but not too wild. At least the bird bones had fallen out. Not that any of it mattered. I ran hot water and washed my hands and face, avoiding the bandage. I dug a brush out of my backpack and tugged it through my hair, then added another layer of deodorant. Feeling slightly refreshed, I returned to the living room.

Tony had just arrived. He was as lean as Rick but shorter, with full-sleeve tattoos on both arms and a gold stud in one ear. He and Wes were laughing and punching each other on the shoulder. Wes introduced us, and we shook hands. Tony accepted a beer from Rick, and we all sat down.

"Together again," Tony said. "I never thought I'd see it."

"You still with Crystal?" Wes asked.

"Yeah, man, she's awesome. And we're having a baby!"

"No way. Congratulations, brother!" Wes said.

"Thanks. We're pumped."

"So what's the story, Wes?" Rick asked. "Why do they want you this time?"

Wes glanced at me, and I took over. It was his story, and these were his friends, but I didn't know these guys. I didn't want to risk that they'd take the wrong side. So I told them about how the government had come for him in the night, while we were at our parents' house, and how they'd come for him again—twice, at Kenneth's house and the hen pen—after Kenneth and I managed to bust him out. Wes looked like he wanted to interrupt, but I kept talking, giving him little choice but to sit and listen like the rest of them.

"They told us they wanted to experiment on him, to see how the symptoms of Gaspereau compare to schizophrenia. But Wes has the right to say no—a right they've violated over and over again. Now they're hunting us like criminals, even though all we want to do is mourn our parents and move on with our lives."

"Fucking government," Tony snorted. "Trust them to ignore the real problem and go chasing some innocents."

"It doesn't make sense," Rick said. "Why would they go after you, especially when you're making it so hard for them? Why not pick on someone else?"

Wes puffed up his chest and opened his mouth, but I cut him off. "There's more," I said, wanting to keep the focus on the big bad government and not on the inconsistencies in our story. "I have a friend who works for the NSA. She's sent us proof that the government was testing biological weapons at a secret lab a few miles from here—and we know there was a leak. We think that's what caused Gaspereau."

"I met this scientist who used to work at the lab," Wes broke in eagerly. "He was in the psych hospital with me. Kept taking about a program called Project Amherst. But something went wrong, he said. And then he killed himself. Or *was* killed."

"Shit," said Tony.

"We think the scientist Wes met was Patient Zero. The government made Gaspereau," I said. "And now they're doing whatever it takes to cover it up. My friend at the NSA was careful, but she's gone silent. I can't get in touch with her, and I don't know why. There's a chance her bosses found out she sent me this info, and that's why they're after us. To keep us quiet." For all I knew, it could be true. Wes wasn't the only one of value to them now.

"Did you say Project Amherst?" Rick asked.

"Yeah," Wes said.

"Does that mean something to you?" I asked.

Rick and Tony exchanged dark looks. "You don't know your Indian history very well if it doesn't," Rick said. "It's a story every American Indian child learns at some point or another: the first use of biological warfare."

Tony nodded. "Dark times, man. When the white man came over, he brought more than guns. He brought diseases that our people had no resistance to. Then one of the generals had what he thought was a great idea. He took blankets that had been used by people with smallpox and gave them to our people. Called it a gift. Wiped out entire nations."

"Oh my God," I said, stunned. They hadn't taught *that* in my history classes.

"I can't remember the exact numbers," Rick said. "But something like ninety percent of the native population was killed by smallpox and other diseases from Europe. No natural resistance, like I said. So we got sick and died by the millions, and then the white man just walked in and took over our lands."

"That's horrible," I said. "But what does this have to do—"

"The general who had the idea for the blankets . . . his name was Amherst."

I sat back in my chair, stunned. "Jesus."

"That sucks, man," Wes said. "But me and Clare aren't like that, you know."

Tony slapped him on the back. "Aw, hell, man, I know that! You're one of the good guys. But you come from a shitty lineage."

"It could be a coincidence, I suppose," I said slowly. "It might be named after some other guy or place called Amherst. But if you're right . . . then that's pretty much confirmation that they were testing biological weapons, don't you think?"

"Sounds like it to me," Rick said darkly.

There was a long silence, and I met each pair of eyes in turn. We had convinced them.

"So . . . you guys gonna help us or what?" Wes asked.

"Fuck yeah," Tony said, jumping to his feet. "What do you need?"

"We need to get to Canada," I said. "Just to hide out until this all blows over. If we stay here too long, they're bound to find us. But if we get caught over there, we can claim refugee status. Your lands straddle the border, and you guys are allowed to cross it, right?"

"Yeah, *we're* allowed to cross it," Tony said. "But not you guys. They check for status cards."

"Don't you know someone at the border who might be willing to look the other way?" I said. "I have money." *If they'll take gold coins and Wayne Gretzky rookie cards.*

"It might have been possible . . . before," Rick said slowly. "But with Gaspereau, they've sealed the border tight. Canada's not letting in anyone from these parts, not even us. Money's not the issue. It's just . . . closed. Even if you claimed asylum, they'd send you back, tell you to go through another crossing. And good luck leaving the quarantine area. I've never seen so much goddamn security."

My shoulders sagged and my chest ached as though he had punched me in the sternum. Not trusting myself to speak, I pressed my fist to my mouth. Wes was sprawled out on the sofa. How much more of this could he take? He'd only just been released from the psych hospital; he needed stability and rest, two things that didn't appear to be in our immediate future.

I took his hand. "Hey. Don't worry. I'll figure it out."

He grunted.

"Sorry we can't help with the border thing," Rick said. "But you can hide out here for as long as you need."

I stood up and paced, hands on my hips. "Thanks, Rick, but we can't stay here. They'd find us sooner or later, or someone would see us and call the cops. We can't give up. There's *got to* be a way out of this mess."

I stopped suddenly, struck by an idea. "Ohhhh." I spun around to face the men on the sofa, the ache in my chest easing. "What do you think the government would do to cover up the fact that they're responsible for Gaspereau?"

That's why Latasha had risked so much to send me that confidential document. It wasn't just interesting information. *It was leverage.*

"Anything, I imagine," Rick said.

"Including leaving us alone?" I asked, getting out my phone.

"Maybe," Tony said. "Or they might just kill you."

"This whole ordeal is going to kill us soon. I don't know about you, Wes, but I'm tired of running. We've got the ammunition. I say it's time to start fighting back."

"Yeah!" Wes said, sitting up straighter. "Let's show those bastards."

"I don't suppose you know much about covering up your tracks online?" I asked Tony and Rick, wishing once again that Latasha was around. I pulled Kenneth's flash drive out of my pocket. I knew Latasha had to have an encrypted copy of this document somewhere safe; it wouldn't be like her not to take precautions. But I had to operate as though she were out of the picture—as much as that thought destroyed me.

Rick and Tony grinned at each other. "I know a thing or two," Tony said.

"If anything happens to Wes—or to me, for that matter—send this to one of the big papers. The *Washington Post*, maybe, or the *New York*

Times. Or *Slate* or something. The papers will protect your identity as a source. Tell them everything I've told you. But make sure you give them the document on here." I handed Tony the flash drive. "If I don't check in with you every five days, that will mean they've caught up to us, and you should go ahead. Does that make sense?"

Tony's eyes were wide, and he was holding the flash drive as though it might blow up in his hands. But when he looked up at me, it was with a new kind of respect. "You're not shitting around," he said.

"No, I'm not," I said grimly. "Mind if I step outside? I gotta make a call."

"I wouldn't go outside if I were you," Rick said. "Bedroom's in the back; you can go in there."

"Wish me luck," I said, kissing Wes on the forehead.

"You'll be awesome," he said.

"Blackmailing the feds?" Tony said, his forehead wrinkled. "You'll need more than luck."

I followed the orange carpet down the hall until I came to a door, which I gingerly pushed open. A fan stood in the corner, and I turned it on. The more ambient noise the better; I didn't want Tony and Rick to find out I'd only told them part of the story. They needed to stay on our side. Then I fished Dr. Hansen's card out of my back pocket.

He picked up on the first ring. "Hello?"

"Dr. Hansen?"

"Yes. Who is this?"

"It's Clare Campbell."

There was a moment of silence, and then he said, "Clare. Good God. We've been trying to reach you. Are you all right?"

"I'd be better if you stopped chasing us," I said. Then I paused. "How is Kenneth—Dr. Chu?"

"He's very upset, Clare, and for good reason—"

"But he's okay?" I asked. "Physically?"

"If you don't count the welt on his head and the bullet wound in his arm, yes, he's fine. But you must—"

"Listen, Doctor, I want to make this quick. Kenneth explained everything—your theory that Wes has the cure, and what you want to do to him. We gave Wes the choice, we really did. I don't want Gaspereau to keep spreading any more than you do. But Wes doesn't want to sacrifice himself—and as his sister and his legal guardian, I'm going to abide by his wishes. So you're going to have to find another way."

"You must be quite isolated not to know what's going on, Clare."

"I know what's going on. I've seen the news," I bluffed. Was there something I didn't know about?

"Last night there were over two dozen suicides. People would rather die than get Gaspereau."

I sat down on the edge of the bed, my mouth open in shock.

"And it's only going to get worse," he continued. "Every day that goes by without a cure, more people are going to die. More people are going to get infected. And in turn, those people are going to infect more people. I'm sure Dr. Chu told you about the symptoms. We can't contain it much longer."

I shook my head vigorously, as though I could shut out his voice. "Then stop chasing us and work on another cure! You don't even know for sure that this will work!"

"I have a high degree of confidence that it *will*," he insisted.

"And I'm supposed to hand over my brother based on your 'high degree of confidence'?"

"It's the best solution anyone has found. We don't have time to play it safe. Right now, this is our *only* hope for a cure."

"I know about the leak."

"I beg your pardon?"

"I know what caused Gaspereau. I know about the lab outside Clarkeston, about Dr. Ling and Project Amherst."

I held my breath.

"Miss Campbell—Clare—I'm not sure what it is you think you know—"

"I have proof," I said. "And if it gets out, it's going to look pretty bad for you. Testing biological weapons in a civilian area? How well do you think that's going to go over?"

"If I can be blunt: you don't know what you're talking about."

I forced some extra bravado into my voice. "I know exactly what I'm talking about. I have a memo from the Department of Defense that proves it, and if you don't leave my brother and me alone, everyone else will know it, too."

"Ah. So that's what this call is about."

"I'm quite serious, Doctor. It's all set up. If anything happens to Wes or me, that letter will be on the front page of the *New York Times*."

"And I'm serious, too, Clare. I don't know how you came by this so-called information"—I sagged slightly with relief; maybe Latasha hadn't been caught after all—"but releasing it would be a mistake. And if you think that's going to dissuade us, you're mistaken. The government cares more about the well-being of its people than its reputation."

Yeah, right.

Dr. Hansen continued. "You want what's best for your brother. That's very understandable, even commendable. It really is, and I wish there were another way. There isn't. It's our job to look at the big picture. And we have an entire country to protect—perhaps the world."

"And what's to keep that entire country from turning on you once they realize this is all your fault?"

"We all have to live with the consequences of our actions. Even governments."

"So you admit it's true?"

He paused, then said, "By telling you this, I will likely lose my job—or worse—so consider it an act of good faith. Yes, there is a USAMRIID lab outside Clarkeston, and yes, there was a very unfortunate accident that led to one of the scientists working on the project being infected with what has now been identified as Gaspereau. But that's where your information ends. Neither USAMRIID nor anyone else was using that lab to develop biological weapons. Rather, they have been working together with the CDC to develop an airborne antidote to several of the biological weapons we know Russia has developed. The goal was to be able to inoculate millions of people in a very short period of time in the event of a widespread attack."

I scoffed. "Are you telling me that's what Project Amherst was doing?"

"Our biological weapons program shut down in '73. Russia's didn't. With tensions increasing dramatically over the last few years, and with Russia's refusal to abide by international laws *and* borders, we needed to take steps to protect our nation and its allies."

When I remained silent, he said, "I'm telling you this because you need to believe we're not the bad guys. The enemy is Gaspereau, and we need to fight it together."

I shook my head. "It doesn't change anything. I can't let you have him. I stand by what I said—I don't care what purpose this lab was intended to serve; the fact is that you still created Gaspereau, and now you want to ruin my brother's life to make up for your mistake."

"Clare, listen to yourself! You are not looking at the big picture. The lab doesn't matter anymore. There won't *be* a government if this disease is allowed to spread unchecked. There will be no one left to blame. The only thing we care about at this point is stopping this disease." His voice hardened. "And we will do whatever it takes to stop it. If you refuse to help us, then you leave us no choice."

"No choice? What are you talking about?"

"There *is* one other way we can stop Gaspereau. But I prayed to God we wouldn't have to use it."

"Why not? What is it?"

"I've just received an executive order from the president authorizing us to euthanize everyone infected with the disease."

CHAPTER TWENTY

For a long moment, I was quite sure I had misheard him. The room blurred around me; the clothes and wallpaper and furniture blended into one swirling nightmare.

"You're going to . . . what?" I stammered.

"I wish it wasn't like this. But sometimes the few have to be sacrificed to save the many."

"You can't!"

"And what would *you* have us do, Clare, since you seem so sure of the right path? Wait until all the hospitals are overrun? Wait until the infected outnumber the healthy? Gaspereau doesn't know borders. Even our soldiers have become infected while enforcing the quarantine. Then they go back to the barracks, and one of them coughs. The hospital has been shut down completely. This isn't a movie, Clare. It's happening. And if we don't do something now, it will be beyond even God's control."

"But . . . you can't just kill . . ." Then I remembered, and doubled over onto the bed. *Maisie.* "Does Kenneth know about this?" I asked, my voice coming out in a moan.

"Right now no one knows about this except you, me, the chief of staff of the army, and the president."

"How do I know you're not lying to me?"

"Because I'm a God-fearing man. I don't know what this will do to my soul, but yes, I *will* sacrifice hundreds of lives in order to save millions. I wouldn't lie about that."

"I can't . . . I have to . . ." I couldn't get the words out.

"Think about it, Clare. Now you know what's really at stake. He would be a national hero. He could stop all of this. It would be an amazing, selfless act."

"I'll . . . I'll call you back," I said. I shoved the phone into my pocket and ran to the bathroom, where I was noisily, violently ill into the toilet.

Wes came running. "What happened?" he asked, bursting into the bathroom. He gathered my hair and pulled it out of my face, and that small gesture was enough to send me over the edge. I collapsed over the toilet seat, sobbing so hard I could barely gasp for breath and retching until my stomach ached. Wes rubbed my back and made shushing noises, as though I'd merely had too much to drink.

"No, no, no," I moaned, my voice echoing into the bowl and sounding strangely hollow. I don't know how long I stayed there, but eventually Wes hauled me to my feet. Rick, who had been standing behind him, handed me a warm cloth and a cup of water. I wiped my face and swilled the water around in my mouth before spitting it out into the sink.

"Thank you," I mumbled, unable to look at any of them.

"What happened?" Tony asked. I walked past them back into the living room and sat shakily down on the sofa.

"Nothing," I said. "I'm sorry . . . I just . . . I just got overwhelmed. With Mom and Dad dying, and all this happening."

"It can't have been nothing, Clare," Rick said. "What did they say to you? Did you tell them about the document?"

"I . . . I did," I said, trying to break through the fog in my head. "They said that there *was* a leak, but that they weren't creating biological weapons. They were working on an antidote. In case the Russians tried to attack us."

"Bullshit," Wes said with a snort.

"That's what I thought at first, but he had no reason to tell me that. He could have just denied that the lab existed."

"They gonna leave us alone?" Wes asked.

"No."

"What the hell do they want with you, man?" Tony asked. "It doesn't make sense. Why aren't they trying to find a cure for this thing instead of going after you?"

I could feel Wes's gaze on me but didn't meet his eyes. "I wish we knew," I lied. "He wouldn't tell me anything more than we already know."

"Well . . ." Rick began slowly. "While you were on the phone, the three of us came up with a bit of a plan."

They all looked rather pleased with themselves. "What kind of a plan?"

"A plan to get us across the border to Canada," Wes said.

"I thought you said there was no way."

"It crossed my mind when you first mentioned it, but . . . I figured it'd be too risky," Tony said. "And it might not work. We don't know what condition it's in."

"What condition what's in?" I asked.

Wes leaned forward, his eyes shining. "The tunnel," he said dramatically, his fingers splayed out in front of him.

I stared at him blankly.

Tony cleared his throat. "Back in the day, before we were the upstanding citizens you see before you, we, uh, may have known some people who would transport certain . . . illicit goods across the border. Or underneath it, if you see what I'm saying."

I saw what he was saying. "There's a drug tunnel here?"

"There was," Tony corrected. "But as far as I know, it hasn't been used in years. It may have caved in, or been blocked on the other side."

"Where does it lead?"

"To a barn just on the other side of the border."

I stood up and went to the window. There was nothing but darkness and my own pale reflection. A few minutes ago, hearing about this tunnel would have filled me with excitement; finally, a way to get out of Clarkeston, a way to save Wes. I would have been halfway there by now.

But things had changed, and horribly so. Now it was no longer a matter of simply waiting for them to discover a cure. For those infected with Gaspereau—hundreds of people, maybe thousands—there would *be* no cure.

How would they do it? Lethal injection? A bullet to the head? I pictured Maisie lying in a hospital bed, her pillows splattered with blood. Wes's reflection watched me in the window. He and I had a way out. Maisie didn't.

"How far away is this tunnel?" I asked.

"Couple miles," Tony said. "We can take you there in the truck. I called a buddy of mine, lives just across the border. He owes me a favor. Said he'd help you guys on the other side."

"You trust him? What if he turns us in?" How long would we have to ask that question?

"He won't. Like I said, he owes me."

I nodded slowly. "Okay. I need to . . . make a couple more calls. Then we'll go."

As soon as I said it, I knew I had made my decision. I was doing the right thing . . . but it was the last thing I wanted to do. I'd been pretending this option didn't exist, but the time for wishful thinking had ended. Some childlike, irrational part of me still clung to the hope that maybe, just maybe, everything would still work out all right.

I went back into the bedroom and called Dr. Hansen. "I'll give you what you need," I said, my voice sounding distant and hollow, even to my own ears.

His sigh of relief was audible. "You're doing the right thing, Clare. Where are you?"

"We'll meet you at my parents' house. No soldiers. No guns. We're coming voluntarily."

"When?"

I glanced at the time. "In three hours."

"Three hours? Why don't you just tell me where you are? I can send someone to pick—"

"Three hours. Tusslewood Street."

There was a pause, then, "Okay."

"There's more. I want a guarantee that you will leave us alone when this is done. Call Al Irvine. He's our lawyer. I want it in writing that neither you nor any government agency will attempt to apprehend Wes, me, Dr. Kenneth Chu, Rob Wilkins, or Latasha Holt. I want complete immunity for us all. I want to see it in writing by the time we meet. Otherwise, no deal."

His pen scratched as he took notes. "Okay. Unfortunately your lawyer has been infected . . . but I can certainly have those papers drawn up by one of ours."

"Fine. What matters is that if you break our agreement in any way, I will release the document in my possession about the lab breach, as well as my recording of our last conversation."

"Recording conversations without consent is illegal, you know."

"So is killing hundreds of innocent people."

He took a deep breath. "Anything else? Wes's medical bills will all be covered, of course."

"Put that in writing, too. That's it." I hung up. The wheels were in motion. There was nothing to do but move forward.

Next I called Latasha. I knew she wouldn't answer, but there were things I needed to say. I waited to hear her voice on the recording: "Hey, you've reached Latasha. Leave it at the beep."

I swallowed hard. "Hey. It's Clare. Things are happening. I can't talk about it . . . I wish I could. I wish we could sit down over a glass of wine and you could tell me what to do. But, for now, I just wanted to say that you are the best friend I've ever had, and I love you very much. And . . . thank you. For what you did for me. I know you risked a lot . . . maybe everything. I just want to know that you're okay. And, um . . . hopefully I'll see you soon."

I ended the call and stared at the phone in my hands. I had to push forward before I lost my resolve.

I deliberated calling Kenneth, but that would be a conversation neither of us wanted to have. Instead, I spent a few moments remembering how his hands had felt on me, how he smelled when he pulled me close, the sound of his voice whispering in my ear. Then I forced myself to stop.

"Let's go," I said as I left the room. I double-checked our backpacks and accepted a couple more bottles of water from Rick. Tony programmed his and Rick's numbers into my phone, as well as the number of his Canadian buddy.

Wes and I climbed into the backseat of Rick's pickup. We crouched down on the floor so we couldn't be seen from the windows. The drive was bumpy and painful in this position, but in a few short minutes the truck came to a stop. I listened, wary of being discovered. "It's okay," Tony said, and we eased ourselves up onto the seats.

We had pulled off the side of a road that seemed to run through a thick wood. Rick and Tony handed us flashlights and kept two for themselves.

"We have to walk the rest of the way," Tony said with a jerk of his head. I had no idea how they'd figured out where to stop. There were no markers, nothing that said this stretch of the road was any different from the rest of it. We followed Tony into the woods. There was no trail, so we were left to pick our way around brambles and climb over fallen logs.

"How long has this tunnel been here?" I asked, more to make conversation than anything else. The silence was unnerving in the dark woods.

"Before our time," Rick answered. "I dunno; maybe the sixties?"

"And it's not being used anymore?"

"Not by us. Maybe some of the younger kids have discovered it; who knows? But if they have, we don't know about it."

"Does the rest of your band know it's here?"

Tony shook his head. "No, and we'd get our asses kicked if the council found out about it. We should have told them, I suppose, but the Canadians used it more than we did. We just used to buy what they brought over."

"Were you part of this?" I asked Wes, already knowing the answer. After all, part of the reason his illness had gone overlooked for so long was because my parents had attributed his increasingly bizarre behavior to his drug use. There were rumors he'd been a dealer for a while, but he'd never confirmed them.

He shrugged and grinned. "I plead the Fifth."

"It doesn't matter," I said, and it was true. Not a whole lot mattered anymore, except getting to the other end of this tunnel safely.

Finally Tony stopped. He and Rick shone their lights at what looked like an old logging cabin. I'd been to my grandfather's old cabin a couple of times, but this one was far more decrepit. The glass was missing in both windows and had been replaced by boards. Even a couple of those were hanging loose, as though they'd given up. The roof was covered in moss. I shuddered.

Wes lit a cigarette, and I glared at him. "What?" he said defensively. "You want me to wait until we're in the tunnel?"

"I don't want you to burn down the forest," I muttered.

"The border's just on the other side of those trees," Rick said, pointing with his hand and keeping the beam of light low. "They have cameras there"—he pointed east—"and there"—he pointed west—"but this is a blind spot. At least, it used to be."

Rick opened the cabin door, which had been slightly ajar. He looked around, his nose wrinkled, then kicked pinecones and branches out the door, cleaning a space on the floor. He bent down and pushed on one end of the floorboards, and the other end lifted up slightly. He wrapped his hand around the loose boards and tugged, but nothing happened. "Tony, give me a hand, will you, man?" Tony joined him. I couldn't see what they were doing around Tony's back, but at last there was a loud creak and a trapdoor lifted up. They set it against a wall and dusted off their hands.

"Pretty sure this hasn't been used for a while," Rick said. "That's a good thing, because it means the cops won't be watching the other end. But it also means it might not be in very good shape. Course, it was never in very good shape to begin with. Not like those swanky tunnels the Mexicans use."

Wes eyed the hole in the ground nervously.

"Think of it as the path to freedom," I told him. "I'll be with you the whole way."

Wes clasped hands with Tony and Rick. "God bless you guys. See you—if we ever make it back."

"We will," I said.

I walked to the edge of the hole in the ground, my heart pounding.

"Wait. You might want these," Rick said, handing us each a headband with a flashlight on it. "You'll need both hands down there."

"Thanks," we both said, trading in our flashlights for the headlamps. Without further ceremony, I dropped into the hole. It wasn't far down, maybe seven feet. I swiveled my head around and found the entrance to the tunnel, which headed north. It certainly wasn't anything fancy—there were no metal or plastic walls, just a long, dirty hole in the ground. We wouldn't be able to stand up inside it, and there wasn't even space for two people to crawl side by side. We'd have to go single file.

My heart fluttered at the thought of being trapped down here. And if *I* was nervous, I could only imagine how Wes was feeling. He landed beside me with a thump and a grunt.

Tony and Rick gazed down at us from above. I gave them both a wave, then pointed my light down the tunnel and said to Wes, "I'll go first. Just follow me and you'll be fine. Let me know if you need to stop and rest or stretch out for a bit; our knees are going to get pretty raw, I imagine."

"I've never been in here before, you know," he said. "I mean, I knew some of the drugs came from Canada, but I didn't ask how they got here. I assumed they smuggled them across the border in their cars or something."

I smiled. "Well, now we know. Remember those snow tunnels Dad used to make us?"

Wes snickered. Every winter, he and our father would dig a network of tunnels through the several feet of accumulated snow on our front lawn. I would explore them only once or twice, preferring to stay inside where it was warm and read my books. But Wes and Dad used to spend hours playing spies or soldiers as they tunneled their way through the banks. "It's just like that, except warmer," I said.

I crouched down and pointed my headlamp ahead. "All we need to do is take one step at a time." I was speaking more to myself than to Wes.

We started crawling. It only took a few minutes for my hands and knees to start aching. Rocks and roots littered the ground beneath us. Then I put my hand on something soft . . . and felt the crunch of bones beneath my fingers.

I screamed and bolted upright, slamming my head on the ceiling of the tunnel and sending a shower of dirt down my neck. "Oh my God, oh my God," I said. My fingers were sticky, and a putrid smell filled the air, almost suffocating me.

"What happened?" Wes asked, pointing his headlamp at my face.

I shuddered violently. "Nothing. I just . . . touched a dead mole or something."

"Cool," Wes said, now scanning the ground with the beam of light.

"Let's keep going." I wiped my hand on my jeans and started crawling again. Every few yards we had to squeeze past a square post topped with a sheet of plywood. My assumption was that these were intended to keep the tunnel from collapsing. I tried not to think of how it would feel to be smothered by dirt and rocks. What if the tunnel ahead had already collapsed? What if we turned back, only to discover that we were trapped in both directions? What would it be like to starve to death underground? Would Wes kill me before that happened? I had the gun; would I need to use it?

"Stop it," I said out loud.

"Stop what?" Wes asked. He was breathing heavily.

"Nothing . . . I was talking to myself. I'm just a little freaked out." Then my light went out.

I stopped dead. The only sound was my breath, coming in short, shallow gasps. The light from Wes's headlamp illuminated the walls around us, but ahead of me there was only darkness. *I'm going to die down here. Then I'll see Mom and Dad. I can say I'm sorry . . .*

"Clare!" Wes scuttled forward and put his arms around me. He pulled me tight against his chest, and I listened to his deep, heavy breaths. "Shhh. It's okay. Just breathe. My light's still working; I'll go ahead. Follow me."

He squeezed past me. I fixed my eyes on the light ahead of him and followed. We couldn't die down here. It was my job to make sure Wes survived.

We stopped to rest after a few more minutes. We lay faceup on the ground and stretched our limbs as much as we could. The air was thick and musty. Wes coughed harshly. I pulled a bottle of water out of my backpack, and we each took several long swigs to rinse our throats.

We didn't rest for long. It was better to keep moving, to get this over with as soon as possible.

Finally, after about an hour, the air felt less heavy in our lungs. The tunnel began to slope slightly upward. And then it stopped.

We were faced with a dirt wall, and for a brief moment I panicked—was the tunnel blocked? Had there been a cave-in? Then Wes looked up, and in the light of his headlamp we saw a wooden door above our heads. Whether it would open remained to be seen. Neither of us could reach it, even on tiptoes, and there were no footholds or ladders.

"Give me the light and hoist me up," I said to Wes. "I'll see if it opens."

I had expected him to offer his hands or knee for me to stand on, but he immediately turned his back to me and dropped to the ground. "Get on my shoulders," he said.

"Are you sure?"

"Yeah, c'mon."

I took the headlamp from him and put it on, then awkwardly clambered onto his shoulders. I grabbed the dirt walls around us to steady myself as he got to his feet, grunting. I had to duck my head to keep it from slamming into the door above. I reached up with both arms and gave it a push. Nothing happened.

"What if it's locked from the other side?" I whispered.

"Try again!" Wes urged.

I pushed again with all my strength, and the wood shifted slightly. "I think it's working!" Again and again I pushed, each time moving the door a little further. Wes panted under my weight. "Almost there," I grunted, and then the door popped open.

Carefully, I lifted my head up to peer out. It was just as Tony and Rick had said. We were inside a barn—a very old one. Moonlight shone through gaps in the walls and ceiling, and the floor was covered in boards that looked like they had once been part of the roof. It was too dark to spy any cameras or other signs of technology, but from what I could see, it looked like a human being hadn't been in this place for years.

"I'm going to crawl up. Then I'll help you, okay?" I said.

"Okay."

I pulled myself up onto the barn floor and rested for a few seconds. Then I started handing broken planks down to Wes. "Make a pile of these to stand on," I told him. I kept tossing them down until he was able to get high enough to crawl out. We lay on our backs on the floor, wheezing.

"You're filthy," Wes said.

"So are you."

It was true; his hair and face were so covered in sweat-streaked dirt he looked as though he'd just smeared mud all over himself. Our clothes were now various shades of brown, and one of my knees was bleeding through a hole in my jeans.

"What now?" he asked, his chest still rising and falling as though he'd run a marathon.

I didn't say anything. I wanted to preserve this moment of solitude, this moment in which we were the only two people in the world. The moon cast an eerie glow. It was as if we had entered another dimension. A speck of dust floated through the air, catching the light of the moon. *That's all we are, really. Just specks of dust floating through time. Our lives mean so little—except to those few other specks who love us. And to those we can save.* I sat up and faced Wes. It was time.

"I guess we call Tony's friend." I dialed the number in my phone.

"'Lo?" a voice answered.

"Is this Dave?"

"Yeah. You one of Tony's friends?"

"Yes. I'm Clare. My brother, Wes, is with me."

"He told me you were comin'. I'm on my way. The old drug barn, yeah?"

"That's right."

"Be there in five."

We waited outside the barn, watching the moon, too tired to speak. My mind churned and roiled like the waves we used to watch on the coast. I ached with exhaustion, but there would be no rest for me. Not yet.

The headlights of a truck approached, and we stood up. A young man got out and walked toward us.

"Dave?" I asked.

"Yeah. C'mon."

We climbed into the back of the truck and bumped along silently. Dave parked in front of a nondescript house on a dark street.

"You want a drink or anything?" he said after we were inside.

"No," I said. "I think we should just get some sleep. Thank you for taking us in."

He snorted. "Tony saved my ass once. He's a good guy. Now we'll be even. I got a futon in the spare room, and your brother can take the couch."

"I'll take the couch," I said quickly.

"You sure?" Wes asked.

"Yeah."

Wes went to the bathroom while I sat down on the sofa and pulled out a pen and notebook I'd snagged from Rick's place. I set them on the coffee table and waited. Wes emerged after a few minutes, looking slightly cleaner. I handed him his bottle of pills from his backpack and some water.

He pulled me to my feet and wrapped me in a fierce hug. "We did it. Thank you."

I fought back my tears. "I love you," I said.

"I love you, too." He kissed my forehead and then went into the spare room and closed the door.

Dave hovered in the kitchen. "So why y'all running? Tony didn't say."

I hesitated. "I'll let Wes tell you in the morning. But we've done nothing wrong."

"Whatever it is, it can't be worse than some of the shit I've done."

I crept over to Wes's door and listened. He was already snoring. Good.

"Listen, Dave. I'm not staying."

"Say what?"

"I have to go back. I just wanted to make sure Wes got here safely. I know it's a lot to ask, but do you think you could look out for him? I mean, he can take care of himself, and I'll wire you some money when I can. For now, take these—you should be able to get them changed at the bank." I handed him a couple of the gold coins I'd taken from my father's safe. "Our uncle will come and get him as soon as the quarantine is lifted."

"Okay . . . but why?"

"I have some . . . unfinished business in Clarkeston. But Wes needed to get out. It's not safe for him there."

"Well . . . do what you have to do, I guess."

"Thanks. I'm going to leave Wes a note to explain."

I turned back to the notebook and wrote:

Dear Wes,

I'm sorry I couldn't tell you, but I have to go back to Clarkeston. I wanted to make sure you got here safely. I'm sorry for leaving in the middle of the night, and I hope you're not angry. But I knew you wouldn't let me go otherwise.

It's really, really important that you don't follow me. You know what awaits you there. But there are some things I have to do back home.

I've given Dave some money, and you can stay here for a while. When the quarantine is lifted, Uncle Rob will come get you. I'm leaving my phone here so you can call Uncle Rob and Tony and Rick. Don't forget to check in with them at least every five days so they know you're okay. But don't tell Uncle Rob or anyone else where you are; not until it's safe.

If—and only if—you get caught by the cops or border guards or anyone, say you want to claim refugee status. They can't send you back without a hearing. If they try, find a church and take refuge there. If you claim sanctuary in a church, they can't come in after you.

I'm so proud of you, big brother. You're kind and funny and imaginative and loyal. You are an amazing human being, and you're going to have a long and happy life. You deserve that.

Don't forget to take your medication.

I love you. God bless you.

~ Clare

I folded the letter before my tears could ruin the ink. "Can you give this to him in the morning?" I asked as I handed it to Dave.

"Yeah. How you gonna get back?"

"Through the tunnel."

"Want me to drive you?"

I shook my head. "No. I don't want Wes to be here alone."

"Then take my bike," he said. "Leave it in the barn; I'll come get it later."

"Are you sure?"

"Yeah."

I followed him into the garage, where a dirt bike stood against the wall. He handed me a helmet and a key. Before I put on the helmet, I called Tony.

"Hello?" he said groggily.

"Tony, it's Clare."

"Clare! Jesus. Did you make it? How's Wes?"

"He's fine. We're both fine. We're at Dave's house; thanks so much for setting it up. But I need you to pick me up on your end of the tunnel. I'm coming back. Wes is staying here."

"What? Why?"

"I'll explain later. Can you come get me in about an hour?"

"Yeah, okay. I'll be there."

I hung up and gave my phone to Dave. "Give this to Wes with the note."

"Does he have your number?" he asked.

"I don't have a number. I'll . . . I'll be in touch." I hoped that was true.

I started the bike and backed it out of the garage.

"Thanks again!" I called. Then I drove away, heading back toward the moonlit barn. The air in my face was like a long drink of cold water. I imagined the salt spray of the ocean misting my cheeks and pretended the wind in my hair was coming off the rolling waves. The stars, so bright out here in the middle of nowhere, sparkled like a thousand tiny fireworks, sending me off on yet another grand adventure.

When I reached the barn, I cut the engine and tossed my head back for another look at the sky. It was perfectly quiet. It was the deep breath before the plunge.

I turned and ran back toward the tunnel entrance, lest I lose my nerve. I dropped back down into the darkness, landing painfully on my ankle. I cried out, but there was no one to hear.

The trip back through the tunnel was even more terrifying—and painful—than before. I counted each crawl to one hundred, then started again. Halfway through I lost all composure and sobbed miserably the rest of the way. *Just keep moving.* It had worked for me so far. I couldn't stop now.

Finally, Tony and Rick pulled me out of the hole. I collapsed on the ground, weeping. They didn't ask questions, not then. Tony lifted me up and put me in the backseat of the truck. Wordlessly, Rick passed me a flask, and I took a long pull of whiskey.

"Where to?" Rick asked.

"Home."

CHAPTER TWENTY-ONE

"You gonna tell us what's going on?" Rick asked as we drove back toward town.

"I had to get Wes somewhere safe," I said. "But there's something I have to do in Clarkeston."

They didn't press me. I wrote a letter to Rob while we were driving. How would he feel when he read it? Angry? Proud? It didn't matter. However he felt, I trusted him to see things through.

I passed the letter up to Tony. "You can read this after you drop me off," I said. "It explains everything. And then—if you don't mind—take it to my Rob. His address is on the letter."

I wrote another letter, this one to Kenneth. It was short and to the point.

You were the best thing to almost happen to me.
I'm sorry I didn't give us a proper chance.
Live without regret.
Give Maisie my love.

~ xo Clare

The drive to my parents' house was silent except for the simple directions I gave them. I wasn't worried about being caught now. I watched the vacant shops pass by, their windows smashed and their signs torn down. A church was advertising a "vigil for Gaspereau," but the parking lot was empty. Banners hanging over the highway signs read "Highway Closed. Quarantine in Effect." Concrete dividers blocked the on-ramps. Barbed-wire fencing surrounded the college dorm building. Men armed with assault rifles stood at the gates.

"I've heard it's a living hell in there," Rick said as we drove by. "Soldiers are deserting just so they don't have to stand guard."

When we pulled up to the house, Dr. Hansen was already sitting on the front step. A sole car was parked on the street. I didn't doubt that other cars were parked on nearby blocks, but at least he had kept his word. No soldiers. No guns. I got out of the car.

"Who's that?" Tony asked out the window, watching Dr. Hansen.

"A friend—I hope. Thanks for the lift. And for delivering my letters. I left my phone with Wes; he's got your numbers."

"You sure about this?" Rick asked. "We can still make a run for it."

I shook my head. "Not this time. You still have the flash drive?"

"Yeah." He patted his front pocket.

"If anything happens to Wes, use it."

I slammed the door, and he drove off. Dr. Hansen was standing now, his hands in his pockets.

"Where is Wes?" he asked.

"He's not coming."

His eyes narrowed. "But why—?"

I held up a hand to stop him. "When I arrived in Clarkeston a few days ago, a man coughed on me at the airport. Right in the face; I could feel the spit land on my cheek. And I shook hands with him. I found out later that he had Gaspereau. His wife caught it from him, so he was clearly contagious. But I didn't get it."

"What are you saying?" Dr. Hansen asked slowly.

"You told me Wes is the cure for Gaspereau. And I believe that I am, too. Both of us were directly exposed, and neither of us got sick. Has that happened to anyone else?"

He stared at me. "No. It hasn't."

"I know you're not the enemy, Dr. Hansen. But neither is my brother. He's made his decision. And I've made mine. You can have me."

Dr. Hansen's eyebrows knitted together. A deep crevice formed in his forehead. "Do you understand what you're saying? We'll have to do some tests, of course. But if it's true . . . well, you understand the implications, do you not?"

"I do. At least, I think so. I know it's risky . . . but there's a chance that . . . that it might not be so bad, right?" My voice broke, and I pressed my fingers to my lips.

"We'll do our very best, Clare. I can't guarantee anything, of course, but . . . are you sure? You have a long, productive life ahead of you. I really think Wes might be the better choice."

"That's not an option. And I can still have a long, productive life ahead of me."

Dr. Hansen watched me silently for a moment. "This is why you wanted the memorandum of agreement."

"Yes. Those are my conditions. Do you have the papers?"

He withdrew a file folder out of his briefcase and handed it to me. I scanned the papers inside. "I want a copy of these sent to my Uncle Rob."

"I'll send them from the hospital. You can watch, to make sure it's done."

I nodded. "Let's go, then."

He led the way to his car. Before I got in, I turned and stared long and hard at the house, fixing it in my memory. It seemed truly empty now, with my parents dead and Wes in hiding. And then Fluff Bucket the cat walked across the lawn and sat on the front step, and for a moment I remembered it as it had once been: my mother cooking in the kitchen, dancing to the Beach Boys on the stereo; my dad reading the newspaper in his easy chair, delivering a running commentary; Wes and I playing G.I. Joe versus Barbie on the living room floor. *That's* what I would remember.

***

I told them to not let anyone see me, but those particular instructions were ignored. Rob was the first to come, right after I'd gotten the results of my tests. Dr. Hansen had immediately done a number of scans as well as a lumbar puncture and brain biopsy. My lower back felt tender. They had shaved half of my head for the biopsy, but they'd used a tiny needle. They only needed enough to confirm that I, too, had what Dr. Hansen had dubbed "warrior cells."

I did.

He gave me a sheaf of releases to sign, but I just laughed at him and handed them back.

"If these meant anything, we wouldn't have had to hide from you," I said.

"All the same, since you *are* volunteering, it will be good to have proof. You're going to be a hero, you know."

I shook my head. I didn't care about being a hero.

When Rob burst into the room, shouting at the guards that they'd have to shoot him to stop him, it was almost like seeing my parents again. He looked like he hadn't shaved since the last time I'd seen him. He grabbed me in a bear hug that made me cry out from the soreness in my back. Then he gripped my shoulders. "What the hell are you doing, Clare?"

I shrugged out of his grip and sat up on the bed. "Did you get my letter?"

"Yes, I got your damn letter. Is it true?"

"Of course it's true."

"So Wes, he's—"

"Best not to talk about it here," I said, unsure of who might be listening. "Everything is in the letter. You'll take care of him, won't you?"

"Of course I will. I have a friend there. He'll go pick up Wes."

"Who? How will Wes—"

"I talked to Wes. He called me."

"He did? How is he? Is he okay?"

"He's fine. He's at your friend's house, he said."

"Did you tell him—"

"About what you're doing? No."

"And you'll help him . . . process it? When the time comes?"

He nodded, then looked at me for a long moment. "I'd like to talk you out of it, but I have a feeling it would be futile. Dammit, Clare. You've got to be the bravest person I've ever met."

I lowered my eyes. "It's not bravery when there's no other choice."

"You had a choice. You could have kept running. You could have let them take Wes. Your parents would be incredibly proud."

I smiled sadly, but said nothing.

"They always were, you know," he said.

I snorted.

He sat down beside me on the bed, and I leaned into him. "Oh, come on, Clare. You were always too hard on them. They didn't know anything about drugs and mental issues—none of us did back then. They did the best they could with Wes—better than anyone could have expected, actually. I know you felt like they didn't love you; like they always put Wes's needs first."

I sniffed. "How do you know that?"

"Because *they* knew it. And they were torn up inside, not knowing how to juggle their troubled child and their extremely gifted one. So they took a chance that you would be okay, that you'd figure it out yourself. You didn't need them as much as he did. Try to see it that way. They didn't abandon you; they trusted you. They knew how strong you were."

I pressed my face into his shoulder to soak up the tears. "I miss them. I thought we'd have our whole lives to sort out our shit. I never thought—"

"Don't beat yourself up," he said. "They knew you loved them. They also knew you needed your independence. And there's nothing wrong with that. They never blamed you. You should have heard them talk about you to anyone who would listen. They loved you something fierce, Clare. You were a free bird—but you were *their* free bird."

There was a commotion in the hallway, and Rob went to the door. "Looks like I'm not the only one who was hell-bent on seeing you."

"Who?" I asked, but my question was soon answered. Rob opened the door and said, "Stand aside, boys. You're not going to keep a doctor from seeing his patient, are you?"

Kenneth entered the room, dressed in full isolation gear. As soon as the door closed behind him, he stripped off his head covering and mask and peeled off the tape that bound his suit to his gloves. Rob slipped out of the room.

Kenneth's eyes were red and swollen. "Clare . . ." he began, his voice shaking. "I can't . . . I had no idea . . . I just . . ." Then he sank into a chair, his face in his hands.

I got off the bed and wrapped my arms around him. "Shhh. It's okay. This isn't your fault. I made this choice. I *want* to do this. For Maisie. For all the other people who are infected. And for Wes—so he doesn't have to."

He straightened up and pulled me to his chest. "I wish it was me," he whispered. "I wish I could do this, instead of you."

I smoothed the hair off his forehead and kissed it. "I know you do. But it seems that Wes and I are the only ones around who have this particular . . . mutation. You know, I've always wanted to have a super-power. I just didn't think it would be something like this."

"I asked to be part of the medical team that performs your proce-dure," he said. "I was declined. They said I was too close to the subject."

I held his face in my hands and kissed his lips, long and softly. "You are. And I'm glad." I smiled at him. "Hey. No one's dying here. Maybe I'll just get some interesting new personality traits."

He seemed unable to speak for a moment. Then he leaned closer to me and whispered in my ear, "A journalist from the *Post* contacted me. They've been in touch with Latasha. She's going to blow this whole thing wide open."

"What?" I said. My heart soared. She was alive.

"She says the world needs to know the truth about Gaspereau. I agree. It was only a matter of time until they found out anyway. It's going to be a crazy shit-storm. I won't be surprised if it goes all the way to the White House."

"But—"

"Don't worry. Latasha, you, and Wes—you're all going to be protected. When this goes public, there's no way the government will be able to go after your brother."

"Good," I said tearily. I kissed him again, harder this time. "You should go," I said finally, looking at the floor. "You don't want me to change my mind."

He didn't have a retort for this. He kissed the top of my head and said, "Don't be afraid." Then he left, and I sat alone, waiting.

It didn't take long. Dr. Hansen came into the room only moments after Kenneth left.

"When do we start?" I said.

"Whenever you're ready."

"I'm ready."

CHAPTER TWENTY-TWO

The first thing I noticed was the lamp beside me. It was the same lamp I'd had as a child. Had someone brought it to the hospital? I turned my head, expecting it to be sore. I was in my old bedroom, in my parents' house. Why wasn't I in a hospital room? I touched my head, expecting to feel bandages, but instead my fingers wove through a full head of hair. A wig? I tugged on it and winced.

"Hello?" I called. "Dr. Hansen?"

The door opened, and Wes came in. "Wes!" I cried, sitting up. It didn't hurt like I'd thought it would. "You're okay!"

"Hey, sis," he said. He was carrying a mug of coffee, which he set down on the nightstand. I jumped out of bed and hugged him close. "How did you get here? Is it safe?"

"Yeah, it's safe," he said. He wore a strange, closed expression I couldn't decipher.

"Why am I here? How come I'm not at the hospital? Did it work?" The last thing I remembered was being wheeled into the operating room as the anesthesia took hold.

"It worked," he said, putting an arm around me. "Gaspereau is gone. You did it."

I collapsed back onto the bed, tears leaking out of the corners of my eyes. It was over. It was actually over.

"So soon?" I asked. "They've given the treatment to everyone?"

Wes nodded. "Yeah. They worked fast. You've been out for a while."

"Oh. Are you angry?" I asked, sitting up again and grabbing his hand. "I wanted to tell you, but I—"

"It's okay," he interrupted. "I'm not mad. They moved you here to recover. Uncle Rob and I are going to stay here with you until you're ready to go back to Seattle."

Seattle. *Latasha.*

"Has anyone heard from Latasha?" I asked. "Where's my phone?"

"She's fine," he said quickly. "She's a hero, actually. Took down the whole fucking government single-handed."

I laughed. That sounded like her. Then I hesitated. "Wait—how long was I out?"

"Oh . . . a while," he said. "I was exaggerating—they're just starting the grand jury thing."

I was surprised Wes even knew what a grand jury was, but I didn't press him. I'd get all the details from Latasha later.

"And Maisie? She's okay?"

"Maisie's great. She lost another tooth. She and Kenneth visit lots. I think he's coming by later today."

My heart swelled in anticipation. But I felt I was missing something, some vital piece of information.

"Wes . . . am I okay? I mean, I feel fine, but I know there were severe risks—"

"You're great," he said quickly. "Like I said, the doctors think you're going to be fine."

That confused me. "Like you said . . . when?"

Wes turned red and jumped up off the bed. "Uh . . . I left my coffee downstairs. I'm going to go get it."

"Okay." I brushed off the feeling. Obviously there was a lot to get caught up on.

Before he reached the door, I said, "Wes?"

"Yeah?"

"Thanks for taking care of me."

He grinned. "It's what I'm meant to do."

I sank back down into my pillows, savoring the smell of the coffee beside me. Latasha was safe. Wes was safe. Gaspereau had been cured. And I still had my memories.

I grinned up at the ceiling, almost delirious with joy. I had hoped against hope that things would turn out this way. My whole life was opening up before me, a vast expanse of sunlight and love and possibility. I remembered Kenneth's last kiss—and laughed aloud with delight, realizing it wouldn't be the last. There could be many, many more. Perhaps—I marveled at how little this thought frightened me anymore—perhaps I would call Clarkeston home once again.

ACKNOWLEDGMENTS

I owe an enormous debt of gratitude to my parents, for encouraging me on this path ever since I wrote my first words, and for inspiring me in so many ways.

Dr. Kim Foster, Dr. Melina Roberts, and Dr. Greg Montgomery helped with the medical research, for which this liberal arts grad is extremely grateful (all errors, of course, are mine). I'd also like to thank the neurosurgeon who wanted to remain anonymous in case she got the details wrong (you didn't).

My first readers gave invaluable feedback. Thank you to Mike Martens, Nell de Jager, Erika Holt, Craig DiLouie, David J. Fortier, Adam Cole, Susan Forest, Janice Hillmer, and Jason Goode.

Paul Lucas, Kjersti Egerdahl, Angela Polidoro, Jacque Ben-Zekry, and the team at Thomas & Mercer have my gratitude for their professionalism and enthusiasm surrounding this book.

As always, I'm so very grateful to my husband and children for their unflagging support.

COMING FALL 2016

BURY THE LIVING

BOOK 1 IN A NEW HISTORICAL FANTASY SERIES BY JODI McISAAC

The first in the Thin Veil series, *Through the Door* is a pulse-pounding adventure that takes readers across the globe and deep into the hidden realms of Celtic lore.

It's been seven years since the love of Cedar McLeod's life left with no forwarding address. All that remains are heart-wrenching memories of happier times and a beautiful six-year-old daughter, Eden. Then, one day, Eden opens her bedroom door and unwittingly creates a portal that can lead to anywhere she imagines.

But Cedar and Eden are not the only ones who know of this gift, and soon the child mysteriously vanishes.

Desperate for answers, Cedar digs into the past and finds herself thrust into a magical world of Celtic myths, fantastical creatures, and bloody rivalries. Teaming up with the unlikeliest of allies, Cedar must bridge the gap between two worlds and hold tight to the love in her heart . . . or lose everything to an ancient evil.

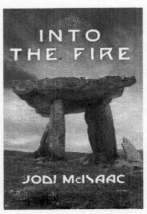

Into the Fire, the second book in the Thin Veil series, is an enchanting blend of Celtic myth, mystery, and adventure that delves deeper into the ancient world first explored in *Through the Door*.

Cedar McLeod would like nothing more than to return to Tír na nÓg, help rebuild the mythical kingdom, and start a new life for herself and her daughter, Eden. But peace isn't what Cedar finds after being reunited with her little girl.

Nuala—who kidnapped and terrorized Eden in her previous bid for power—has returned and is making a persuasive claim for the vacant throne. The devastation such a ruler would bring upon both the kingdom and the human world is unthinkable. With no one else to stake a convincing counterclaim, Cedar steps forward . . . but first she must prove her worth beyond a doubt.

Her opportunity comes when she is charged with finding an ancient treasure, the Stone of Destiny, and returning it to its rightful home. It is a quest that will lead her to question her beliefs and push her loyalties to their limits. If she succeeds, Cedar could grant her new world and her new family a chance to flourish again. If not . . . destruction may be the only path ahead.

Brimming with page-turning adventure, *Among the Unseen*—the exciting conclusion to Jodi McIsaac's Thin Veil series—weaves an enchanting, captivating spell.

Life just keeps getting more complicated for Cedar McLeod. As the recently crowned queen of Tír na nÓg, she's trying to understand her magical new kingdom, even as she misses her life back on Earth. It doesn't help that a dear friend has just betrayed her—a betrayal that almost cost Cedar and her family their lives. And things aren't easy at home, either, as Cedar's seven-year-old daughter, Eden, lost and lonely in Tír na nÓg despite her special powers, has become painfully distant.

Cedar vows to do whatever it takes to protect her family once and for all, and starts rounding up those who plotted against her. But then a new disaster breaks out: a mysterious sickness is plaguing the Unseen, Ireland's magical creatures, including those Cedar knows and loves. With enemies still on the loose and without knowing whom she can trust, Cedar must race against time to reverse an ancient curse, in a journey that will take her from Tír na nÓg to Earth . . . and beyond.

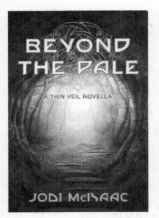

Discover the beauty and tragedy of Tír na nÓg leading up to the events of *Through the Door* in this ninety-page prequel novella *Beyond the Pale*, available as an e-book.

Kier believes she has the perfect life—and the perfect love—in the Irish otherworld of Tír na nÓg. But when she is unwillingly wed to the High King in an arranged marriage, her lover takes matters into his own hands in an unexpected and horrifying way. Now, she must do whatever it takes to protect her husband and her kingdom from the man she loves—even if it means losing everything.

To learn more, follow Jodi McIsaac on Twitter (@jodimcisaac) and Facebook (/jodimcisaac), and visit her website, jodimcisaac.com.

ABOUT THE AUTHOR

Photo © 2015 F8 Photography

Jodi McIsaac grew up in New Brunswick, Canada. After stints as a short-track speed skater, a speechwriter, and a fund-raising and marketing executive in the nonprofit sector, she started a boutique copywriting agency and began writing novels in the wee hours of the morning. She loves running, Brazilian jujitsu, and whiskey, and is an avowed geek girl. She currently lives with her husband and two feisty daughters in Calgary.